WINGS OF FIRE

WINGS OF FIRE

THE POISON JUNGLE

by
TUI T. SUTHERLAND

SCHOLASTIC PRESS
NEW YORK

All rights reserved. Published by Scholastic Press, an imprint of Scholastic Inc.,
Publishers since 1920. SCHOLASTIC, SCHOLASTIC PRESS, and associated logos are
trademarks and/or registered trademarks of Scholastic Inc.

The publisher does not have any control over and does not assume any
responsibility for author or third-party websites or their content.

No part of this publication may be reproduced, stored in a retrieval system,
or transmitted in any form or by any means, electronic, mechanical,
photocopying, recording, or otherwise, without written permission of the
publisher. For information regarding permission, write to Scholastic Inc.,
Attention: Permissions Department, 557 Broadway, New York, NY 10012.

This book is a work of fiction. Names, characters, places, and incidents
are either the product of the author's imagination or are used fictitiously,
and any resemblance to actual persons, living or dead, business
establishments, events, or locales is entirely coincidental.

Library of Congress Cataloging-in-Publication Data available

ISBN 978-93-90189-17-5

Printed in India

First printing, August 2019
This reprint edition : June 2023

Book design by Phil Falco

To Hazel

Tsetse Hive

Beetle Lake

Vinegaroon Hive

Hornet Hive

Cicada Hive

Mantis Hive

PANTALA

Tsetse Hive

Beet

A GUIDE TO THE
DRAGONS

Cicada Hive

Mantis Hive

Yellowjacket
Hive

Wasp
Hive

OF PANTALA

Bloodworm
Hive

HIVEWINGS

Description: red, yellow, and/or orange, but always mixed with some black scales; four wings

Abilities: vary from dragon to dragon; examples include deadly stingers that can extend from their wrists to stab their enemies; venom in their teeth or claws; or a paralyzing toxin that can immobilize their prey; others can spray boiling acid from a stinger on their tails

Queen: Queen Wasp

Lake Scorpion

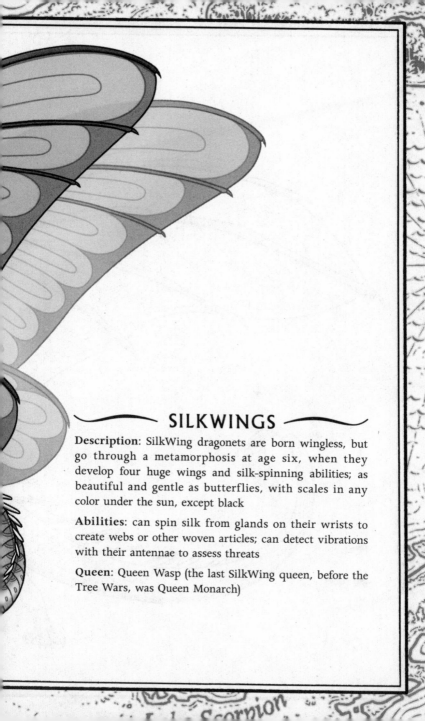

~ SILKWINGS ~

Description: SilkWing dragonets are born wingless, but go through a metamorphosis at age six, when they develop four huge wings and silk-spinning abilities; as beautiful and gentle as butterflies, with scales in any color under the sun, except black

Abilities: can spin silk from glands on their wrists to create webs or other woven articles; can detect vibrations with their antennae to assess threats

Queen: Queen Wasp (the last SilkWing queen, before the Tree Wars, was Queen Monarch)

LEAFWINGS

Description: wiped out during the Tree Wars with the HiveWings, but while they lived, this tribe had green and brown scales and wings shaped like leaves

Abilities: could absorb energy from sunlight and were accomplished gardeners; some were rumored to have unusual control over plants

Queen: last known queen of the LeafWings was Queen Sequoia, about fifty years ago, at the time of the Tree Wars

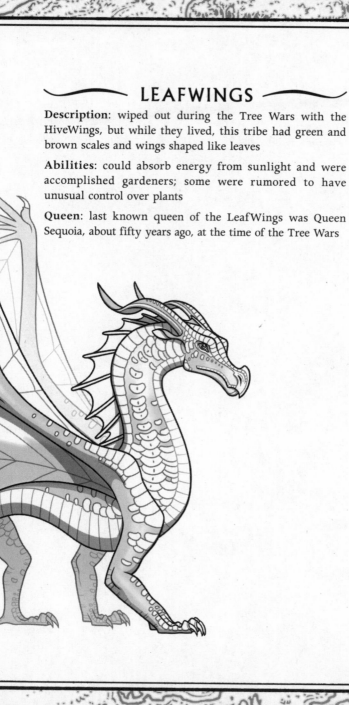

Tsetse Hive

Beetle Lake

Vinegaroon
Hive

Hornet Hive

Cicada Hive

Mantis
Hive

THE
LOST CONTINENT
PROPHECY

Turn your eyes, your wings, your fire
To the land across the sea
Where dragons are poisoned and dragons are dying
And no one can ever be free.

A secret lurks inside their eggs.
A secret hides within their book.
A secret buried far below
May save those brave enough to look.

Open your hearts, your minds, your wings
To the dragons who flee from the Hive.
Face a great evil with talons united
Or none of the tribes will survive.

WINGS
OF
FIRE

PROLOGUE

The HiveWing city loomed out of the savanna, impossibly tall and imposing and indestructible-looking, and honestly, its big smug aura would have been enough reason to burn it down, in Bryony's opinion.

But it was also, bonus, full of their enemies.

Not to mention that it was made from trees that had been stolen from her own tribe, the LeafWings, long before she hatched. She had never known those trees herself, but she *should* have. They should have lived hundreds of years, whispering to their seedlings and slowly reaching toward the light. Instead they had been murdered, ground up into splinters, and mixed into the mash HiveWings called "treestuff." Every Hive was made of it.

Which is why every Hive is going to burn.

Eventually. This one was a bit of a trial run. Bloodworm Hive — even the name gave her the creeps. She was glad her leaders had chosen one so palpably horrible; she might have felt a tad less enthusiastic about burning the prettier Jewel Hive they'd flown past a few days ago.

Then again, maybe not. All she had to do was picture the dragons inside and even the sparkly Glitterbazaar became instantly more sinister.

But it didn't matter; they were here, behind a greenhouse outside Bloodworm Hive in the middle of the night, moments away from executing their great mission.

"I think it's kind of funny that all the Hives have greenhouses," she said to Hemlock and Pokeweed. "It's like, the HiveWings wiped out all the trees thinking they were *sooo* clever, and then after they were done, they realized, oops, plants are kind of useful, actually; maybe we should make some little houses and grow a few."

She brushed one of her leaf-shaped wings across the panes of glass. "Easy enough once they also stole the SilkWings' fire, I guess," she added.

Hemlock and Pokeweed, as usual, were being stoic and boring and ignored her by staring grimly off into space, as if they were too busy envisioning heroic things to trouble with conversations. She rolled her eyes, crouched beside them, and peeked into the jar Belladonna had left them.

Bryony had seen fire before, once when lightning hit a tree and burned it to charred ash. But she'd never seen it like this, a long thread curled quietly inside stone, glowing like a bit of captured sun. It was so *small*.

Especially compared to the giant Hive in front of them.

"How can this possibly work?" she whispered. *How can this tiny bit of fire bring down a whole city?*

"We follow the plan," Hemlock said. He gestured at the bags of dittany and other flammable plants they'd brought with them from the jungle.

"This would be easier if we had Sundew with us," Pokeweed pointed out in his deep, slow voice. "I don't understand why she isn't here."

"She's busy," Hemlock said curtly.

"Doing what?" Bryony asked, although she knew perfectly well he would continue to not tell her anything about his daughter's mystery activities.

"I thought she was going to help," Pokeweed said again. "I *thought* the plan involved flaming ivy growing up the walls."

"It will," Hemlock said, lifting his claws and flexing them significantly.

Pokeweed gave him a dubious look. "Maybe we should wait for her," he said. "Maybe she'll come soon."

"Pokeweed," Hemlock said, finally letting a bit of exasperation slip into his voice. "Don't be annoying."

"Hm," Pokeweed grumbled. "That's nice."

"The plan is fine." Hemlock picked up the jar and cupped it between his talons. The glow lit up his face from below, casting his eyes into shadows. "We have what we need."

"Not being annoying," Pokeweed muttered. "Being sensible."

Another dragon appeared around the corner of the greenhouse, and for a moment, Bryony tensed, ready to fight.

But it wasn't a HiveWing. This dragon had goldenrod-yellow spots on his wings, but the rest of his scales were shades of gray, pale and dark overlapping, like a chinchilla. Or a snuggled-up pile of chinchillas.

She'd only known this SilkWing for a day, but every time she saw him, she thought of small adorable furry things.

"Grayling!" she whispered.

"Hi, Bryony," he whispered back, smiling.

"Is it done?" Hemlock interrupted.

"We did the best we could," Grayling said. "All the SilkWings who sleep in the Hive have been warned to stay near an exit and keep their dragonets with them so they can evacuate first. We have members of the Chrysalis assigned to retrieve our eggs and the dragonets going through Metamorphosis right now. And we've sent messages along the webs that connect this Hive to Jewel Hive and Mantis Hive." He hesitated. "If we had one more day —"

"We don't," Hemlock said, not unkindly, but with absolute finality in his voice.

Grayling's gaze went to the long bridge of silk overhead that stretched toward Mantis Hive. It glimmered a little, as if some of the starlight was caught in the silvery filaments.

"Do you really think the whole city will burn?" he asked. "And the webs along with it?"

"We're not going to set the webs alight on purpose," Bryony answered. "But if the Hive burns down like we're hoping . . ." She didn't have to finish the sentence. It was pretty clear what would happen to the webs that were woven to the top levels of the Hive.

When Sundew had first told them about the underground movement of SilkWings called the Chrysalis, Bryony had thought someone must have cracked her very hard on the head. She had grown up side by side with Sundew, who was only a year younger than her. They had both been raised with the absolutely certain knowledge that SilkWings were weak and timid and never stood up to anyone.

And then when Sundew said they needed to *warn* the Chrysalis before burning Bloodworm Hive . . . well, that was truly epic nonsense. Wouldn't someone go straight to tell the HiveWings? Wouldn't that ruin the whole plan?

But then they found Grayling and a few other dragons from the Bloodworm Hive Chrysalis. And now Bryony couldn't even think about what would have happened if they'd burned it without getting the SilkWings out first. She'd never have known Grayling at all; he might have died, and she wouldn't have known she'd lost him.

"All right," Grayling said, shaking himself. "Then how can the Chrysalis help?"

"You would do that?" Bryony asked, surprised.

A spark kindled in Hemlock's eyes. "You could burn it from the inside, too," he said. "That would be very helpful."

Grayling looked up at the Hive — no, not the Hive, Bryony realized. He was looking at the webs where he and his family lived, the home they had spun for themselves. The only home they knew. This mission, if it succeeded, would leave them lost in the savanna, with no idea where they'd end up.

"You don't have to do anything," she said, earning herself a frown from Hemlock. "It will be massively dangerous."

He met her eyes and tipped his head to the side. "I've wanted to fight back against the HiveWings almost since the day I hatched," he said softly. "They let my father die and they sent my brother away to Tsetse Hive. Lady Bloodworm is one of the cruelest of Wasp's sisters; that's why the Chrysalis here has so many members. I'm ready to do something real. I think we all are."

"Excellent," Hemlock said. "Let's choose locations and plan our timing."

"We all have to act fast and as synchronized as possible," Bryony said to Grayling. "Queen Wasp will be inside all these dragons the moment she realizes what's happening. By then it has to be too late for her to stop it."

"I'll show you the plants we have for burning," Pokeweed said lugubriously.

"I can do that," Bryony jumped in. "You and Hemlock review the interior map of the Hive we got from the Chrysalis." She brushed Grayling's wing with her own and beckoned him over to the supplies.

As she described each plant — how quickly it would catch, how long it would burn, which ones would spray burning oil — she caught Grayling watching her with a strange expression in his eyes.

"What?" she said, putting down a bundle of dead palm fronds they'd gathered that morning along the shore of Dragonfly Bay.

"It's just . . ." He hesitated. "I'm just amazed at how much trouble your tribe has gone to — all these plants and all this work — just to save us."

Bryony tried not to show how startled she was. "To save you?" she echoed.

"The SilkWings," he said. "You could have left us to rot in Queen Wasp's talons, after we abandoned you during the Tree Wars. But you didn't. You came back to set us free."

Oh, the guilt! Bryony felt it stabbing all her internal organs at once. How could she tell him that she'd never once thought about the plight of the SilkWings before she met him? That their mission was vengeance, not rescue?

"It's n-not —" she stammered. "I mean, we — we're doing it for ourselves. Honestly. Please don't think of us like heroes or saviors or anything."

He flicked his tail, nearly toppling a neat pile of dry grass. "Maybe as friends, then?" he asked.

"That works for me," she said. "I'm sorry we're burning down your home."

"It's more like a cage anyway," he said. "Where are you going to go after it burns?"

"We found some underground caves to hide in for a few days," she said. "Belladonna said we had to lie low so we wouldn't lead Wasp back to everyone else."

"Oh," he said, running his claws over one of the palm fronds. "Any chance there's room in there for a small friendly SilkWing?" She smiled at him, and he made a "sorry about this" face. "Or . . . a couple hundred of them?"

"I'll talk to Hemlock about it," she promised. She could see the older LeafWing beckoning them, his talons holding down the scribbled map of the interior of the Hive.

"Thank you," Grayling said.

She twined her tail around his. "Let's go set a fire."

Tsetse Hive

Beetle Lake

Vinegaroon
Hive

Hornet Hive

Cicada Hive

Mantis
Hive

Yellowjacket
Hive

Wasp
Hive

Bloodworm
Hive

PART ONE
ROOTS AND SPROUTS

CHAPTER 1

Sundew sometimes liked to imagine that she could fly all the way around the world without stopping, using nothing but her fury to keep her going.

When she got tired, she'd think about all the things that made her angry.

HiveWings.

HiveWings.

HiveWings.

Queen Wasp.

The murder of the trees.

The attempted murder of my entire tribe.

HiveWings.

Mother and Father . . .

No, those weren't allowed on this list.

HiveWings. Sundew imagined stabbing her claws into their necks, ripping their smug expressions off their faces, choking them with strangler vines, releasing fire ants into their eyeballs . . .

A flash of yellow and black caught her eye, and she whipped her head toward it with a hiss.

"Sorry!" Cricket dropped to a different air current and called up, "I didn't mean to startle you!"

"You didn't," Sundew snapped. It was sort of difficult to rage-fly on the power of hating HiveWings when there were two HiveWings flying right alongside her, being *extremely* noisy and distracting. Also when one of those HiveWings was sort of practically almost a friendish kind of dragon, maybe, and the other was the size of a large mango and madly in love with Sundew.

"SNUDOO!" cried the little dragonet tied snugly to Cricket's chest. Bumblebee reached her tiny talons toward Sundew. "MRBLE SNUDOO!"

"Is that tiny lizard trying to say my name?" Sundew asked, alarmed. "How did THAT happen?"

"She's very smart," Cricket said proudly.

"Not if she thinks she wants *my* attention," Sundew pointed out. She turned her head north again, beating her wings harder.

There was a dark line on the horizon ahead. They were almost there.

The Poison Jungle. Home. Or Never-home, as some of the

LeafWings called it, but the only home Sundew had ever known. Her tribe's true home, the rest of the continent, covered in vast ancient forests, only existed in stories of the old days and dreams for the future.

Sundew breathed and flew.

Each wingbeat brought her closer.

Closer to the thorn-sharp, fangs-bared, twisted safety of the Poison Jungle.

Closer to the dragon she wasn't allowed to think about.

She felt the pouch she kept over her heart thump once, twice, again, in rhythm with her wings. It was the only pouch, out of the many wrapped around her, that didn't hold venomous insects or useful plants.

Inside it was nothing but a small jade frog.

Which didn't help with the not-thinking-about. It served, in fact, the opposite purpose.

But Sundew still brought it with her everywhere. As long as her parents, Belladonna and Hemlock, didn't know what it meant, they couldn't do anything about it.

"Um — Sundew?" Blue asked nervously from her left. She tilted her head toward him. It was weird to know a SilkWing, after years of scoffing about how beautiful and useless they were. Even weirder, he'd turned out to not be useless at all. *Flamesilk. I should have been a flamesilk. If I had the power of fire . . .*

Well, I sort of do, now that we have Blue.

That thought made her uncomfortable, and she wasn't sure why. She bared her teeth at a passing starling, and it nearly fell out of the sky in fright.

Blue's wings glimmered azure in the rays of the setting sun. "Um. Isn't the Poison Jungle . . . really dangerous?"

"Or is that a lie?" Swordtail asked from her other side. "Like, maybe LeafWings spread stories exaggerating how dangerous it is so that no one else would go there? That would make sense; I bet that's it."

Sundew laughed. "How could *we* spread stories?" she said. "We haven't communicated with any SilkWings or HiveWings since the end of the Tree Wars fifty years ago. We were supposed to be extinct. That was kind of your whole goal, remember?"

"Not *our* goal," Blue protested in distress.

"No, everything you've heard about the jungle is true," Sundew said to Swordtail. "Queen Wasp sent a few expeditions to the Poison Jungle looking for resources and trying to make sure no dragons were hiding from her there. Almost all of them died; the rest are the ones who brought the stories back to you."

She frowned. "One of the expeditions was sent to burn down the jungle, because Wasp wanted no more trees anywhere. *None* of *those* dragons survived." She flicked her tail. "We helped the jungle make sure of that. No one who comes for the trees again will be allowed to live."

"But then how have you survived?" Blue asked. "How can there be a whole tribe living in a place that's so dangerous for dragons?"

"We didn't have a choice," Sundew answered. "It's easier when you grow up knowing what to avoid and how to treat snakebites and where the quicksand is. Nowadays we only lose a few dragons a year to the carnivorous plants."

"The what now?" Swordtail said, his voice rising an octave. "CARNIVOROUS WHATS?"

"Yeah, *you* will *probably* get eaten," Sundew said with a shrug. "They always get the loud flappy ones. And that HiveWing dragonet is cobra lily food for sure."

"ZAMEE!" Bumblebee shouted from behind them.

"I am not enjoying this conversation," Swordtail observed.

"Do we have to go to the place with the certain death?" Blue asked.

"Yes, because it's my home," Sundew said. "And also the only place you'll be safe from Queen Wasp after burning down her greenhouse of mind-control plants." *And also because there's a dragon there who I'm definitely not thinking about and certainly do not think about all the time.*

"We'd be safe across the ocean, wouldn't we?" Cricket offered, flying back into Sundew's line of sight. "In the Distant Kingdoms?"

Sundew laughed. "If you would all like to fly out to sea in search of an imaginary continent, go for it." She thought, but did not add: *Except for you, Blue. You belong to the LeafWings now.*

The group fell silent as they drew closer to the edge of the Poison Jungle. The Snarling River, dark and swift-flowing, marked the boundary, but the jungle was always prowling across the line. Pitcher plants and cobra lilies grew thick along the shores on both sides, and every time Sundew flew this way, she saw more plants extending their tendrils across the water, more twisted little thorn trees starting to muscle their way up on the wrong side.

If we set it free, the Poison Jungle could devour the continent for us, and all the HiveWings, too.

If I set it free. I could unleash the jungle and send it forth to strangle our enemies.

I won't, though. I don't want a Pantala covered in poisonous, dragon-eating plants. I want the Pantala of the old stories: the giant forests that stretched from shore to shore.

She closed her talons into fists.

But if I can't have that, feeding all the HiveWings to overgrown bladderworts is a solid plan B.

Sundew was over the river when she realized the others had stopped, hovering in midair to stare at the trees. She swung around and flew back to them.

"They're so big," Cricket said in an awestruck voice. Her gold-orange wings hummed like a cloud of dragonflies. The late-afternoon sunlight caught in her glasses, reflecting the rippling water below. "I didn't know trees grew so enormous. Some of them look as tall as the Hives! How old are they? Can you tell? Would they all get that big if they lived that long? Are they *all* dangerous? Oh, please tell me you have books about all these plants!"

"*I* want to know how you can fly in there when everything's so close together," Swordtail declared, squinting at the tangles of vines, fallen trees, giant spiderwebs, and thickets of plants that wove impassable barriers between the trees.

"It feels like one vast creature with a million eyes," Blue added softly. "I can almost hear it breathing . . . like it's waiting for us."

The others stared at him, and even Sundew, who was used to the creepy aura of the Poison Jungle, felt a trickle of ice run through her veins.

"Arglerarrrgh flort," Bumblebee announced, jabbing Cricket's chin with one of her claws and breaking the spell. "Eeeepow? Snudoo?" She reached hopefully toward Sundew.

"I think 'eeeepow' means 'eat now,'" Cricket explained with a sigh. "She's been yelling it for the last half a continent."

"EeeeeeeeeeeeePOW!" Bumblebee demonstrated with expansive arm gestures, trying to wiggle out of her sling. "EEEEEEEEEpow!"

"You can wait until we get to the village," Sundew said sternly. "Don't make that face at me. No whining, or you can wait until tomorrow morning."

Bumblebee flopped slowly over backward so her head and wings drooped toward the river below. "Eeeeeeeeeeeeeeee*never*," she said, mournfully and distinctly.

"Awww," Cricket said, tucking the dragonet back into place and patting her head. "She's such a quick learner." Bumblebee snuggled into her chest and gave a loud, dramatic sigh.

Sundew turned to Swordtail. "We keep the outer layers of the jungle as wild and impenetrable as possible," she said. "For obvious reasons."

"Obv — oh, she means you," he said to Cricket. "The obvious reasons are your murdery tribe and your evil queen."

"Swordtail, come on," Blue said, drawing closer to Cricket.

"Your tribe isn't exactly welcome here either, SilkWing," Sundew pointed out. She had a feeling she was going to get a pretty strong reaction when they got to the LeafWing village. But it was Belladonna's fault for leaving and setting a Hive on fire instead of waiting for Sundew to meet her, as she'd promised. If she didn't want Sundew bringing strangers into the jungle, she should have stayed in one place till they came.

Sundew looked up at the press of jostling tree trunks that rose before them. "Flying gets easier farther in," she explained. "But for now, we climb. Follow me, stay close — and *don't touch anything* I haven't touched first."

She arced her wings and caught an air current that smelled faintly of salt and distant whales. It lifted her up and up, toward the swaying tops of the trees.

Up here, the branches were like thousands of long spider monkey arms. They reached and caught one another, bending back and looping around, fuzzy with pale green moss or marked with the scratches of dragon, jaguar, and tamarin claws.

The spot where the makahiyas grew was well camouflaged; other plants with similar leaves had been planted all around it up and down and along the wall of foliage. But Sundew never had any trouble finding it. She could have flown to it with her eyes closed. She could sense the vibrations of the makahiya leaves like quiet music in her head; they were higher and trembled more than the vibrations of other plants.

Sundew slowed down and brushed her tail lightly across the center of the makahiya cluster. At once the long, oval, fern-like leaves began folding together, pair after pair along the stems like butterfly wings closing up. As they closed, they revealed a gap in the branches behind them, just large enough for a dragon to fit through.

"Whoa," Blue whispered. "I've never seen a plant do that before."

"Oh, I think . . . they're called 'touch-me-nots,' aren't they?" Cricket asked Sundew.

"That's one name for them," Sundew answered.

"Oooooo," said Swordtail. "That sounds super dangerous! Touch me not — or you will DIE!"

Sundew snickered, and Cricket covered her snout to hide her smile. "Actually," Sundew said to Swordtail, "this is probably the only plant up here that *won't* kill you."

"Hmm," he said skeptically, squinting at the folded leaves as he followed Sundew through the hole.

Stepping into the jungle always felt like plunging underwater, if that water was actually thick green soup, in a cauldron, boiling, and full of insects. Sundew hissed at a mosquito the size of her ear, and it veered away in search of more docile prey. Behind her, Cricket let out a yelp and lifted one talon to reveal a crushed mess of yellowy-orange ooze that had probably been a tree slug.

"Oooom-yum?" Bumblebee inquired, reaching for it. "Eeee?"

"*No,*" Cricket said. "GROSS, Bumblebee!"

"GWOSE!" Bumblebee cried, waking up an anaconda as thick as Sundew's tail in the next tree over. The snake raised its head slowly and narrowed its eyes at the little dragonet.

"Shhh. Let's move," Sundew whispered. She ran lightly along the branch and leaped to another, then scrambled up to one that crisscrossed above them. The trees shook as the other dragons tried clumsily to follow her.

Sundew could sense the message spreading through the trees. *Something new.* Leaves whispered to leaves; roots and networks of underground filaments flickered the news along like twigs in a current. *Watch listen be safe caution stand guard.* She didn't have time to dig her talons into the dirt and shape the story. She had to hope she could get her dragons to the village quickly, and then she could take a moment to talk to the trees.

"You're like a monkey," Swordtail panted, catching up to her when she stopped to wait for them. "I mean — in a good way — like a — very fast — jumps — good jumps — not foodishly — I mean, not in a dinner way — just, so fast." He wheezed to a stop.

Cricket balanced along the branch to a spot behind him, digging in her claws in a way that made Sundew wince. The trees wouldn't like that. But Bumblebee kept lunging sideways, nearly out of her sling, reaching for bright flowers or shining beetles, so Sundew could see why Cricket needed to hold on tight.

Bringing up the rear behind her was Blue, who looked as if he was trying to swallow the jungle with his eyes.

"It's scary, like being high up in the webs," he said thoughtfully, "but loud, like the inside of the Hives, except the buzzing isn't in a language you can understand."

"And the smell is way worse," Swordtail observed.

Sundew bristled. "No, it isn't! The smell of hundreds of dragons trapped in one structure is *much* worse! This is what plants and fresh air and freedom smell like!"

"Isn't it also what rotting plants smell like?" he asked. "And dead animals? And . . . I don't know what else . . . swamp gas?"

"*You* smell like swamp gas!" she said furiously.

"I'm sorry," Blue interjected. "I only meant it's interesting. I'm trying to map it onto something I've felt before, but it's so different from anywhere I've been."

"Yeah, sorry," Swordtail agreed, giving Sundew an abashed look. "It's not that bad. Some of it is kind of cool. Like that flower right below us — look, Blue, it's like an enormous wild pink open book. I mean, SO pink! And it actually smells kind of —"

"DO NOT —" Sundew shouted as he leaned toward it, sniffing.

But it was too late. Swordtail's nose brushed the pink surface, and the plant's jaws snapped shut around him, yanking him off the branch and swallowing him whole.

In an instant, Swordtail was gone.

— CHAPTER 2 —

"— touch the Venus dragon-trap," Sundew finished with a sigh.

Cricket shrieked, and eight more dragon-traps snapped shut all around them, excited by the noise. The HiveWing jumped back and crashed into Blue, nearly knocking them both off the branch.

"Swordtail!" Blue shouted. *"Swordtail!"*

"I was about to point those out," Sundew said. "One of the most dangerous plants in here. Never touch those. Never *never*." She gave Bumblebee a very stern look. *"Never,* small dragon, do you hear me?"

"Snabble *poof*," Bumblebee said in an awestruck tone, staring at the spot where Swordtail had been.

Blue scrambled around Cricket. "Swordtail! Can you hear me?" He reached toward the overstuffed plant below them, where Swordtail's long blue-and-orange tail dangled, flailing, from between the trap's jaws.

Sundew smacked Blue's knuckles. "What did I just say?" she barked. "NEVER TOUCH THEM!"

"How do we get him out?" Cricket asked frantically.

Muffled yells were coming from inside the plant. The sides bulged as Swordtail thrashed and struggled, but Sundew knew that there was no way for a dragon to escape on his own once he was inside.

"SWORDTAIL!" she shouted. "STOP MOVING!"

Of course, he was yelling too loud to hear her.

"Basic carnivorous plant safety lesson number one," Sundew said to the others, but mostly to Bumblebee's wide-eyed face. "If you fall into a dragon-trap, go as still as you can. If the plant thinks you're just a rock or tree branch that fell in by accident, it'll open back up and drop you. But if you FLAIL AROUND LIKE AN IDIOT," she shouted at Swordtail, "then it will KNOW YOU'RE A DELICIOUS SNACK FOR SURE."

"And then what?" Cricket asked, wide-eyed.

"Then it releases its digestive juices and eats you," Sundew said. "Obviously." She swatted at Blue as he tried reaching for Swordtail again.

"SWORDTAIL!" Cricket and Blue yelled in unison.

"It's pretty definitely figured out he's alive by now," Sundew said. She pointed to the long hairs along the edges of the plant's mouth, which were starting to lock firmly together. "It won't drop him even if he does shut up long enough to hear us. But it's a slow process — it'll take at least half a day before it kills him."

"Can't we slice it open and cut him out?" Cricket asked, raising one of her talons to flex her claws.

Sundew shook her head. "They've adapted for that. It takes forever to saw through the shell of a dragon-trap. Plus they grow in clusters like this on purpose, so if you try, another one will get you." She pointed to the gaping pink jaws hanging from the trees all around them, particularly the one leaning over Swordtail's plant, ready to swallow any dragon who tried to help him.

Blue paced up and down the branch. "Swordtail!" he called again. "We'll get you out, I promise!"

"So what do you normally do?" Cricket asked Sundew. "Your tribe must have found a way to rescue dragons from being eaten."

Sort of. If having me counts as "finding a way." Sundew had been studying the nearest plants as they talked. There was a promising kudzu vine choking one of the trees below them, or a thorny greenbrier vine system tangled through the branches just behind the dragon-trap cluster. The sharp-dark stems prickled in the corners of her mind, coiled and dangerous. If she could get to one of them . . . but then she'd have to reveal her secret abilities to Blue and Cricket.

They're going to find out pretty soon anyway. And it's the only way to save Swordtail.

"I can —" she started.

There was a flash of bright orange light and heat beside her. A long thread of flamesilk flew out of Blue's wrist and slithered around the dragon-trap's leaves and stem.

"Stop!" Sundew yelled. She lunged across Cricket and grabbed Blue's arm, slamming it down to the branch. "WHY ARE YOU ALL IMPOSSIBLE?" She whirled and saw the fire already beginning to catch and spread down the length of the dragon-trap stem, toward the tree where its roots were. As the stem burned through, the squirming bulb of the dragon-trap drooped and lolled sideways, setting off three more plants as it knocked into them.

Sundew leaped up to a higher branch and seized a cluster of giant bromeliads. A small blue tree frog jumped out of one of them and gave her a reproachful look as she ripped the flowers free. Inside each cluster of leaves was a pool of water, some the size of her cupped talons, some much bigger. She swooped down and poured them over the fire.

It sizzled and hissed at her. Half the flames went out, but one end began sprinting faster toward the tree. The smoke was already thick and curling into her eyes, making them water. All the nearest dragon-traps had drawn back as far as their stems would allow. Leaves all around her curled away from the fire; she could feel the tree screaming deep in her nerves.

I need a fire-resistant plant — something full of water or sap — or giant leaves I can use to smother the flames. Sundew glanced desperately around and spotted a chokecherry tree on the jungle floor, far below her. She leaped through the smoke to the trunk of the burning tree and pressed her talons against the bark, sending her power down through the wood, through the roots, through the mycelium threads under the soil, into the chokecherry tree.

The chokecherry tree burst upward, growing at the speed of an erupting volcano. Its branches smacked other plants aside; its roots burrowed deep and fast to keep it steady. In a matter of heartbeats, the top of the tree was level with Sundew's head and the berries on it were enormous, the size of her fists.

She grabbed talonfuls of berries and smashed them onto the branch below the fire, smearing the juice around and around. The flames reached the wet barrier and slowed, prodding the goop in a disgruntled manner.

More water splashed down on the fire from above. Sundew looked up and saw Cricket with her claws full of bromeliads. Bumblebee was buried deep in her sling, her snout covered by the striped fabric. Cricket poured out the stored rainwater in the flowers, methodically covering all the flames until, at last, they were extinguished.

Sundew rested her forehead against the tree, checking it for damage. Apart from the one burnt limb and the smoke clogging its leaves, the rest of it was shaken but unharmed. The dragon-trap, however, was definitely dead.

She turned toward it and realized that Blue was holding up the head and trying to pry open the jaws at the same time, mostly unsuccessfully. Cricket hovered beside him, supporting the weight of the plant and Swordtail. The other dragon-traps, which had been scared back by the fire, were slowly inching toward them again.

Sundew flew over to Blue. She could hear Swordtail coughing inside the plant.

"That was *incredibly* stupid!" She snapped her tail back and forth. Her insides felt as though they were boiling with anger, as though the flamesilk had gone straight into her veins as well. "You could have set this whole jungle on fire!"

"I'm sorry!" Blue said, and at least he looked like he meant it, unless the tears in his eyes came from the smoke in the air. "I panicked! I only wanted to save Swordtail — I had no idea it would spread like that."

"You should have thought about it! You just saw Wasp's greenhouse go up in flames!"

A fellow LeafWing would have roared back at Sundew. A dragon from her tribe would have bristled, defended himself, argued, stormed around, pointed out all the ways she was wrong. Most conversations in her village ended in fights, or started with a fight, or at least involved some shouting.

But Blue nodded and wiped his eyes and apologized *again*. "You're right. I'm really, really sorry, Sundew."

Which made it kind of impossible to keep yelling at him. The ball of Sundew's anger bounced back inside her and started mutating into something useless and distracting, like guilt or pity or something. She scowled down at the dragon-trap, which was starting to crack open where Blue was pulling on it.

"I bet your flamesilk is hard to control, isn't it?" Cricket asked breathlessly, trying to hold up the still-smoking plant.

"Yeah," Blue said. "So it was extra stupid of me."

"We'll help you practice with it," Sundew said, wondering if she could really offer something like that. There wasn't a LeafWing alive who knew anything about managing flamesilk. "But for now, promise me you *won't use it* in the jungle unless I tell you to."

"I promise," he said. "I really promise. Can you help me get Swordtail out? He must be so scared."

"NO! NOT SCARED!" Swordtail half yelled, half sputtered through the crack in the plant's jaws. "This plant is in big trouble! I'm going to slice it up from the inside! I'm going to give it such a stomachache! It'll seriously regret trying to eat ME!"

"You deserved it!" Sundew barked at him. It was a relief to have someone she could be mad at without feeling bad. She hooked her claws around the top edge of the plant's mouth and motioned for Blue to take the bottom edge. "You basically fed yourself to it!"

"I did not — that is — it — I was just smelling it!" Swordtail growled.

Sundew flapped her wings, pushing herself backward as hard as she could. "The smell is designed to attract dragons," she conceded. "But only dragons with no brains in their heads! Who like constantly causing trouble for their traveling companions! I *said* you would get eaten right away and I was right!"

With a ripping, crackling sound, the jaws finally parted. Swordtail hauled himself out and back onto the first branch, coughing and blinking rapidly. The others let go of the dragon-trap, and the head broke off from the blackened stem, tumbling away to the forest floor.

Sundew could sense the hunger of the surrounding

dragon-traps. As the smoke faded into the air, they were getting bolder, rustling closer in their stealthy way.

She shoved Cricket and Bumblebee back onto the branch, and Blue clambered after them.

"I've never seen such a pileup of idiocy," she said. "Now *really* stay close to me and *really* don't touch anything!"

"I feel like we could have gotten a bit more of a warning," Swordtail objected with a cough as they started walking again. "Like, it'd be pretty helpful if you'd point out: *that's* a carnivorous plant and *that* one is super flammable and *that* one can kill you."

"All right," Sundew said, waving at the entire jungle around them. "*These* are dangerous plants and *most* of them are carnivorous and *all* of them can kill you. Do not sniff, touch, eat, poke, lick, or set fire to *any of them*, or you will probably die, and next time I will let you."

"She doesn't mean that," Cricket whispered to Bumblebee, who chirped sleepily back at her.

"It must have been pretty awful when your tribe first got here," Blue said.

Sundew did not dignify that with an answer, since she was pretty sure it would involve more yelling at him, and apparently she didn't really enjoy yelling at Blue. (Yelling at Swordtail, on the other hand, was always satisfying.)

They climbed in silence for a little while, hopping from

branch to branch as they descended through the jungle. It was a prickly silence, though; Blue had an aura of guilt around him, Swordtail kept muttering under his breath, and Sundew could feel Cricket's eyes on her. She knew her well enough by now to guess that Cricket was trying really hard to hold back a question, and that pretty soon she would fail.

"Sundew," Cricket burst out as they passed a cluster of glowering giant hogweeds.

"Arrgh, what?" Sundew said, casting a glance over her shoulder at the HiveWing. Cricket's glasses were fogged up from the humidity, and she kept swiping at them with Bumblebee's sling.

"It's just . . ." Cricket hesitated, and Sundew realized what she was going to ask. Even in the midst of fighting the fire with bromeliad pools, of course Cricket would notice what every dragon around her was doing. Especially if it was something weird and unscientific.

Cricket tilted her head at Sundew. "Did you . . . make a *tree* grow?"

CHAPTER 3

Sundew winced.

Her gift was no secret inside the tribe, but Belladonna had been very clear that she wasn't supposed to let any HiveWings or SilkWings find out about it. Sundew had already risked exposing it twice — once when she grew the vines that helped Blue and Luna escape the flamesilk cavern, once when she used seaweed to help her transport an unconscious Swordtail across Dragonfly Bay. She'd gotten away with it both times; she'd even managed to avoid Cricket's questions.

But there was no way to get around the Poison Jungle without using her power. She couldn't even walk through the LeafWing village without dragons asking her for help with their plants. Cricket and the others would know everything soon anyway.

"Yeah," she said to Cricket. "I do that sometimes."

"Grow *trees*?" Cricket asked. "Like . . . really tall trees out of nowhere before anyone can blink?"

"Not out of nowhere," Sundew said. "I can only help along whatever plant is already there. I can't make plants or seeds appear. If I could, I'd have been throwing down oak trees and beech groves and pine forests all over Pantala by now."

"But that's amazing," Blue said. "Why didn't you tell us? Because you didn't know if you could trust us," he answered himself immediately. "Because you wouldn't want Queen Wasp to find out."

"As if we would ever tell Queen Wasp!" Swordtail objected.

"Oh!" Blue said. "I remember reading something about this! LeafWings who could control plants — I remember thinking that sounded like magic and wondering what I would grow with it if I could."

"Can all LeafWings do this?" Cricket asked.

Sundew shook her head, but she was rescued from any further questions by an eruption of roars from the jungle below.

The others jumped, and Bumblebee woke up and poked her head out of the sling. "RAWR?" she inquired. "Bammo slammo eeeeeeenow?"

"Everyone shush," Sundew said, crouching low to the branch. "Especially you," she whispered to Bumblebee.

"YOUUUSHH HA HAA SO SHH," Bumblebee declared proudly. Cricket produced a berry from somewhere and the little dragonet seized it and stuffed it whole into her mouth, which would keep her quiet for at most ten seconds.

Thick leaves hid them from what was happening below, but Sundew could clearly hear at least three dragons bellowing and a fourth roar that didn't sound like a dragon to her. She rested her ear against the bark of the tree and tried to get the tree's sense of what was going on. But whatever it was, the tree was apparently not threatened and therefore not interested.

"Come ON, Mandrake!" one of the dragons bellowed. "Strangle it or something!"

"It's moving too fast!" Mandrake's voice shouted back. "If it would just — can we back it over to — or next to that —"

"Can't I *please* just kill it?" yelled the third dragon. "We could be home and cooking it by now! This panther will die of old age before Mandrake finds the *perfect* vine in the *perfect* place and figures out what to do with it!"

Oh, poor Mandrake. Sundew could guess exactly what was happening now. She'd seen enough of the hunts this hapless dragon had been dragged into by his father and sister.

"Stay here," she whispered to the others. Sundew swung lightly down through the branches, slipping carefully through the leaves and avoiding the spiderwebs as well as she could. In a moment, she found a spot near the trunk with a view of the jungle floor, where, if she kept still, the clusters of giant rattling seed pods should keep her hidden.

Now she could see Mandrake darting helplessly around the clearing, grabbing at plants but letting them go without using them. His father and sister watched from the low branches of the nearest trees, with matching critical expressions on their faces. The panther slunk after him, snarling, its teeth bigger than Mandrake's claws. Its black fur rippled over huge muscles. Only the biggest, strongest, scariest mammals could survive in the Poison Jungle, so all their panthers were unnecessarily gigantic and terrifying.

Terrifying to dragons like Mandrake, that is. Not at all terrifying to Sundew, who was in charge of hunting their prey for every big tribe feast. *How dare they have Mandrake do it instead*, she thought with a flare of anger. *Are they having a feast without ME? Don't they care where I am? Aren't I their precious savior of the world or something?*

Then again, her last fight with Belladonna had been quite dramatic. It would be just like her mother to spite her by burning down a Hive and celebrating with an all-tribe panther feast while pretending she didn't care whether Sundew was there or not. She knew Sundew would have to come back eventually. Sundew had nowhere else to go.

But if I did . . . if I could just fly away . . . would I?

Sundew's talons went to the pouch with the little jade frog in it.

I could have left. Belladonna doesn't even know I could have left them. But I didn't, because I have a purpose, and that purpose is vengeance. I hatched for one reason: to destroy our enemies.

That's why I will always come back. Not for Belladonna or Hemlock. I come back so that one day I can be the one who wipes out the HiveWings forever.

A tiny face clamoring "SNUDOO!" poked its way into her thoughts, and she scowled.

Or . . . all the HiveWings except two, I guess.

Below her, the panther pounced experimentally toward Mandrake. Mandrake shrieked and threw a seed pod at it before running off to the other side of the clearing. Nettle sighed loudly and rolled her eyes.

"He has to learn how to do this," Wolfsbane said to her.

"Why?" she complained. "I could do it so much faster without any magical powers. And if we need the magic, we have Sundew."

"We don't have Sundew right *now*," her father pointed out. "She might have to go on another mission like this one, and what if we're attacked and Mandrake has to step up?"

"Then we're all going to die," Nettle said flatly.

"I can *hear* you," Mandrake protested, "and it is *not*

helping." He dug his talons into the leaf mulch underneath him and closed his eyes.

By all the trees, Sundew thought. *Don't close your eyes, Mandrake! Not when there's a panther stalking you!* This was why Mandrake was never assigned to offensive plant magic. He always had to FOCUS and BREATHE, even in the middle of an actual emergency.

Well, Sundew couldn't let him get mauled by a panther, even if that might make her life a little easier. She sent her magic down through the trunk and into the ground and through the roots and the mosses and ferns to the thicket of thorn tangles behind the panther. As it crouched, growling, ready to spring at Mandrake, she felt into the root system that extended below the panther's paws. Just before the giant cat leaped, a new thorn bush burst out of the ground and slammed into the panther's underbelly. Thorns stabbed and tangled the panther's fur as they sprouted, trapping the animal in place. With a furious yowl, it tried to struggle, but its movements only ensnared it further.

Across the clearing, Wolfsbane and Nettle goggled at the panther in bewilderment. Sundew had to cover her snout to keep from laughing.

Mandrake cracked one eyelid, then opened them both, looking startled and pleased.

"Whoa. Did I do that?" he asked.

"Son!" Wolfsbane crowed. "Look at you! That was incredible!"

"Uh-uh," Nettle said, resettling her face into its usual sneer. "No way. Sundew! Sundew, you can't fool me. I know you're here somewhere!"

Sundew held her breath, wondering if she could brazen it out. Wolfsbane and Mandrake squinted up into the trees, and of course, right into that moment of silence, a very loud, high-pitched voice howled, "SNUUUUUUUUUUUUUUUDOO OOOOOOOOOOOOOO!"

"What was that?" Mandrake asked, looking spooked.

"Sounded like a dragonet," said his father.

"Sounded like proof that I'm right," Nettle barked. "Come on out, Sundew!"

Sundew sighed. There was no hiding the wrestling and shushing noises coming from above, or the "EEEEEEE EEEEEEEEEEE NOOOOOOOWWW" wail that followed. DRAGONETS. ONE HUNDRED PERCENT THE WORST.

She swung down from the tree and thumped to the ground in a cloud of damp leaf fragments.

"Hey, Mandrake," she said with a nod.

"Oh," he said, his wings drooping. "It *was* you."

"Pardon me for making sure you didn't become *her* feast instead of the other way around!" Sundew growled, flicking her tail at the panther.

"I *knew* it," Nettle said.

"Sorry — I mean — thank you," said Mandrake. "I was just excited for a moment."

"I know," Sundew said, "but you *have* to learn to feel the plants with your eyes open." She glared at Wolfsbane. "Especially if your irresponsible family is going to keep trying to get you killed."

"I was watching him," Wolfsbane said dismissively. "Sundew, *what* is that cacophony up there?" He pointed up with his eyebrows raised, as though there was anything unfamiliar about the sound of a hungry dragonet throwing a temper tantrum.

"You can come down!" Sundew shouted to her friends. "Go to the trunk and work your way down slowly — don't touch anything but the tree!"

Nettle's mouth dropped open again. "Who is that?" she demanded. "Someone who doesn't know our jungle? Did you bring STRANGERS into our trees?"

"Don't be a drama queen," Sundew said sharply. "They can help us."

"Do your parents know about this?" Wolfsbane asked, which was only the most irritating question in the universe, and one Sundew was very sick of hearing. Belladonna and Hemlock had gone ahead and burned down a Hive without asking her first, so it served them right for her to bring

HiveWings and SilkWings into the jungle without *their* permission.

Swordtail hit the ground first, his talons sinking into the layers of moss and dead leaves with a squelch. He looked a little the worse for wear after his tussle with the dragon-trap, but still very clearly a SilkWing.

Nettle was about to snap something furious, when Blue climbed down behind Swordtail, and she lost her powers of speech. There was *nothing* that color blue in the Poison Jungle. He was a kind of shiny that Sundew's tribe wasn't used to.

But even Blue's beautiful wings couldn't distract the LeafWings from the appearance of Cricket, cradling Bumblebee.

Nettle flared her wings with a violent hiss. Wolfsbane whipped a long thorny vine off his tail and held it ready to fight. Even Mandrake growled softly under his breath.

"It's all right, calm down!" Sundew said. "They're with me."

"That doesn't make it all right!" Nettle cried. "HiveWings in *here*?! What is wrong with you? Queen Wasp will be right behind them!"

"No, she won't!" Sundew snapped. "She can't mind-control these two. She doesn't know where they are, or where we are. Nothing has changed! Except *now* we have a flamesilk."

Wolfsbane let out a little huff of surprise and pointed at Blue. "That one?"

Sundew hesitated and was furious at herself for hesitating. Why did she feel weird about this? "Yes," she said. She felt a twinge of that weird feeling at the nervous look on Blue's face. *But he doesn't have anything to worry about*, she told herself. *He can be useful to us, and we'll protect him from Wasp. Win-win.*

"I wouldn't say you '*have*' a flamesilk," Swordtail said pointedly. "I mean, he *is* a flamesilk and he's here, but he has himself. No one else has him, I mean. He is not for having. He's his own dragon!"

"Hmmm," Wolfsbane said, ignoring him and studying Blue with fathomless brown eyes. "So why not kill the others and just keep this one, Sundew?"

"Because they're all useful," Sundew said quickly. She tried to make her voice sound as aggressive and no-nonsense as she could. "Especially the HiveWing. She's immune to the mind control, and we think she's figured out how Wasp does it."

"What about him?" Nettle asked, pointing at Swordtail. "He looks unnecessary."

"All right, maybe *useful* is the wrong word," Sundew amended, earning an offended look from the blue-orange-white dragon. "But we can't kill him without upsetting the flamesilk. Not worth it."

Blue blinked and sidled a step closer to Swordtail. His antennae had unfurled into thin trembling stems over his head, like tentacles of ivy looking for a place to land safely.

"I *am* useful," Swordtail protested. "I have *many* uses. I am smart and I know things and I can fight HiveWings and I am *in* the *Chrysalis*, hello, which everyone seems to forget, secret revolutionary over here, and I am also, by the way, extremely good company."

"And the dragonet?" Wolfsbane asked Sundew.

"An experiment," she said. "We think she's immune to the mind control, too."

"You *think*?" Nettle demanded. "That's quite a risky experiment, you idiots."

"It's going great so far!" Sundew flared.

"You get away with everything because you're Belladonna's daughter and you're soooo special!" Nettle shouted. "But you've gone too far this time, Sundew! No one will stand for this!"

"Let's go ask Belladonna what to do," Wolfsbane said, resting one talon on Nettle's shoulder.

"Fine." Nettle shook him off. "But I know what she'll say. We'll be back soon to execute your new pets!" She folded her wings and hissed at Sundew one more time before turning and marching away.

"Wait for us here," Wolfsbane said.

"I'll stay with them," Mandrake offered. Wolfsbane gave a faint shrug and followed Nettle into the undergrowth.

Sundew sat down with a snort of disgust. This wasn't how she'd planned to arrive. *She* was supposed to be the one who explained all this to Belladonna. Not that she wanted to. But she didn't want stupid Wolfsbane to do it! He'd get it all wrong! But it didn't matter. Belladonna wasn't the boss of Sundew. Except in the literal, she-ran-the-whole-tribe sense. But Sundew was going to save the world and wreak furious vengeance on those who deserved it, so there wasn't anything Belladonna could do to her or her friends. Not if she wanted a part in the vengeance! *Just try me, Mother.*

"Uh," Blue said. "That . . . didn't sound like it went very well."

"Really? That was a pretty average conversation with Nettle," Sundew said. She took a breath, searching the greenery with her mind. There — a bush covered in small pale globules. Her power slipped through the roots and stems to grow just one of the branches out until she could reach it. She took one of the sticky white berries and threw it at the panther.

It snarled and snapped the berry out of the air. A moment later, the panther keeled over, dead.

"Aw, cool," Mandrake said with a flick of his wings,

which were dark green with thin gold stripes on top and mahogany brown underneath. "But everyone can still eat the panther, right?"

"Yeah. I use these on prey all the time," she said, tossing one to him. "Harmless to dragons, deadly to mammals. No idea why."

"Really?" Cricket said. Mandrake handed her the berry, and she gave it a fascinated look.

"EEEEEEEEEEEEE?" Bumblebee asked, leaning out of her sling hopefully.

"Maybe not this," Cricket said to her. "Just to be safe."

"Here, these are all right to eat," Sundew said, unearthing a tuber from the dark earth and flinging it to Cricket.

"Snudooooo," Bumblebee cooed with a worshipful look.

"Maybe she thinks 'snudoo' means 'food,'" Sundew guessed.

"Pretty sure she knows it's you, the hero who provides all the best food," Cricket said, tucking the root into Bumblebee's tiny talons. The dragonet wrapped her little arms around the tuber and began gnawing on it with great determination.

"Excuse me. Should we be running away?" Swordtail asked. "Maybe hiding? Boss? Don't you think hiding us might be a good idea?"

"No, you nitwit, we're trying to get to the village, not hide from it. Getting there was the whole point. Nobody's going to execute you," Sundew said impatiently. "Not until I tell them to anyway. They need me."

"Because of your power?" Cricket guessed.

"They need yours, too," Sundew pointed out to Blue. "So tell them exactly what you want. Don't let them walk all over you."

"Oh, but . . . all right, but loud dragons are hard to deal with," he said. "Are all LeafWings that, um . . . shouty?"

"Everyone but me," Mandrake answered with a nervous laugh.

That's not true, Sundew thought, touching her jade frog lightly through the pouch. *But he's never met the others.*

"The one nice LeafWing," Swordtail said. "Sounds like a good dragon to know."

"I'm Cricket, this is Bumblebee, that's Blue, and that's Swordtail," Cricket said. She tilted her head at Mandrake. "Who are you?"

"I'm Mandrake," he said, smiling his nonthreatening crooked smile at all of them. "Sundew's fiancé."

CHAPTER 4

Cricket whirled to stare at Sundew.

"Her *what*?" Swordtail echoed.

"I thought we agreed not to use that word," Sundew grumbled at Mandrake.

"Well, 'future husband' sounds weird," he pointed out.

"So does 'fiancé'! Super weird!" She snapped a dying branch off the nearest bush and broke it in her talons over and over until it was a pile of splinters.

"But — you — this dragon?" Blue said, bewildered. "I just . . ."

"Didn't picture your one true love being someone like this," Cricket finished for him.

"Nobody said anything about true love!" Sundew yelped at the same time as Mandrake stammered, "No, no, that's not at all, no, we are not that, no."

Cricket and Blue exchanged puzzled glances, which made Sundew want to poke them quite hard with her claws. Just because they were all melty and silly over each other didn't mean everyone else in the world got to be that way.

"But . . . I thought . . ." Cricket started, and Sundew suddenly had a horrible flash of memory.

Oh no.

She'd said something to the nosy HiveWing a few days ago, about how she understood Swordtail's obsession with Luna because she had a "one true love," too.

A thing she hadn't even *thought* about blurting out, because she'd never expected to see Cricket standing here, in the Poison Jungle, right in front of Mandrake, about to spill the biggest secret Sundew was keeping from her tribe.

"NOPE," she shouted before Cricket could finish her sentence. "Wrong! Bad! No thinking! Whatever you thought, stuff it back in there!" She bumped Mandrake's side and did a weird hopping sidestep that was definitely not going to convince anyone of her sanity. "We're just betrothed. It's not weird! It's normal fine!"

"Oh my goodness," Blue said, blinking.

"What is happening right now?" Swordtail asked.

"All right, I'm sorry," Cricket said. She took a step back from Sundew, tilting her wings calmingly. "I totally misunderstood."

She hadn't, and she didn't, and she knew it. Sundew couldn't read other dragons the way she could read plants, but Cricket was like a wide-open encyclopedia, and at the moment, her pages were turned to "Mystery I Am Biting My Tongue About for Now But Will Definitely Solve Eventually." Which did not bode well for Sundew's secret.

"So. How can you have a fiancé?" Cricket asked. "Aren't you the same age as I am?"

"I'm six," Sundew said, "but ever since we hatched, the plan has always been for us to get married eventually. We both have the strongest leafspeak in the tribe. Which means our dragonets should be even more powerful, and that's what the tribe needs to defeat the HiveWings and restore the trees."

Unless I can do it all myself. Then I could be with a dragon I choose.

Mandrake was nodding. "Sundew's leafspeak is much stronger than mine, though," he said. "The strongest our tribe has seen in centuries."

"That's why Belladonna and Hemlock got together to have me," Sundew said. "They had the strongest leafspeak in the last generation."

"The tribe has been working toward having a dragon like Sundew ever since the Tree Wars," Mandrake added.

"Ohhhh," Cricket said, as though several answers were finally clicking together in her head.

"When did my parents get back?" Sundew asked

Mandrake. She wanted to know AND she also very much wanted to get off the subject of her future marriage.

"Not long before you," he said. "Maybe half a day? And only Belladonna and Odollam. Hemlock and the other two were going to ground near the, uh, the target." He cast a nervous glance at the other dragons.

"They know," she said. "We saw the fire. From a distance, I mean."

His eyes lit up. "Oh wow! Was it amazing? Belladonna said they torched the whole thing. Flames brushing the clouds! HiveWings screaming with rage!"

"We weren't that close," Sundew said. "We just saw the smoke. I don't know if the whole Hive burned down." *And I wouldn't trust Belladonna's report.* Her mother had a tendency to exaggerate, especially when it came to grand plans against Queen Wasp.

"The whole Hive," Blue echoed, gazing up into the trees. "And all the webs connected to it."

Mandrake had the grace to look a little abashed. "Was that your Hive?" he asked.

"No," Swordtail answered. "You guys burned down Bloodworm Hive, and good riddance. Good riddance to all of them."

Sundew saw Cricket flinch and Blue gently rest his tail on hers.

"BLEH!" Bumblebee announced suddenly. She threw the tuber at Swordtail's head, bonking him on the snout. "NOMOBLEH! GIMMEEGO! EEEEEMEGO!"

"Hey, ouch, you violent little larva," Swordtail yelped.

"Bumblebee, calm down," Cricket said, trying to wrestle the dragonet back into the sling. But the little HiveWing was too furious to be handled. She yowled and threw out her yellow-and-black-striped wings and flung herself around wailing until she managed to topple out of Cricket's arms onto the leaf mulch.

Immediately she popped up and sprinted over to Sundew, as well as she could sprint. It was more of a waddle, if one were going to be strictly accurate. Bumblebee collapsed on top of Sundew's foot and batted her woebegone amber eyes up in Sundew's general direction.

"Snudoo," she sniffled. "Snooooooooobleemee."

"Whatever a snoobleemee is, it's not my problem," Sundew informed her.

Bumblebee clutched her ankle as Sundew tried to pull away. "Hubblesnubbleooble," she said piteously. "Eeeeeeeeeeeeeeesnorf."

"How starving can you be?" Sundew demanded. "We'll be in the village soon, and there's plenty of food there."

Bumblebee's pinprick claws dug into Sundew's scales as she clambered up onto the LeafWing's shoulder and snuggled into the curve between her wing and neck. "Pennyfoo," she said confidently.

Sundew had never held a dragonet, or carried a dragonet, or ever had anything climb on her (apart from unpleasant insects), as far as she could remember. Her mother had outlawed pets in the village, because they wasted resources and distracted dragons from their mission. Dragonets were strictly supervised and kept to their own area, for their safety — and also probably because Belladonna didn't like them any more than Sundew did.

All her front-of-brain thoughts told her to peel off the baby HiveWing and give it back to Cricket. She did not need to walk into her tribe with a tiny enemy plastered to her neck, burbling cheerfully. Also, she shouldn't let Bumblebee get any more attached to her. Also also, what if Queen Wasp *did* jump into Bumblebee all of a sudden? Then the dragonet would be in the perfect position to strangle Sundew.

I'm not scared of Wasp! she scolded herself. *I can protect myself from a dragonet! And I don't have to prove anything to anyone in my tribe! So what if they don't like that I've got a HiveWing on my shoulder? I AM going to let her stay there, just to show them I DON'T care!*

"This is stupid. We don't have to sit here and wait for Wolfsbane," she said, resetting her wings to keep Bumblebee in place. "I don't need permission to go into my own village! Come on." She marched toward the trees.

"But, Sundew," Mandrake protested, "it'll only be a moment. Don't make them mad!"

"They're already mad!" she retorted. "They're going to be mad no matter what we do! And it's not like we're going to spend the night in the jungle. We're going in. Follow me, and don't ask questions," she said, giving Cricket a stern look.

"Even — I mean, yes, Sundew," Cricket said.

"Bring the panther," Sundew said to Mandrake. She sent a message to the thorn vines, and they relaxed, releasing the big cat's body enough that Mandrake could haul it over one shoulder and stagger along behind them.

The outer perimeter of the village was a short walk away. It looked like an upside-down nest, a huge emerald-and-chocolate-colored living dome made of interlocking vines and shrubs that soared up and up between the trees. The barrier enclosed the entire village, protecting the dragons inside from all the ways the jungle might try to sneak in to kill them. Hemlock, Belladonna, and Sundew's grandmother had started it, with their limited leafspeak, but Sundew had perfected it.

She tested it as they approached, sending her senses along the roots under her talons and out through the weaving branches to search for any holes or weaknesses. There was a patch where the leaves were thin; after a moment of pressing the edges with her mind, she found an infestation of caterpillars that were nibbling their way through the roof.

Oh, no you don't. Nobody eats my work! You will die for this, caterpillars!

She summoned another vine to coil across the thin spot, blending in with the other leaves. Except this one was full of toxic sap; when the caterpillars tried to eat it, they would be poisoned. Or they would see their friends dying, wise up, and go find a different plant to infest.

It was very satisfying. If only all Sundew's problems could be solved that easily.

"Wow," Cricket said as the whole barrier came into view, rising far over their heads. "How did you — er — I mean, I really wonder how dragons could build something like this, and how long it would take, and which plants were used, and how it survives, but notice how I am totally not asking, although I am definitely listening, should anyone around here maybe feel like talking about it."

"I'll give you a tour later," Sundew said, hiding her amusement.

Of course, Sundew could go in and out of the barrier anywhere she wished, just by communicating with the plants. But for the sake of appearances, when anyone was watching, she went through the main gate. Unless it was super annoying, and that depended on who the guard on duty was.

A long, elegant dragon sat in coiled stillness by the entrance, as poised as a carnivorous plant, waiting for her prey to pass by. Sundew squinted at her and saw streaks of pinkish red along her horns and the veins of her summer-green wings. She exhaled with relief. They were in luck; it was Cobra Lily, one of Sundew's favorite dragons.

Cobra Lily was the opposite of Nettle. She was never annoying or judgmental, and she rarely shouted. When Cobra Lily got angry, it was a deep, cold, icy anger that she held on to for the rest of her life, and only friends like Sundew knew it was there. Sundew had once seen her slip a deadly manchineel fruit into another dragon's lunch as payback for insulting her sister two years earlier. He'd survived, but only barely.

Cobra Lily was kind of awesome.

"Hello, beautiful," Cobra Lily said languidly as they came up. "You've got a little monster on your neck."

"You have no idea," Sundew agreed. "How's the village? Did I miss anything?"

"Boring without you." Cobra Lily leaned down to nudge Sundew with her snout. "You were gone *forever*. I nearly murdered Nettle just to make something interesting happen."

"I can't imagine anyone objecting to that. Anyway, I know, but wait till you see what I brought back." Sundew moved Bumblebee to her back so she could sort through her pouches.

"Spies and slugs, by the look of it," Cobra Lily guessed, eyeing the other dragons over Sundew's shoulder.

"The Book of Clearsight," Sundew said as she hauled it out and put it in Cobra Lily's talons. "And the secret of Wasp's mind control. We think." She brought out the length of vine she'd cut off the plant in Wasp's greenhouse. "Any idea what this is?"

Cobra Lily studied it for a moment before turning her eyes back to the book. "Never seen it before," she said.

That was disappointing. Cobra Lily was always top of the class; Sundew had hoped she'd be able to solve the mystery quickly. But there were other LeafWings Sundew could ask.

Thump went the little jade frog over her heart as she tucked the vine away again.

"Belladonna said this was useless." Cobra Lily flipped through the pages of the Book, scanning Clearsight's prophecies.

"It's not! No way!" Cricket burst out. "Because now we know the truth! Did she tell you what's in there? And how it changes everything?"

Cobra Lily leveled her cool gaze on Cricket. "Why is your prisoner talking to me?" she asked Sundew.

"She's not my prisoner; she's . . . I don't know, an ally, I guess. And she's right. I mean, we nearly got killed stealing it, so it better not be useless! I can't believe Belladonna said that." Sundew growled softly. Was Belladonna trying to downplay Sundew's successful mission?

Cobra Lily handed back the book. "Cool. Good luck explaining *them* to everyone else."

A moment later they were inside, or at least, into the detoxification chamber. Cricket looked around in puzzlement at the tightly woven branches that surrounded them. The space where they stood was barely big enough to fit four dragons (and one tiny dragonet) squeezed in together. It was *meant* for three, but of course Swordtail squashed himself in as well. Mandrake, on the other talon, was politely waiting outside for his turn.

"Get off my tail," Sundew said, shoving Swordtail away. "Bumblebee, close your eyes." The dragonet tilted her head quizzically, and Sundew reached up to cover the little HiveWing's face with one of her talons.

"Why are we all — AAAAAAAABGLBGLBE!" Blue shrieked as a cascade of water poured over them. Cricket threw her wings over her head, and Swordtail blundered back onto Sundew's tail, so she had to push him off again.

As quickly as it had come, the water was gone, sluicing away through a channel that led outside the barrier.

"That's to wash away any seeds that might have been trying to sneak in," Sundew explained. She pointed at the clusters of thorn balls and tiny winged seed pods that were spinning away on the surface of the dirty water. "The Poison Jungle is always trying to get through, and it has many tricks. But so do we! Bet you feel stupid now, seeds!" she shouted at them.

"The . . . seeds feel stupid?" Blue asked, blinking.

"Well, they SHOULD," Sundew said. "I've told them a MILLION times to stay out of here, but it's the one order they can't seem to get through their thick heads. Pods? Bark? Argh, there isn't a dragonspeak word for it."

"Maybe the instinct to spread is too strong," Cricket said thoughtfully. "It's survival to them, sticking to whatever will carry them the farthest, trying to plant themselves wherever they can. I mean, is it disobedience if they can't help it? How would a plant teach its seeds to fall off our feet before we enter the village? That would be so amazing if it could, though. Some kind of warning system, maybe? But it would have to know that going inside the village would kill it, somehow . . ."

She trailed off as Sundew pushed open the chamber door and they all stepped through into the murky green light under the dome.

This was the village. Sundew's home. The safest space in the Poison Jungle: a circle cleared of all the deadliest plants so that LeafWing dragonets had half a chance of surviving to adulthood. Instead of menacing strangler vines, dragon-traps, or deadly sandbox trees looming overhead, there was open air all the way to the roof of the dome, as high above them as the tree canopy. It was high enough for dragons to fly — and for dragonets to learn to fly — without the danger of anything snaring their wings or dripping poison on their scales.

Sundew was kind of unreasonably proud of this feature. Belladonna had started the walls, but she'd never managed to complete the overhead enclosure on her own, so it had only become truly safe in here once Sundew came along. Fatalities, especially among the dragonets, had dropped significantly.

But of course we can't talk about that. We can't take a moment to say, hey, things are a little better, aren't they? We can only talk about the HiveWings and our fury and all the things we're going to do to them. No time to pat you on the head or say "Thank you, Sundew."

She took a deep breath. Stepping into the village always made her heart beat faster and her ears lie flat, as though she was preparing for battle. It should have been the other way around. It should have been the jungle that set off her danger sensors. But in here, Sundew knew that her mother was always a few steps away — that they were always only moments from a fight.

"SUNDEW!"

Case in point.

Belladonna came thundering out of the meeting house, her wings billowing like storm clouds. She flew down the steps and landed with one claw already in Sundew's face.

"How *dare* you bring enemies into our village?"

"I told her to wait outside!" Wolfsbane cried, aggrieved. "Hey, I told you to wait outside!"

"Yeah, not sure where you got the idea that you can tell me to do anything," Sundew said to him. She batted her mother's claw aside. "And *you* might remember, Mother, that working with these dragons was your idea in the first place."

"Out there!" Belladonna yelled, pointing vaguely out of the jungle. "Not in here! WHAT IS THAT ON YOUR NECK?!"

"This is Bumblebee," Sundew said. She had to admit she was kind of enjoying how much she'd thrown her mother for a loop. "Isn't she cute?"

"Me mum me," the dragonet said, curling her tail around Sundew's neck and edging a little closer.

Other LeafWings were gathering, whispering, arguing in hushed tones all around them. One of them pointed at Cricket, and there was a ripple of scowls across all the green and brown faces.

"These are our allies," Sundew announced in a raised voice. "Anyone who hurts a scale on their bodies will find his or her eyeballs on the wrong end of a bombardier beetle."

She turned back to Belladonna. "Cricket, as you know, is immune to Wasp's mind control. And Blue is a flamesilk. They helped us get the Book of Clearsight — as *you* requested — and now they need a place to hide from Wasp. Seems like the least we could do, right?"

"A flamesilk?" one of the LeafWings called.

"Prove it!" called another.

Sundew grabbed Blue's wrist to stop him, but he'd remembered her lecture and was already shaking his head.

"Not in here, you bees for brains," she spat at the offending LeafWing.

"He doesn't have to prove it," Belladonna said regally. "We know what he is. It was his flamesilk we used to burn down Bloodworm Hive."

Blue gasped and pulled away from Sundew as the dragons around them went, "*Ohhhhh,*" in hushed, pleased tones.

"Wait, what?" Cricket said. "Blue's flamesilk? But . . . how?"

They didn't know. They never put it together. It hadn't occurred to Sundew that this would be a surprise to them.

Maybe an unforgivable surprise, judging by the looks on their faces.

"Is that true?" Blue asked.

"Sundew," Cricket said. "How did your parents get their claws on Blue's flamesilk?"

CHAPTER 5

"I gave it to them," Sundew said defiantly. "Of course I did. So what?"

Blue sat down and clutched his head. *"When?"* he cried. "How did you even have any?"

"I gathered some when you first came out of your cocoon," Sundew said. "Don't you remember? I put it in a stone jar. I wasn't sneaky about it."

"But you were with us from then until we escaped Jewel Hive," Cricket said. "Weren't you? I thought you didn't see your parents in all that time."

"I saw them the night after I got Blue's flamesilk," Sundew said. "While you were all asleep in the carpet stall outside the Glitterbazaar. I got up early and met them to give them my report — and the flamesilk, as they'd requested — and to ask for more time, as *you* requested, which they said no to again — and then came back and rejoined you before you woke up."

"Why didn't you tell us?" Swordtail demanded.

"I don't report to *you*," Sundew pointed out. "Belladonna was my mission commander."

"Not that you follow my orders very well either," Belladonna observed.

"I can't believe this," Cricket said to Sundew. "I keep thinking you . . . but then I keep being wrong."

Their expressions gave Sundew a squiggly feeling that she wanted to stab and stab and stab until it was dead. "How can you possibly be surprised?" she asked. "Where did you *think* they got the fire to burn down Bloodworm Hive?"

"I didn't think it was from *me*," Blue said. He buried his face in his talons. Cricket sat down next to him and spread one of her wings over him. "You took such a little bit."

"You only need a little bit of flamesilk if you have the right materials," Belladonna said briskly. "Although of course more is better. Which is why you're going to be so useful for the rest of the war."

Blue shuddered. "No *way*," he said. "I don't want to be useful for killing anyone!"

Belladonna's look was almost pitying. Sundew could *almost* see a dragon in there who felt guilty about what she wanted to do, and who maybe understood why Blue didn't want to do it. But that dragon was never going to be the one everyone else saw.

"You can't imagine we'd let a weapon like yours fall into our talons and *not* use it," Sundew's mother said. "Try to think of what we're doing as 'freeing your tribe' rather than 'killing the other one.' Does that help?"

"No!" Blue cried.

"If you want his cooperation," Sundew interjected, "you're going to have to take care of his friends. Safe harbor for both SilkWings and both HiveWings. And I do mean safe — no mysterious leaves in their food, no fire ants in their beds. If you want the flamesilk to help you, you have to take care of them just as well as you take care of him."

"But, Sundew —" Blue started, then yelped as Swordtail trod on his foot.

"What she said," Swordtail talked over him. "Exactly that, especially the no fire ants, please."

Belladonna sat back on her haunches and regarded them with narrowed eyes for a long moment. "Hmmm," she said. "Very clever, Sundew."

Sundew managed by the skin of her teeth not to say "Really?" in an excited little dragonet voice. She'd outwitted her mother! It was just like she'd said to Blue; he had to realize he had the power here, and together they could use it. They just had to be smart. And maybe he wouldn't want to use his flamesilk at first, but she could convince him . . . or figure out a way to use it that he wouldn't have a problem with.

"Yes," Belladonna said, flicking her tail and shooting Sundew an approving look. "Bringing us hostages to leverage in case the flamesilk was reluctant. Very, *very* clever. I knew we'd raised a smart little warrior."

Sundew's jaw dropped. That wasn't — she hadn't — that was not how this was supposed to go! Cricket and Bumblebee weren't *leverage*! There were even minutes when she liked Swordtail, every once in a while. She certainly hadn't meant to turn them over to her mother as hostages.

And maybe Belladonna knew that. Maybe the betrayed look on Cricket's face was exactly the reaction she'd been hoping for. Or maybe her mother really did think Sundew had tricked all these dragons into walking into her claws.

Either way, Belladonna saw them as her prisoners now.

Sundew's rage pulsed under her scales. She wanted to flay something. She wanted to upend all her pouches over Belladonna's head and let the insects devour her. She wanted to scream and tear down the barrier and let the jungle come surging in.

"I meant what I said," she hissed. "Anyone who harms these dragons will answer to *me*. That includes you, Belladonna."

"All right, dear," her mother said dismissively. WHICH WAS THE WORST. Sundew was going to STRAIGHT UP STAB HER just for that tone of voice, never mind everything else. Belladonna turned and waved one talon at Wolfsbane. "Let's put them all in Pokeweed's nest. He'll be hiding out with Hemlock for who knows how long."

"We'll take Bryony's, too," Sundew said. She knew which nests were free; she knew which dragons had been sent to burn the Hive. And she wasn't going to let Belladonna pen up Cricket and the others in one tiny place. It didn't have to feel like prison, even if it kind of was.

Even if this whole place feels like a prison to me sometimes.

From the moment she'd stepped back into the village, Sundew's claws had been twitching. She was so close to where she really wanted to be. She'd been gone for so long and she'd managed to focus on the mission for all that time . . . but now all she wanted to do was blast a hole in the barrier and run to her dragon.

She touched the pouch with the jade frog in it. *Not much longer. Don't make a stupid mistake now, with everyone watching.*

"Get them settled and come report to me," Belladonna said to Sundew. "I particularly want a full explanation of *that* thing." She flicked one claw at Bumblebee.

"We'll get the feast ready," Wolfsbane said, hurrying to where Mandrake had dropped the panther.

Bumblebee grabbed Sundew's ear and whispered, "EEEEEEEEEEEEEEEEEEE?" into it.

"Yes, come on, we'll find you something." Sundew turned toward the food stores.

"Wait," Swordtail said, jumping forward. "Sundew, ask about Luna."

Sundew was pretty sure her tribe hadn't found Luna; if they had captured another, more willing flamesilk already, they wouldn't be reacting this way to Blue. But she had promised to ask. She lifted her chin and looked up into her mother's sharp green eyes.

"Has anyone seen another SilkWing? She was blown out to sea several days ago — we wondered if she came ashore in the jungle."

Belladonna turned to look at one of her lieutenants, who shook her head. "Those are the first SilkWings I've ever seen," Byblis said, pointing at Blue and Swordtail. "We haven't run into any strange dragons in our territory." She started to say something else, hesitated, and then shook her head again. "No. We haven't brought anyone unusual into our village."

There was a very slight, barely perceptible emphasis on *our*.

Sundew heard it, and she knew what that meant, and that the smart thing to do would be to wait and get answers her own way later. But unfortunately, Cricket heard it, too, and she pounced.

"Did you say 'our village'? What does that mean?" she asked. "What were you going to say?"

Byblis shifted on her talons, stirring the leaf mulch under her claws. "Nothing," she said. "No confirmed reports. Only rumors. I don't bring every silly rumor back to our commander." She bowed her head toward Belladonna.

"Rumors of what?" Swordtail nudged Sundew's side. "Make them tell us, Sundew!"

"I must admit I'm curious as well," Belladonna said archly. "I give you permission to share, Byblis."

"Well . . . all right." The other LeafWing looked very uncomfortable. Byblis was one of Belladonna's most loyal dragons. She was in Sundew's earliest memories, following her mother's orders, watching over Sundew, making sure all the rules were followed. Byblis needed rules. She liked everything to fit into squares. She never set foot outside the barrier unless she was on a specific mission, and then she came right back. Sharing an unsubstantiated rumor without evidence to back it up must have felt like rubbing nettles on her palms to her.

"A few of the guards on patrol mentioned that there was . . . increased activity . . . over *there*," she said. "More noise, voices raised. Agitated trees. The ones with leafspeak said there was a whisper of something new, but you know how plants can be; they often don't know what they don't know. We believe we noted slightly more prey being caught. Nothing definite, mind you. But . . . *potentially* consistent with the possibility of one or more strange dragons perhaps having arrived . . . *there.*"

"Where?" Swordtail cried. "What are you talking about?!"

"Are you saying there's another village in the jungle?" Cricket said, glancing at Sundew. "Who lives there? More LeafWings?"

Belladonna snorted. "They don't deserve to be called LeafWings. *We* are the LeafWings! We're the ones who are still fighting for our future! We're not giving up on our tribe and rolling over like pillbugs! LeafWings. Pah." She stabbed her claws into the ground, dragged out a flailing earthworm, and sliced it into pieces.

"Mother has a *bit* of a complex about the other tribe," Sundew explained.

"We call them SapWings," Byblis added. "By order of the commander."

"My *order* was to *never speak of them,*" Belladonna hissed. "They might as well not exist, for all the use they are to us." She scrabbled up the dirt and reburied the carved-up earthworm bits.

"But Luna might be there!" Swordtail asked. "We should go ask! Sundew, can we go ask?"

"No one is going anywhere," Belladonna commanded. Sundew frowned at her, and perhaps something in her look got through. "Tonight, I mean," Belladonna added, a little reluctantly. "It's too dark for anyone to wander around in the jungle, especially brainless outsiders who can't wait to get eaten. I will consider sending them a message in the morning. *If* everyone behaves." For some reason, she looked at Sundew. Sundew gave her a matching glare.

"Luna's a flamesilk, too!" Swordtail said quickly. "She's way more likely to help you than Blue is! If the SapWings have her, you should definitely try to get her back here!"

Belladonna rubbed her chin. "Hmmm," she said. "An interesting point, butterfly dragon. I will include that in my considerations." She turned to go back into the meeting house in a definitive, this-conversation-is-over kind of way.

As soon as she was gone, Bumblebee tugged on Sundew's ear again. "EEEEEEEEM," she said vehemently.

The food nets were full to overflowing, most likely in preparation for the feast. Sundew walked Bumblebee over to them and let her pick out a mango, then a piece of dried capybara, then a bowl of river snails (which Bumblebee took one bite of and promptly flung at Sundew's face), and then another mango, and then she had to wrestle the dragonet away from the food and drag her back to the others.

"HrrrmbleGRRR," Bumblebee growled. She flopped onto

Sundew's shoulder and set her tiny teeth into a piece of capybara, which Sundew suspected was a second strip the dragonet had smuggled away somehow.

Blue and Cricket and Swordtail had fallen silent as she came up to them. They were all looking at her as if they weren't quite sure whether she was Sundew, the dragon who'd been helping them and protecting them and saving their butts for the last several days, or a dragonet-eating crocodile instead.

"The nests are this way," Sundew said, stomping past them. She didn't have to explain herself. She was a LeafWing! Besides, they were her prisoners when she met them. They should be grateful that now at least they were valuable prisoners.

And she'd helped with their problems, too, hadn't she? She'd helped save Blue's sister, even though it made Belladonna grumpy. It certainly wasn't Sundew's fault that Blue had immediately lost her again. Sundew had also helped Swordtail find the Chrysalis, and she'd helped with Cricket's starry-eyed "let's save the tribes with truth! and flyers!" plan. She'd done all kinds of dangerous nonsense for these outsiders! How dare they be all aghast that she was still a LeafWing, loyal to her tribe, at heart?

I don't need them to like me. I don't need anyone to like me except one dragon.

"Here," she said, stopping at Pokeweed's nest. It was a ramshackle assortment of branches woven into a sort of egg shape. Sundew wasn't even sure if it would keep out the rain. Pokeweed was a big dragon who didn't care much about his own physical comfort. He lived to destroy HiveWings; that was all. But at least his nest was big enough to fit two sleeping dragons comfortably.

"Blue and Swordtail can take this one," Sundew said. "Cricket and Bumblebee in that one." She pointed to Bryony's nest, which was close by, and much tidier than Pokeweed's. The two of them were near the outer edges of the village, along a path lined with nests that led to the meeting house.

"What about you?" Blue asked. "Aren't you going to stay with us?"

Sundew squinted at him. Hadn't he just been giving her an "oh, you're a monster" face?

Maybe I misread it. That was Cricket's expression . . . but maybe Blue's was just sad face, and I mistook it for hating-me face?

"I have my own nest," she said, flicking her tail toward the woven sphere where she slept. She'd been so thrilled when she turned two and Belladonna and Hemlock had given her permission to move out of theirs and build her own. It had taken her a while to notice that no other dragonets left their families before the age of five. But she didn't dwell on that. After all, she saw plenty of her parents all day long during training and lessons. She *liked* the peace and quiet of being completely alone at night.

I do like it. Besides, it's much easier to sneak out of the village this way.

"Of course," Blue said.

"How will we remember which ones are for us?" Cricket asked, pacing around the cluster of nests. "They all look the same."

Sundew scrunched her eyebrows quizzically. They looked *nothing* the same. The branches came from different plants or were woven in different ways and . . .

She took a deep breath. *Help one more time, and then I can leave them to Belladonna if I want to.*

Sundew reached into the ground with her leafspeak. She found a tendril and followed it back, calling roots to her, until a vine curled through the soft dark earth and climbed up, weaving around the doorway of Bryony's nest. Purple morning glories burst from the buds as it settled in place.

"There," she said. "Think you can figure it out now?"

"Thank you," Blue said.

"So cool," Swordtail breathed.

"Sundew —" Cricket started.

"I have to go report to Belladonna." Sundew disentangled Bumblebee from her neck and passed her into Cricket's talons. The dragonet protested sleepily, breathing capybara breath into Sundew's snout, but it didn't take long before she was curled up in Cricket's arms with her eyes closed.

"It's just . . . aren't you our friend?" Cricket asked. "There's so much you didn't tell us, like about the flamesilk or the other village or the secret plans to burn the Hives or the dragon you're going to marry . . ."

"Maybe not everything is your business!" Sundew flared. "Maybe you don't *need* the answer to *every question in the world*. Maybe I was a little busy helping you investigate Queen Wasp and burning down greenhouses and keeping you alive!"

"It's not her fault, Cricket," Blue said, leaning against the HiveWing's side. His shimmering blue-purple scales were dimmer in the green light that filtered through the dome, but his flamesilk glowed like fireflies under the scales on his wrists. "She was trying to help by bringing us here. She's been working on her tribe's plan her whole life — she's only known us for a few days. It makes sense that she didn't tell us everything. And you know she didn't want them to burn Bloodworm Hive."

"Do I know that?" Cricket asked. "Sundew, can you protect Blue if he doesn't want them to use his flamesilk anymore?"

"Of course I can!" Sundew shouted, and they all jumped back. "By all the trees! It's like you cannot keep straight in your heads who are the good guys and who are the bad guys here! When it is very obvious! ARGH AT YOU!" She whirled and flung herself at the path toward the meeting house.

As she stormed off, she heard Swordtail say, "She's right. I have no idea if her mom is the good guy or the bad guy or what right now."

Sundew did *not* let herself think, *Neither do I.*

She did *not* let herself worry about who was honest with her and whom she would rescue from a burning Hive and whether being manipulative was normal for a mom and a leader and what was going to happen next to Blue and his friends.

She gave her report. She showed Belladonna the length of vine from Wasp's greenhouse. Belladonna recognized it from the days they'd spent hiding there, but neither she nor any of the dragons she summoned knew what it was either.

Sundew also explained what they'd learned about Wasp's mind control, just as she'd promised Cricket she would. And as she'd predicted, Belladonna didn't care. The entire HiveWing tribe was still trapped in Wasp's power. It didn't matter how they got that way. They still had to be defeated, every last one of them, and the only decision left to make, according to Belladonna, was which Hive to burn next.

After giving her report, Sundew stopped by the weapons storehouse, where Mandrake, as usual, was sorting and taking care of the hazardous insect collection. He was always happiest in here, tending to the bullet ants and venomous centipedes.

Sundew took off her empty pouches and reorganized her weaponry and supplies between the rest of the leafy bags, then resettled them around herself.

"Do you want to restock?" Mandrake asked. He gestured at the wall of neatly labeled boxes. "More sleep lilies? Or smoke leaves?"

"Not tonight," Sundew said. "Maybe tomorrow." She was too tired to plan a new set of weapons, and she didn't know what the next threat would be anyway.

Sundew sat through the feast, but she didn't feel like eating panther or dancing with Mandrake or smiling at any of the dragons who came to congratulate her on a successful mission. As glowing night blooms lit the village, she watched her fellow LeafWings sidle up to Blue and Swordtail, testing out questions, slowly letting them in. She saw Cricket try to join the conversations, and she saw all the LeafWings turn away from her with their wings curled and teeth clenched. She saw the looks they gave Bumblebee as the little HiveWing dragonet ate everything she could reach, and she saw how Bumblebee seemed to sense it and grow smaller, staying close to the shelter of Cricket's wings.

Don't make every problem your problem, Sundew. Not right

now. Just get to midnight, and deal with everything else tomorrow.

And then, finally, finally, the feast ended. The LeafWings started crawling into their nests. Two dragons took up their posts outside the village entrance. Blue paused in front of Sundew as they headed down the path to the nests.

"Are you sure you don't want to stay with us tonight?" he asked.

She shook her head. She wanted to be with someone who made her feel more like herself, not dragons who made her feel like an untrustworthy snake. Swordtail waved from the doorway of Pokeweed's nest, and she nodded back.

She climbed into her own nest and watched through the branches as the village went quiet.

Finally, finally, finally the time came.

Almost midnight.

Time to go.

Sundew slipped out of her nest and padded stealthily to the far side of the barrier from the entrance. The plants here knew her very well. They'd been trained to grow in a way that looked impenetrable to anyone else, but as she approached, they sensed her and leaned away from one another, bending and twining until there was a hole in the barrier just big enough for a small LeafWing.

She hopped through and let it close behind her. The jungle night was noisier than the day, between the insects and night-prowling predators, the declarations of the frogs and the skittering clouds of bats overhead. She used her leaf-speak to clear the way, warning off the dragon-traps and sundews. She knew this route by heart, better even than she knew the names of her fellow LeafWings.

Soon she was at the pond. Dark water rippled in front of her, reflecting slivers of light from the three moons.

Sundew set the small jade frog on the boulder in the center of the pond, climbed the nearest safe tree, took a deep breath, and curled herself on a branch to wait for Willow.

CHAPTER 6

It was the frog's fault, really, that Sundew had discovered the SapWings when she was only two years old.

Not the jade frog. This was an actual frog, small and brownish green with orange flecks across its knobbly back. A frog that hopped into Sundew's bowl of taro, snarfed up the sugar-sprinkled grasshopper she'd been *saving* for dessert, stuck out its tongue at her, and then jaunted off into the jungle as if it aggravated dragons every day with no consequences.

Well, THAT was not going to stand. NO, SIR. THIS time, there would MOST DEFINITELY BE CONSEQUENCES, FROG.

She chased the frog to the thorn-vine fence, Belladonna's original version of the barrier, where it popped through a gap in the leaves and vanished into the jungle.

Now, dragonets under four years old were not technically allowed outside the safety perimeter of the village on their own. But Sundew was not like the other LeafWing dragonets. And really, she was *almost* three, which was *practically* four. And plus also, what was she supposed to do? Just LET the frog taunt her like that?

Besides, she knew the jungle better than any of the other dragonets. She was a Venus dragon-trap slayer! She had battled cobra lilies and sundews and pitcher plants and beaten them all! She had mighty superpowers! No one could stop Sundew, chosen one, daughter of the leaders of the LeafWings! Especially not on a QUEST FOR VENGEANCE.

This frog was going DOWN.

Sundew glanced around to make sure no one was watching — most of the adult dragons were in a council meeting, so it seemed fairly safe — and then hurtled over the fence.

The jungle on the other side of the thorns looked a lot like the jungle on her own side, except maybe the plants were bigger and grew more thickly entwined. She spotted the miscreant frog right away. It was squatting in a patch of wet leaf mulch, chewing in a *very* self-satisfied way. Chewing *her grasshopper*.

"AHA!" Sundew roared, pouncing on it.

Her claws squished into the disintegrating leaves and mud, but somehow missed the frog, which leaped several feet into the air and bounded off through the undergrowth.

"NO!" Sundew shouted. "You will PAY FOR THIS!"

She shot after the frog, ducking under snapping plant teeth and weaving through thickets of strangler vines that tried to tighten and ensnare her. She was moving too fast for them, but not fast enough to catch the frog, who could bounce right over quicksand that she had to go around. At one point, she lost the frog and had to freeze for a moment — and then it made the mistake of leaping away again, and she was after it at once.

Sundew was surprised when they broke through into a clearing and she realized the sky was turning purple. She didn't think she'd been chasing the frog for *that* long . . . but she hadn't been paying attention to anything except the flicker of its legs up ahead. One of the moons was already climbing the sky.

Belladonna and Hemlock were going to be furious.

Not as furious as I am, she thought. *With THIS FROG, who caused all this TROUBLE in the FIRST place and must FEEL MY WRATH.*

She slowed down as she slipped out of the trees, realizing there was a pond in the clearing, fed on the far side by a small silvery stream. A boulder as smooth as obsidian stuck up out of the water near the middle of the pond, and some of the far trees leaned down toward it like parent dragons feeding their little ones. Not particularly like *Sundew's* parents, that is, but like a few other parents she had seen among the tribe.

The frog had paused by the edge of the pond, half-buried

in the mud. Sundew could see its eyes rolling back toward her and its throat pulsing rapidly.

She crept forward on stealthy talons, placing each claw silently, crouching close to the ground, and holding her wings perfectly still.

Here I come, frog. Prepare to die.

One step . . . another . . . closer . . . and . . . POUNCE!

Her claws closed on mud and thin air. The frog disappeared into the pond with a smug *plop!*

"ARRRRRRRRRRRGH!" Sundew roared, shaking the leaves on the trees overhead and making several dragon-traps snap shut on nothing. "You SLIPPERY, flea-brained, smirking, BUG-EYED SON OF A HIVEWING! I am going to DESTROY YOU!"

Even in her rage, she knew better than to leap into an unfamiliar body of water without checking for waterwheels and bladderworts first. She whipped around, wrenched a large branch out of the nearest tree, and started furiously stabbing the water with it. Droplets flew up and drenched her face and wings, and the underbrush rippled with tiny animals scurrying away from the enormous splashes she was making.

She checked the sharp end of the branch. No impaled frog. No tangles of deadly underwater plants either, but that didn't mean there weren't any. If she went into the water and got drowned by a hungry waterwheel instead of fulfilling her great stupid destiny, her parents would strongly disapprove.

BUT THE FROG. IT COULDN'T GET AWAY WITH THIS.

"Come out and face me like a reptile!" Sundew shouted. "I'm going to bite off your legs and feed them to a tarantula! I'm going to pour piranhas into this pond and tell them all to eat you slowly!"

"By all the trees," said a voice above her. "Who *are* you talking to?"

Sundew jumped back, startled.

A pale green dragon sat on the boulder, blinking down at her. She had definitely not been there a moment earlier.

Also, she was a dragonet, out beyond the safety perimeter, just like Sundew.

Also, Sundew had never seen her before, which didn't seem possible in a group as small as the LeafWings.

Also, she had the deepest brown eyes Sundew had ever seen.

"My archnemesis," Sundew growled in response to her question. "Who is hiding in this pond but NOT FOR LONG because I am going to DESTROY HIM. Or her. Whatever it is."

The new dragon tilted her head to study the water. "Wow. What did this terrible, extremely doomed fiend do to you?"

"It STOLE my GRASSHOPPER, which I was — you know what, it doesn't matter," Sundew said, noticing the amusement that was sneaking onto the stranger's face. "What it DID is not the point; what I am going to do TO IT is COMPLETELY JUSTIFIED, trust me. I just have to catch it first."

"Are we . . . we're not talking about a dragon, are we?" the stranger asked.

"Nnnnoooo," Sundew admitted.

The other dragon wrinkled her snout thoughtfully. "A crocodile? A monitor lizard? Oh, a Gila monster! Those things are *cranky*. I nearly got in a fight with one last two moons night, because I stepped on its tail, but I obviously didn't mean to! Hey, maybe it's the same one!"

"It's not," Sundew snapped. She scowled at the water. "It's . . . a frog," she said at last. "But a VERY BAD frog who deserves STAMPING ON."

"Oh, no. That's — oh dear." The stranger covered her face as though she was overcome with sympathy, but Sundew could see her shoulders shaking.

"Don't you laugh at me!" she yelped. "You would understand if you'd seen its stupid smug face! I can't *stand* smug faces. I just want to SMUSH THEM ALL FLAT. You should have been here five heartbeats sooner, then you could have seen it SMIRKETY SMIRKING its way into the pond."

Sundew glanced around at the dimming sunlight. "Where . . . *did* you come from anyway?"

The stranger waved one of her wings at the trees behind her. "From the village, of course, silly."

But the village wasn't behind her. It was quite a long way in the opposite direction.

"Um. What?" Sundew asked, which wasn't exactly the incisive line of questioning she'd been planning on.

"Who are you?" the other dragon asked. "I feel like I should really know you already."

Sundew drew herself up and made her fiercest face. It was one thing for Sundew to not know this stranger, but it was inconceivable for this stranger to not know *her*. "Yes, you should! I'm *Sundew*. Who are *you*?"

The dragon tilted her head. Her scales were dappled with darker green leaf shapes, like the shadows of long oval leaves. Her eyes looked like they were smiling. Her whole *face* was doing a weird crinkly sparkly thing that made Sundew's face want to do the same thing. Crinkling and sparkling! What kind of weird brain magic was this?

"Sundew, really? That's an unusual name," she said.

"No, it's not!" Sundew snapped. "I mean, it is, technically, because I'm the only one who has it, but everyone's heard it, so it's very well-known, which means it can't be unusual, by that definition, I mean, is my point, and besides, YOUR name is the weird one, it's . . . just, SO WEIRD . . ." The brain magic was doing something to her words, too! She frowned as severely as she could. *Stop crinkling, face!*

"I haven't told you my name yet," said the other dragon, sparkling even more.

"Well, I BET IT'S WEIRDER THAN SUNDEW." Sundew fluffed out her wings.

"I'm Willow," said the dappled green dragon with the perfect face.

"There, see, I was right," Sundew said. "Like, who ever knew anyone named Willow, NOT ME."

Willow tilted her head, looking confused. "What do you mean by 'well-known'? I've . . . never heard of you. Should I have?"

Sundew flicked her tail and accidentally knocked a startled lizard into the pond. "I'm the daughter of Belladonna and Hemlock!" she said. "You know! The whole plan? I'm the one who has to save Pantala?"

"Save Pantala from what?" Willow asked.

Sundew's jaw dropped. "From THE HIVEWINGS!" she cried. "Don't you know anything? Where have you been? Who *are* you?"

"Oh!" Willow's front talons flew to her face. She stared at

Sundew as though a lightning bolt had dropped out of the sky and asked for directions. "I know why your names are weird! You're a *PoisonWing*!"

"A what?" Sundew barked, but Willow had already flown off the boulder to land beside her. She circled Sundew, studying her wings and tail with wide eyes. Up close, she carried a scent of mint and chocolate and new rain.

"But how can you be? You look just like us!" Willow said. "Maybe a little prettier." She met Sundew's eyes and ducked her head, doing that full-face smile crinkle thing and trying to hide it at the same time. "Maybe a lot."

Which was a weird and wrong observation, because Willow was the one with the river-deep eyes and the sparkle face and THAT WASN'T THE POINT, SUNDEW.

"I'm not a poison-anything," Sundew said. "I'm a LeafWing."

"But you're one of the offshoots, aren't you?" Willow asked. She stopped circling and sat down, checking the ground below her for anything thorny first. "The scary dragons with all the dangerous-plant names?"

Sundew stared at her. "Offshoots?" she echoed. "I thought . . . we were the only ones. The only LeafWings left."

Willow's sparkly look dimmed a little, as though someone had thrown cobwebs over her starlight. "Oh . . . no," she said. "There's us. The rest of us. The, um . . . sorry, I'm not sure how else to say this . . . the real LeafWings? The ones who stayed with Queen Sequoia and are still loyal to her."

"Queen Sequoia is still *alive*?" Sundew said, startled.

"Wow," Willow said. Her wide-eyed look was sort of unreasonably adorable. "I can't believe they keep us a secret from you! We learn all about the PoisonWings in school."

"What do you learn?" Sundew asked, curiosity warring with anger. Did Mother know about this? If so, how DARE she hide anything from Sundew! "What do they tell you about us?"

"Oh, you know . . . how some dragons wanted to keep fighting the Tree Wars, so they split off from the rest of the tribe when we reached the Poison Jungle. And then they started naming their dragonets after deadly plants instead of giving them tree names, like LeafWings always have. And how they've been plotting revenge on the HiveWings all these years. Queen Sequoia met with their leader last moon cycle — she's always trying to convince her that it's safer to stay here and lie low until Queen Wasp dies."

Met with their leader — there was only one dragon that could be.

Belladonna. Sundew's mother. Sundew wondered which "hunting expedition" or "council meeting" had been the lie Belladonna had tossed her way to hide her secret meeting with the LeafWing queen. The queen who was still alive, even though Sundew and the other dragonets had been taught that she died during the Tree Wars.

Willow was still talking. "I mean, can you imagine how dumb it would be to go poke one of the Hives? As long as they think we're extinct, we're safe. But if we let them know we're still out here?" She shuddered.

"Excuse me," Sundew said, bristling. "So your suggestion is we let them win? We let them steal our continent and revel in our extermination? We just accept living *here*?" She waved her wings at the Venus dragon-traps overhead, which had been slowly leaning down toward them, closer and closer as the conversation went on. Sundew dug a rock out of the mud and threw it at the nearest plant. It snapped shut and drew back, and the others around it bristled.

"It's not that bad here," Willow said. "Right? I mean . . . I think it's better with, um . . . interesting company." She gave Sundew that crinkle-sparkle smile face that made all the words in Sundew's head run around bumping into one another like disoriented moths.

Do NOT smile back at her, Sundew. She is fundamentally wrong about your entire life purpose! WHAT IS YOUR FACE DOING, SUNDEW?

"We deserve to be out *there*," Sundew said, trying to focus on everything she'd been taught. Belladonna had trained her to summon her anger at a moment's notice; that was a safe place to go when Sundew's other emotions got too complicated. "Wasp could live for another hundred years, or she could be replaced by someone equally bad. We can't just sit around and wait for history to sort itself out. We *have* to fight! We have to *make* things better with our own claws!"

Willow blinked at the fist Sundew was making, and then she reached out and took it between her own front talons. She smoothed out the tension and laid one palm over Sundew's, her scales warm and light as a fern frond. Sundew could feel Willow's heartbeat, going only about half as fast as Sundew's.

"Shhhh," Willow said softly. "You don't have to do anything right this second. Just be here. Breathe."

No one had ever told Sundew to "breathe" before. Her first instinct was to scoff that she already WAS breathing and she did it rather often and was quite good at it, thanks very much. But there was something in Willow's face, in her eyes as she gazed down at Sundew's talons, that made her impossible to scoff at.

They stood like that for a moment. One of Willow's graceful wings was a breath away from brushing Sundew's, like a butterfly hovering just over a leaf. Sundew wondered if the butterfly was as aware of it as the leaf was. She wasn't sure if her heartbeat was slowing down or Willow's was speeding up, but at some point, she realized they had synced.

"Don't you think *thump* is a terrible word?" Willow said thoughtfully. "I mean, that's what most dragons would say our hearts are doing, but it doesn't *feel* thumpy to me. *Pulse* doesn't seem right either. *Beat* sounds too violent. It's not quite tapping. There should be a better word for this."

"For two heartbeats finding each other?" Sundew said, as quietly as she could, trying not to break the spell.

Willow gave her a shy sideways smile. "I hope so."

Sundew didn't know what to say. Belladonna would have told her to push the other LeafWing into the pond and yell at her about the Tree Wars and how important it was to go kill Wasp. She would have pointed out that Sundew had a duty to marry Mandrake and raise superpowered danger-babies to destroy their enemies. Belladonna would have said there was nothing more important than their vengeance, and that Willow was not worth talking to.

But Belladonna was a liar, and Willow was the only dragon who'd ever given Sundew this all-over-inside-sparkles feeling.

She let her wing brush Willow's lightly. "Guess what, I've made a decision."

"You have?"

"Yes." Sundew cleared her throat and made a portentous face. "I have decided to spare that odious frog's life in your honor."

"Oh!" Willow laughed. "That's too bad. *I* had just decided to camp out by this pond until it emerges so I could murder it for you."

"What?!" Sundew couldn't stop herself from laughing, too. "No one has ever offered to murder a frog for me before!"

"Well, no one has ever offered to *not* murder a frog for me before," Willow said. "It's very magnanimous of you."

"That's me," said Sundew. "Ever so magnaganimous."

"Can you come live with us?" Willow burst out. "Come be a LeafWing and meet Queen Sequoia and forget about fighting and see me every day?"

That was the first time she'd asked, but it wasn't the last. Nearly every time they met, Willow offered again to bring Sundew into the other village, to give her a home and teach her how to be a peace-loving SapWing (a name Willow never used and quite disliked).

But every time, Sundew had had to say no.

No. I have a purpose.

No, my tribe needs me. Your tribe needs me to do this, too, even if none of you realize it.

No. I have to save the world first.

"I'm sorry," she'd said that first time. "I can't."

Willow had looked away, wings sliding slowly down, but

Sundew had caught her talons before she could pull away entirely.

"But can I see you again?" she'd asked. "Tomorrow night? And the night after that? Maybe also the one after that and the one after that and the one after that? I can sneak out; it's easy."

Willow had laughed again, and the next night she'd given Sundew the jade frog. *Our signal,* she'd said. *So I know if you're there. Leave it on the rock, and I'll come find you.*

In the ensuing four years, Sundew had convinced her mother that even the youngest dragonets needed to know about the SapWings, instead of only learning about them when they turned four. But Belladonna never took her to her meetings with Queen Sequoia, nor did she ever tell the council what they talked about. She'd forbidden Sundew to go to their village or try talking to any of them. She seemed to find Sundew's interest in them suspicious, and she hated hearing about them in any case.

So Sundew kept Willow a secret. Her secret.

This was the longest they'd gone without seeing each other. She'd told Willow it might be a while, but she'd been gone even longer than she expected. And she hadn't told Willow why, or where she was going.

A light rain started to fall, misting through the leaves

above Sundew. She wasn't sure how much time had passed. Only one of the moons was visible through the canopy now.

Will she still come? What if she's given up watching for the frog?

But at last the shadows around the pond rippled and one glided up to the boulder and then down to the moonlight in front of her, becoming the silhouette of the only dragon Sundew ever looked forward to seeing.

Sundew leaped out of the tree and bounded over the grass into Willow's wings.

CHAPTER 7

"You were gone *forever*!" Willow said, clasping Sundew's front talons in hers. "I have so much to tell you! I've been waiting and waiting and checking the boulder every night and it was dreadful and I didn't like it and let's never do that again! I was half afraid Belladonna must have found out about us. I started to wonder whether I needed to mount a daring rescue operation — blast through the barrier! Knock the other PoisonWings aside! Tear down your prison and sweep you away to safety! Wouldn't that have been so heroic?"

Sundew twined her tail around Willow's. "The most heroic, romantic thing ever, but totally unnecessary. You know Belladonna couldn't keep me locked up, even if she wanted to."

She reached her leafspeak into the earth, sending her power along the roots until she found what she wanted, and summoned a spray of violets from the ground. They sprang up, small and beautiful and purple, right beside Willow's claws.

"Show-off," Willow said affectionately. This particular clearing was probably the most colorful spot in the jungle, thanks to the clusters of flowers scattered all over it, which Sundew had grown for Willow in the last three years. "So what have you really been so busy with? I had this awful nightmare that you left the Poison Jungle and ran into Wasp. It felt so real, I almost told Queen Sequoia about it, but she's always reassuring us that Belladonna wouldn't endanger the rest of us by . . . that she'd at least tell . . . Sundew?" she said, her voice faltering at the expression on Sundew's face. "What is it?" She let go of Sundew's talons and covered her mouth. "Oh no . . ."

"I did leave the jungle," Sundew said. "Don't freak out."

"But you weren't seen," Willow said. "*Nobody saw you*, because you were careful, right?"

"We *were* careful," Sundew said slowly. "I mean . . . *we* were careful . . ."

"Who's we?" Willow asked. "What does that mean?"

"Belladonna, Hemlock, and I made it to Wasp Hive without any trouble," Sundew said. "But we couldn't get inside at first. And then we ran into these . . . other dragons."

"Oh no, oh no," Willow whispered.

"But it was all right!" Sundew said quickly. "Two of them

were SilkWings, and the other is a HiveWing who can't be mind-controlled and she's on our side. Now, I mean. We kind of dragged her onto our side, but I think she was heading that way anyhow. Technically she's really on this one particular SilkWing's side, but he might be with us, unless Belladonna has ruined it, but the point is, they were fine and wanted to help. Well, agreed to help. In a couldn't-say-no but basically agreeable-ish sort of way."

"I'm going to have a heart attack," Willow said. "So you met some allies and came straight home? Safely? Without being seen?"

"Well . . . no," Sundew admitted. "We . . . kind of stole the Book of Clearsight."

"WHAT?" Willow shrieked, sending an explosion of sleeping birds catapulting into the night sky.

"Shhhhhhhhhhhhhhh," Sundew said, reaching to cover Willow's snout. "We had to have it! We needed to take away Wasp's secret knowledge of the future. Or at least, we needed to know what it says, too. Right? Isn't that one of Sequoia's eternal arguments, that we can't do anything against Wasp because she has this all-knowing book to warn her of our every move?"

"Yes, but that's insane," Willow said. "That book must have been the most heavily guarded object in the most heavily guarded Hive in Pantala."

"It was," Sundew said. "But not anymore! Ha ha! Now it is MINE!"

"No *way*," Willow said. "You really did it? Did you read it? Are you now the most all-knowing dragon in all the land? The future spread out before you! All the secrets of what's to come!"

"So," said Sundew, "no."

"No?"

"Turns out, the whole Book mystique was an enormous lie. Clearsight did leave a few prophecies, but they petered out over a thousand years ago. *Nothing* Wasp told us was true."

Willow stared at her in the moonlight. "Wow," she said softly. "Didn't you once guess that? A couple years ago? You said, 'What if none of it is real? What if there never was a Clearsight and everything we've been told about the Book was made up by a sinister HiveWing somewhere along the way?'"

"Did I say that?" Sundew flicked her wings, pleased with herself. "Well, I was half right. It looks like Clearsight was real, but so were the lies and the sinister HiveWings all over the last thousand years."

Willow took a deep breath. "OK," she said. "So that's amazing. You snuck into the Hive, into the Temple, stole the Book, got back out again, and came straight home without being seen. Right?"

"Um," said Sundew. "No."

"No?! Sundew!"

"Not exactly. I mean . . . we did sneak *into* the Hive without being seen. And the Temple. The actual stealing and running away went . . . less well."

"By all the trees," Willow said. "You *were* seen? Sundew, tell me you weren't seen!" Her wings were shaking. Sundew grabbed her front talons again.

"It's all right! I'm here, aren't I? I made it back safely. I even brought our new allies with us. One of them can shoot fire! A fire-blasting dragon *and* the Book of Clearsight — that's a pretty successful mission, don't you think?"

"But HiveWings *saw* you. So they know we're not extinct. Oh, maybe no one will believe them!" Willow said. "It'll be like seeing ghosts or scavengers — a dramatic story to tell at parties, but no one takes it seriously. Right? Maybe the others will think they were hallucinating. Having wild visions! Imagination run amok! And everyone will laugh at them and say, 'Ha ha, LeafWings, they're all dead! You goof! We scoff at your hilarious story and definitely are not even remotely considering going out with an army to hunt down and kill the rest of the tribe. Because there aren't any left! LeafWings, how amusing.' This could happen. That's probably how it will be. I mean, how many HiveWings saw you, after all? One? Two?"

Sundew scrunched up her face.

"Three?" Willow said nervously.

"More like . . . all of them?" Sundew admitted.

"ALL OF THEM?"

"You have *got* to stop shouting," Sundew said. "Your village isn't that far away. And I'm not up to dealing with any dragons who aren't you tonight."

"You can't possibly mean *all* of them," Willow said.

"Well," Sundew said, "in the sense that Queen Wasp possessed the entire population of Wasp Hive, summoned them to the Temple, had them all attack us, and then watched me escape, I think technically, yes, all of them is pretty accurate. Oh wait! Actually, only all of the ones in Wasp Hive. Not the other Hives. So that's only one out of nine Hives, like, so, really only one-ninth of the HiveWing population. See? You were right. Not all of them, after all."

"All the dragons in Wasp Hive," Willow said faintly, "with the queen in their heads, attacked you and saw you and watched you escape with the Book of Clearsight."

"Yes," Sundew said. "Now you've got it. It was a very impressive escape, if I do say so myself."

"So," Willow said, "basically we're all going to die."

"No!" Sundew cried. She reached up and brushed her claws gently along Willow's face. "No, we're not, Willow. We're going to *win* this time."

"How can you possibly think that? Even if we could win eventually, war means dead LeafWings, especially war against Queen Wasp. And we can't win, because nothing is different from last time except there are fewer LeafWings to start with!"

"That's not true," Sundew said. "Things are completely different." She started counting off on her talons. "We have a flamesilk. We have the Book of Clearsight and know the truth about it. Our half of the tribe has been preparing for war for fifty years and have lots of new weapons. The SilkWings are restless and oppressed and unhappy — I mean, not all of them, I think, but enough to have formed an underground anti-HiveWing movement, so they won't just blindly go along with Wasp this time. Also, the HiveWings will be too scared to come fight us in the Poison Jungle. *And* we know the secret of Queen Wasp's mind control." She let go of Willow and tugged the vine out of its pouch. "It's a plant. This plant. She must eat it or something, and she injects it into HiveWing eggs to put the dragons inside under her power."

She held it out, and Willow sniffed the leaves, then ran one claw lightly along the prickled stem.

"I don't know it," she said. "If it grew here, surely you'd be able to sense it, wouldn't you?"

"I tried." Sundew had been trying, from the moment they

stepped into the jungle. She'd been sending her leafspeak out into the jungle, tracing along root pathways and tangles of underground mycelia as far as she could go. "A couple of the oldest trees did that 'hmm' thing they do when something seems familiar, and once I thought I heard a relative of this plant echo back from somewhere far away. But I lost it, and none of the trees could tell me where it might be."

"There are dragons we could ask in my village," Willow said. She hesitated, then touched her forehead to Sundew's for the length of five heartbeats. "I think you need to come to my village, Sundew. I think it's time."

Time to meet the SapWings. To see how the other tribe lives. What it's like to be a village of cowardly dragons instead of warriors for justice.

Time to finally see Willow's home.

"I can't." Sundew let go and stepped back. "I'd be betraying my tribe. Belladonna would be furious . . . and wouldn't you get in trouble?"

"Not as much as you will," Willow said. "I mean, a lot of dragons will be mad. But we *have* to tell Queen Sequoia about all this, don't you see? She needs to know about the Book, and the flamesilk . . ."

Sundew started to interrupt, then stopped herself, but Willow knew her too well to miss that.

"What? Is there something else?" she asked.

"Maybe . . . one more thing," Sundew said. "She'll *probably* want to know about the Hive we burned down."

Willow opened her mouth, then closed it again, then opened it again, like a really adorable but totally flabbergasted dragon-trap in the rain.

"Sorry, I didn't get to that part," Sundew said. "Hemlock took a few other dragons to burn down one of the Hives. I only saw it from a distance, but there was a lot of smoke, so I think it must have worked."

She decided not to mention burning Wasp's greenhouse as well. She'd let that come up later, at a more natural and hopefully less tense point in the conversation.

"Then we don't have any time," Willow said, taking a step back toward her village. "I thought we'd have a moment to plan, but that's an act of war, Sundew. Wasp is probably on her way here right now with the whole brainwashed HiveWing army behind her."

"Doubtful," Sundew scoffed. "And I still can't —"

"I agree with Willow," interjected a new voice. An enormous, long-necked LeafWing emerged from the trees behind Willow, ducking her head to avoid the lower branches and dangling dragon-traps. Her tail was scarred with claw marks and dragged in the pond as she came toward them. Sundew saw, with horrified fascination, that she was missing an ear and half of one of her horns. This was a dragon who had been in battle and fought hard. This was also a dragon who had been alive for a very long time — a dragon who could still remember the ancient forests before the Tree Wars.

And from the way she walked, and the way she tilted her head to look down at them, and the way she held her wings like majestic jewels, this was a royal dragon.

The royal dragon.

"Hello, Belladonna's daughter," said Queen Sequoia. "Willow is correct that I need to know everything. I think it is high time you joined the real LeafWings."

— CHAPTER 8 —

"Your Majesty!" Willow gasped.

Sundew found herself bowing her head instinctively, and she quickly jerked it back up again. She was a true LeafWing — or a PoisonWing, as the SapWings called them — and more important, she was Sundew and she bowed to *nobody*.

Queen Sequoia smiled faintly. "You have exactly your grandmother's stubborn expression. I saw it many times during the Tree Wars."

"My grandmother?" Sundew echoed, surprised. She'd heard of her, of course, all the time, but she'd died before Sundew hatched.

"She was my best general." Sequoia sighed. "And my most loyal, until I finally gave her an order she couldn't follow: give up and run away. That's when she left me and started your group instead." She turned, offhandedly sweeping a noisy toad into the pond with one talon, where it sank with a startled *glorp*. "Come. We will be safer in the village."

I shouldn't. I should turn and run home. Belladonna will LOSE HER MIND if she discovers I've run to the SapWings to tell tales on her.

She wasn't sure whether it was the idea of Belladonna's apoplectic face or the air of authority around Queen Sequoia, but she found herself following the queen with Willow by her side.

"Did you tell her about me?" Sundew hissed at Willow. "Did you bring her here?"

"Sundew," Willow said patiently, in the tone of a teacher reminding her students that three plus three always equals six. "I wouldn't do that, and you know it."

She did sort of know it, but there was a part of her that was still mad that she'd been caught like this, and she wanted someone to blame. Sundew scowled. *I can blame Queen Sequoia. What was she doing spying on us? How dare she! I will definitely tell her how I feel about that in as mad a voice as I like. I don't have to treat her like a queen! I can yell at her if I want to! Maybe not right this second. Maybe later. When I FEEL LIKE IT.*

"Don't be scared," Willow whispered.

"I'm not scared!" Sundew snapped, loud enough for the queen to glance over her shoulder at them. She lowered her voice. "When am I ever scared? What do I have to be scared of? She's just a big dragon. She doesn't even have an army. I'm *not* scared."

Willow stopped and took one of Sundew's talons. In the dark, Sundew felt the smooth familiar weight of the jade frog come to rest in her palm. She tucked it back into her pouch, brushed her wing along Willow's, and felt her heart rate start to calm down.

"I'm sorry she followed me, but I'm not sorry you're coming to the village," Willow said, starting to walk again. "There's something I can't wait to show you."

"You did say you had something to tell me," Sundew remembered sheepishly. "What is it?"

"I mean, *I* think it's exciting," Willow said. "Maybe not as much to you, after all your almost dying and war starting. But guess what? There are strangers in our village! Three of them! And you'll never believe where two of them come from! It's amazing. Wait until you see them."

"Is one of them a SilkWing?" Sundew asked. "One of the SilkWings I brought to the rainforest is looking for his sister." She stopped herself just in time from adding, *And our spies thought you might have her.* She was quite sure that Queen Sequoia was listening to them, even though she was several steps ahead.

"Actually, yes, the third one is a SilkWing," Willow said. "Aww, I hope we can reunite them."

Sundew flicked her wings, surprised and pleased. What were the chances that Luna would have blown ashore here? And survived and been rescued by the SapWings before Sundew's tribemates or the dragon-traps or the cobra lilies or the snakes got her?

That would solve a few problems, if we could give Luna to Belladonna instead of Blue. A willing flamesilk ally would be a much better bargain than hostages who have to be coerced into helping us. Then Blue and Cricket could do whatever they want to do next, and if they don't want to be my friends anymore, that's just fine.

But first Sequoia would have to agree to give up Luna. What if she has her own plans for using flamesilk?

"And the other two?" she asked.

"You'll see." Willow flashed her an unmistakable grin, sparkling even in the darkness under the trees. Sundew felt a funny shiver in her chest, as though her heart had shaken raindrops off its wings.

Even after everything I just told her, even though she thinks I've endangered her tribe and restarted a war she doesn't want . . . she still loves me.

In Sundew's life, love mostly came in the form of yelling

and criticism and judgment. Her parents "loved" her, and showed it by telling her everything she did wrong, correcting her mistakes, and starting shouting matches whenever they were the slightest bit aggravated.

It still confused her sometimes when Willow did none of that. It was confusing her right now. Wasn't Willow angry at her?

She'd never seen Willow get angry.

It was kind of unsettling, honestly. Sundew had thought about it for years and eventually came to the conclusion that Willow must just hide her anger really well. But did that mean it would erupt one day, all of a sudden, and burn down their relationship? These were the things Sundew worried about at night.

She'd expected to find a wall or barrier or fence like the one she'd built around her own village, but instead the SapWing village crept up around them, like termites. The first sign was that all the dragon-traps disappeared. Sundew had never walked through a stretch of jungle with no dragon-traps in it — nor, she realized, were there any sundews, or pitcher plants, or anything else that ate dragons.

Sundew was looking so carefully for carnivorous plants that she missed the first few leaf houses, but then, they were overhead, and it was dark.

Suddenly she noticed a cluster of phosphorescent moss in a tree up ahead, and as they approached, she realized it lit up the interior of a kind of leaf globe tree house, perched in the higher branches.

"Whoa," she said, stopping without realizing it. Willow nudged her forward again, and then Sundew spotted more and more of them. The trees were full of the leaf houses — not so different from the nests in her village, except that they were in the sky, covered in leaves, and much bigger than her own. She guessed each would fit at least six dragons comfortably, at least of the ones she saw.

Now she heard voices, too: here and there the murmur of dragons talking, and not far away, someone singing a lullaby. She heard a dragonet chirping and his parents sending him back to bed. She heard the soft rustle of dragons leaping from tree to tree, possibly tracking the queen's movements — *and mine*, she guessed, her claws curling into the dirt.

Willow and Sequoia spread their wings at the same time, and Sundew followed suit. They leaped into the air and led her to the largest tree house of all, a structure that spiraled all the way around an enormous baobab, with several levels, balconies, and rooms built out along the massive branches. Sundew couldn't see all of it in the dark, but from the night blooms that were lit up in a few rooms, she was able to see dark-purple-and-white clematis vines twining all around the columns and bright red trumpet creepers dangling from the ceilings.

They landed in a room on the top level with a smooth polished wood floor that must have taken a lot of work to make so slippery and shiny.

A young LeafWing was waiting for them, curled on a mahogany throne, sewing sheets of speckled paper together to make a book. She looked a little older than Sundew, with large brown eyes and deft dark green claws.

"Hazel," Queen Sequoia said reprovingly as the dragon looked up. "What have I told you about bookmaking at night?"

"It's . . . an efficient use of my time?" Hazel guessed with a mischievous grin.

"You will ruin your eyes." The queen tugged the pages out of her talons as Hazel protested. "And then we'll either have to steal glasses from the HiveWings or have a blind queen, and I don't like either of those plans."

Sundew gave Willow a startled look.

"That's the queen's great-granddaughter," Willow whispered. "Princess Hazel, next in line for the throne."

Oh, right — Willow had mentioned Hazel a few times. Mostly in the context of why Queen Sequoia refused to restart the Tree Wars. Something about not wanting to lose any more dragons.

"I think glasses are cute," Hazel said breezily. "And we won't have to steal them if the scouts are right about the PoisonWings capturing a real flamesilk today!"

"*Hazel,*" the queen said in a warning tone. "This is Sundew. Belladonna's daughter."

Hazel's jaw dropped. She stared at Sundew for a long, awestruck moment.

"That's how you were supposed to react when you met me," Sundew whispered to Willow.

"*The* Sundew?" Willow gasped, widening her eyes theatrically. "The one and only Sundew? The one who *almost* slew the great and terrible grasshopper-stealing frog menace of the jungle?"

Sundew bopped her on the nose with her tail, and Willow dissolved in giggles.

"Am I allowed to say hi?" Hazel asked her great-grandmother.

"Yes, of course," Queen Sequoia said, a little impatiently. "Especially if it gets you off my throne, go on. Chairs are for old dragon bones, not bendy little saplings like you."

Hazel bounded off the throne and skidded across the floor to Sundew's feet. "Hello! I'm Hazel — sorry, you know that. I hear about you all the time! Belladonna thinks *you* should be queen instead of me; do you think so, too? She's so scary! Sorry, I know she's your mom. Ack, I'm saying all the wrong things." She drew herself up and did a rather impressive imitation of Queen Sequoia's regal expression. Even her voice went hilariously fancy. "Welcome to the LeafWing village. We are delighted you could join us. Tea?"

"Oh, you don't have to be queen-face Hazel for Sundew," Willow said.

"Yes, she does," Queen Sequoia called just as Hazel was starting to relax her wings. She snapped them back into elegant arches immediately. "It's good practice, and none of us know Belladonna's daughter as well as you apparently do, Willow."

"Oh . . . I . . . we met . . . um," Willow stammered.

"By accident," Sundew said. "It was my fault. Not that we have anything to apologize for! Whoever said we couldn't know each other? I mean, that would be a stupid rule."

"I believe that is Belladonna's rule," Sequoia said, rubbing her forehead. "Isn't it? No fraternizing between PoisonWings and LeafWings?"

"We're not PoisonWings," Sundew snapped. "And even if it is her rule, it's still stupid and she didn't even make it until after I met Willow and she can't tell me what to do or who to like anyway, it's none of her business."

"It's a little bit her business," Sequoia pointed out. "As both your mother and your commander. But I'm not actually remotely interested in you and Willow or how you met or why she's been sneaking out and staring wistfully at an empty pond for the last several nights." She pointed one long claw at Sundew. "I heard you say something about a book, a flamesilk, and a burned Hive. The full story. Now."

Sundew didn't *have* to tell her; technically this wasn't *her* queen, if the tribe had officially split in two. But then again, if she had to choose between obeying this queen or following her mother's orders, she kind of liked the idea of choosing this one. And she did need help identifying the vine, if she was still following Cricket's daft plan of trying to un-brainwash the HiveWings.

Plus, it would make Belladonna so mad, and she fully deserved it.

So Sundew told the queen everything — the whole story about leaving the jungle, hiding in the greenhouse, meeting Blue and Cricket, stealing the Book, rescuing Blue, sneaking into Jewel Hive, finding the Chrysalis, spreading the truth about the mind control and the Book, Cricket kidnapping an egg for some reason, escaping, figuring out that the mind control was connected to a plant, watching Bloodworm Hive burn from a distance, and then taking advantage of the tribe's distraction to burn down Wasp's greenhouse of mind-control plants.

"And then we came home," she finished. "And nobody followed us and everything is fine. Mission accomplished. All good. Vengeance on track."

The queen leaned back into her throne with a weary expression. Sundew wondered how old she was. As old as she looked? The Tree Wars were only fifty years ago, and she'd been a young queen when Wasp tried to steal her power and usurp her tribe, if Sundew remembered her history correctly.

"I can't believe Belladonna did it," Queen Sequoia said in a thin voice. "After all our conversations! After everything I've said to her! Her mother was so loyal, but that *viper* —" She snapped her jaw shut suddenly and took a deep breath through her nostrils.

"Great-grandmother?" Hazel said.

"DO NOT TALK TO ME I AM CALMING DOWN," Sequoia barked.

The three younger LeafWings looked at one another, then back to the queen. Sequoia was staring so hard at a knot on the end of her throne that Sundew thought it might burst into flames. She kept breathing in and out, extremely loudly, through her nose.

"Are you —" Hazel started.

"NO I AM NOT," Sequoia growled. "SHUSH."

Hazel sighed. "This could take a minute," she whispered to Sundew.

"Does this happen a lot?" Sundew whispered back.

"Only when she's *really* mad. Usually she can squash it pretty well without this whole theatrical interlude."

"I can STILL HEAR YOU." Sequoia thumped the side of her throne with her tail. "I am TRYING to COUNT until I FEEL CALMER and less like MURDERING EVERYONE."

Sundew tilted her head at the queen. "Count?" she echoed, glancing at Willow.

"That's why all her meetings with Belladonna take so long," Hazel joked. "Because she has to take deep breaths and count to calm herself down after everything your mom says, or else she might end up strangling her."

"She should try!" Sundew said. "Why doesn't she just yell at her? Or us?"

Willow gave her an alarmed look. "I don't want her to yell at us!"

"But then maybe she'll feel better," Sundew pointed out.

"Well, *I* wouldn't!" Willow said. "I'd feel awful! And I bet she would, too. Does yelling make you feel better? It's only ever made me feel worse."

"Oh my goodness," Sundew said. "I must hear every story about you yelling at someone right this minute."

Willow scrunched her nose at her. "I was very little, it was only once, and I still feel guilty about it."

"Well, *I'm* sure they deserved it," Sundew said loyally.

"Great-grandmother tries very hard not to yell at her subjects," Hazel said in her queen-face voice. "She was a more impulsive, angry dragon back during the Tree Wars, and she has come to believe it got several of her subjects killed. She has made an effort to become a wiser, calmer ruler, thanks in large part to the implementation of this counting-to-ten strategy."

"She must be past ten by now," Sundew said. "*I* could have counted to nine hundred in this time."

"Not with a trio of aggravating twigs chattering like magpies in the background," Queen Sequoia interjected sternly. She took another deep breath. "I am calm. Everything is fine."

"I just want to say," Sundew blurted, "that I for one am very glad you were an angry dragon when the Tree Wars started, because it meant you fought back against Wasp's power grab and didn't just roll over for her like Monarch did. I'm *glad* you fought for our tribe and protected us from her. I would *hate* for the LeafWings to be stuck where the spineless SilkWings are right now. So thank you for being a mad dragon and I say keep it up and let's go fight some more!"

The queen gazed down at her for a long moment, and then a flicker of a smile crossed her face.

"I think Belladonna made a mistake leaving you out of our meetings for all this time," she said. "You're considerably more persuasive than she is."

Sundew fluffed up the frill along her spine and beamed. *Take that, Belladonna! I knew I should have been invited! Just like I've been saying!*

"But no," said Queen Sequoia. Sundew deflated as she went on. "My LeafWings are not getting involved in another war."

"Do we have a choice?" Willow asked. "Won't Wasp come after all of us now, after what happened to Bloodworm Hive?"

"I suspect she'll be even angrier about her greenhouse than the Hive," Sequoia said thoughtfully. "Especially if that was her only supply of this mystery plant, and she needs it to control her tribe. Let me see that vine."

Sundew pulled out the cutting, which was looking a little the worse for wear after going in and out of her pouch several times. She stepped forward and draped it over Sequoia's outstretched talons.

Something happened to the queen's face. It was fast and hard to catch in the dim phosphorescent light, but Sundew thought she saw recognition and horror flash through the queen's eyes. Her claws closed around the vine compulsively, crushing it slightly, and then she released it again and took another deep breath.

"You know it!" Sundew said. "You've seen this vine before!"

"I'm . . . not sure," Sequoia said. She rose abruptly to her feet. "I need to consult my books. Go away and come back after dawn. All three of you," she added with a stern look at Hazel.

Sundew kind of wanted to ask for the vine back, but she had a pretty strong feeling the queen would say no, and then what would she do — try to wrestle it out of the massive dragon's talons?

I'll get the truth out of her when we come back, though, she thought as they all took a step back toward the edge of the balcony. *She definitely knows that plant.*

"Can I take Sundew to meet the new dragons?" Willow asked.

"Yes, yes," the queen answered, waving them off.

"They're asleep, you nut," Hazel pointed out with a grin at Willow that made Sundew absolutely wild with jealousy.

"Then we'll just peek at them," Willow said. "Come on, Sundew!"

The new dragons, it turned out, were only a few levels down the same tree, in two side-by-side interior rooms that Sundew noticed were not prison cells, *exactly*, but were not exactly wide open to the rest of the village either. She also couldn't help but notice the vines of thorns and toxic sap that wound around the doorways, or the four LeafWings stationed nearby, casually playing pickup twigs in the hall in the middle of the night. They gave Willow and Sundew suspicious looks but went back to their game with a shrug when they saw Hazel with them.

"The SilkWing is in there," Willow whispered, pointing to the first doorway.

Sundew peered inside, her heart thumping. This whole time, she'd felt confident that Luna was all right. Her sense of Luna, from the short time they'd been together, was that Luna could absolutely take care of herself. But Blue and Swordtail had worried so much and so incessantly that it must have rubbed off on her a little, because now she felt a tremor of weird excitement as she peered into the dark room. Luna, at last! Safe and sound! So everyone could shut up about her and focus on the mission!

Except . . . it wasn't Luna.

She couldn't see the sleeping SilkWing very clearly, but she could see that the wings were a dark color, maybe blue or purple, not the pale pearly green that Luna's were. And there was no flamesilk glow from this SilkWing's wrists.

"What's wrong?" Willow said softly.

"Not the dragon we're looking for." Sundew shook her head with a sigh. Blue was going to be disappointed. Swordtail was going to be worse; he was going to be SUPER ANNOYING about it. But Luna *had* to be all right. She must have just landed . . . somewhere else. "Where did you find her?"

"Trapped in a Roridula not far from the border," Willow said. "She's lucky we got there before it ate her."

"I wonder what a SilkWing was doing *inside* the Poison Jungle," Sundew said thoughtfully.

"Escaping from HiveWings, I think," Willow said. "Now, come see the others." She tugged on Sundew's elbow and led her to the second doorway. Sundew found herself holding her breath as she looked inside.

For a moment, she didn't know what she was seeing. There were two dragons, asleep back-to-back with the bigger one's wing tented over the smaller one. The smaller one seemed to be greenish, like a LeafWing, but the wing she could see was an odd shape, not leaflike at all. And the other dragon was . . . not green . . . maybe blue? Like a SilkWing . . . but with only two wings?

Strangest of all, they were both kind of glowing.

She squinted at them.

Yup. Little patterns in their scales had a faint glow to them, all along their wings and across their snouts and down their tails. As though they had rolled in phosphorescent moss, except it seemed to be really part of them.

"What *are* they?" she breathed, awestruck.

"They call themselves SeaWings," Willow whispered. "And they come from the Distant Kingdoms."

—— CHAPTER 9 ——

Willow and Sundew spent the rest of the night in a pile of leaves in Hazel's room. Willow offered to take Sundew back to her own home, but she was clearly nervous about waking her dad and explaining Sundew to him in the middle of the night. So they decided it would be easier to sleep in the queen's tree house and deal with grown-ups in the morning instead, with daylight to help, and after the queen spoke to them.

Sundew fell asleep almost as soon as she lay down next to Willow, the long days of flying and stress catching up to her all at once. She had a moment to breathe, a moment of feeling Willow's tranquil heartbeat through their scales, a moment to think, *Stay on guard, I don't know this village, there are strangers all around me, except Willow, I have Willow, right beside me . . .* and then she was out, in a darkness beyond dreams.

She slept well past dawn, as she realized when she finally awoke to find the sun shining cheerfully, already ambling up the curve of the sky.

She sat up quickly and blinked at Hazel, who was perched in her hammock, reading a book.

Hazel's room was bright and airy, studded with open windows and balconies so the breeze flew through it, but sheltered from the rain by an overhanging roof of large round leaves. Three desks took up half the room, even when they were shoved into the corner to make space for the leaf pile Sundew had slept in. Each desk was covered in a mess of bookbinding supplies made from jungle ingredients: some kind of sap glue dripping over the sides of its pot, tree fiber threads draped everywhere, and bark for the covers scattered about, dyed in colors from deep berry red to summery daisy yellow to a swirl of purple and pearl white.

Bright red trumpet creeper flowers poked through the roof, and Hazel had hung small paper dragons and clouds from every leaf stem, so there was a little blizzard of them flying overhead.

Sundew blinked again and looked over her shoulder to see Willow still asleep beside her. Willow had one wing flung out to the side, the way a baby dragonet might sleep, and her cheek was pillowed on her front talons in a cute smushy way.

Focus, Sundew!

Or pause for a moment to be happy. That's what Willow would say to do. After all the craziness with SilkWings and sneaking through Hives and dealing with strangers, I'm back with her at last, where I can just be myself.

She sighed. *All right, moment over.*

"Hazel," she said, and the princess finally looked up from her book. "Aren't we late to meet your great-grandmother? Weren't we supposed to be there at dawn?"

Hazel's wings lifted and fell in a shrug. "She sent a messenger that she wasn't ready yet. She'll call us when she wants us, don't worry."

Sundew frowned at her. "And what am I supposed to do until then? Just sit around this village like an orchid waiting to be stomped? Dragons will be looking for me! Also I have things to do!" She thought of Blue and Cricket and Bumblebee and Swordtail. Would they worry about her? Or would they think she'd abandoned them, as would be typical of her according to them apparently?

I hope someone feeds Bumblebee, she caught herself thinking, and then she wanted to smack herself. That dragonet would 1,000 percent make sure someone fed her; she didn't need Sundew for that. None of them needed her.

"You're doing the most important thing," Willow said sleepily. "You're investigating the mind-control plant *and* warning us that the HiveWings know we're here. That's pretty important, if you ask me."

"The HiveWings don't know we're *here*," Sundew pointed out. "They know we're still alive, but they don't know where."

Willow propped her chin on one talon and gave Sundew a skeptical look. "You don't think they'll guess pretty quickly? Hmmm. Where could those dragons who like trees possibly be? Oh, perhaps in the only bit of forest left on the whole continent, which also happens to be the only place we haven't been able to go for the last fifty years, what a coincidence."

Sundew felt unease ripple under her scales. Was Willow right? Would it be that easy for Wasp to find them? She'd assumed Wasp would come after them eventually . . . but also that she'd waste some resources searching the whole continent first.

"It doesn't matter if they guess right," she huffed. "The Poison Jungle will fight them off! Even if they arrived at the Snarling River today, they couldn't get through to either of our villages. The jungle will eat them alive."

"I hope you're right," Willow said. "Hey, while we wait, let's go talk to those SeaWings! Don't you want to meet them?"

Sundew's scales prickled with excitement and nerves.

She'd nearly forgotten about them while she slept. Dragons from the Distant Kingdoms! She couldn't believe it, but Cricket was right — it was a real place, where dragons really lived.

"Yes," she said. "Let's do that right now."

"We can take them some breakfast," Willow said, sitting up and stretching. "Hazel, want to come, too?"

The princess shook her head. "I'm at a really good part," she said apologetically, holding up her book. "You know Great-Grandma usually never leaves me alone for this long, so I want to take advantage of it while I can."

"I get that," Willow said. "See you later!"

"Bye," Sundew mumbled, following Willow out of the room. They flew down to the kitchen level, where two busy dragons waved at Willow and made puzzled faces at Sundew but didn't stop their whirl of chopping and peeling and preparing. Willow scooped up two halves of a coconut, gave one to Sundew, and filled them both with strips of dried mango and raw fish.

"It seems like most of the dragons in the palace know you," Sundew observed.

"I guess," Willow said, glancing around at the chefs. "I mean, everyone kind of knows everyone. There aren't that many of us in the tribe, after all."

Because the HiveWings tried to wipe us out. And then half of us left to form our own tribe, Sundew thought, with an odd twist of guilt under her usual anger.

"Do you come here a lot, though?" Sundew asked, watching Willow dig out and open a barrel of macadamia nuts. "To the palace, I mean? . . . Maybe to see Hazel?"

Willow crinkled her snout at Sundew. "Hazel *is* a friend of mine," she said, "like all the dragonets our age in the village. But if what you're *really* asking is 'Hey, Willow, have you by any chance fallen in love with some other dragon while I abandoned you to go start a war and frolic with SilkWings?' the answer is no, I haven't, you're still the only dragon for me, even when you ask silly veiled questions." She tossed a nut at Sundew, which bounced off her nose before she caught it.

"Oh," Sundew said. "Well then. Good. Fine. I mean, that *wasn't* what I was asking, but since *you* brought it up, that's great and good and fine with me."

"And?" Willow prompted.

"And . . . thank you for the macadamia nut?" Sundew guessed.

"And you're still the only dragon for me, too, Willow, light of my life, I promise I will never fall for a beautiful SilkWing and leave you." Willow put one talon dramatically to her forehead.

"By all the trees!" Sundew said. "Of course! That's obvious! That's so obvious. I don't need to say that, do I? You know all that. I mean, *obviously*. As if! Leave you for a SilkWing! BLEH."

Willow giggled. "I know," she said, "but you should say it all the time anyway."

"I can't imagine you would take me seriously if I said things like 'light of my life' all the time," Sundew said, balancing the coconut and its contents carefully as she spread her wings and flew off the balcony with Willow.

"I will always take you exactly as seriously as you deserve," Willow said, grinning.

"That is not a comforting answer, light of my life," Sundew said. Willow started laughing so hard, she nearly dropped her coconut.

A different set of not-quite-exactly-guards were gathered outside the strange dragons' rooms. These four were bent over a map of the jungle around the village, pointing out spots where unwanted plants were trying to get in and comparing stories of their valiant battles with dragon-traps.

They glanced up at Willow and Sundew but didn't move to stop them or even ask what they were doing there as they landed.

"Can anyone in the village just stop by to see the weird dragons?" Sundew asked.

"I suppose so," Willow said. "But I probably visit them the most, because I'm the one who found them."

"You ARE?" Sundew blinked at her in surprise.

"Didn't I mention that?" Willow said. She flicked her wings back and batted her eyelashes. "I *rescued* them! From a GIANT anaconda! If it weren't for me, they'd be super dead! And then we'd have nothing but the remains of two interesting corpses to study." She sighed.

The bluer dragon poked her head out of her room. In the daylight, it was a little harder to see the dots of phosphorescent scales around her eyes and along her snout bones, but her deep blue color, unusual wing shape, and — Sundew noticed for the first time — webbed talons were much more obvious. "Willow!" she said brightly. "I always know it's you when I hear someone talking loudly about heroic anaconda rescues. I will forgive you for the corpse comment because you come with food."

"Hi, Tsunami," Willow said, passing her one of the coconuts. "This is Sundew, my girlfriend."

Unexpected tiny starbursts of joy exploded all through Sundew's body, from her toes to her wingtips. They had never told anyone that before! Hearing Willow say it out loud, casually, to a totally random dragon, was probably the second-greatest moment of Sundew's life, right after meeting

Willow. She wondered what the blue dragon must think of meeting a LeafWing wearing whatever incredibly giddy expression she probably had on her face.

"Hello, Sundew. What kind of tree is that?" Tsunami asked, backing into the room so they could enter. The other dragon lay on his side by the wall. He looked slightly ill, but he lifted his head curiously to see them.

"It's not a tree: it's a plant that eats dragons and other animals," Willow explained. "She's one of the PoisonWings I told you about."

"That's not what we call ourselves," Sundew said quickly. "We're LeafWings, real LeafWings."

"She might be able to answer some of your questions," Willow said to the dark blue dragon, "because she's just been to the Hives."

"Oh!" Tsunami said, looking at Sundew more intently.

"Hi," croaked the other SeaWing. "I'm Turtle. Sorry I'm not getting up. I don't feel very well."

"He swallowed a *lot* more of the Gullet River than I would recommend," Willow explained. "I'm sure he'll be all right in another day or two. The ginger tea has been helping, hasn't it, Turtle?"

"Hrm," he more or less agreed, flopping his head down again.

"Poor dragon," Willow said. "You know, I told them to turn around and go straight back to their continent, but it's a good thing they didn't. I don't think Turtle would have made it."

"Grmbph," he groaned.

"You really came all the way from the Distant Kingdoms? How did you get here?" Sundew asked Tsunami. She could practically hear Cricket banging off the walls of her brain, yelping questions. These dragons from the Distant Kingdoms would absolutely make her lose her mind. She'd probably be even worse about them than she was about her beloved mysterious reading monkeys.

"We swam," Tsunami said. She held up one of her webbed talons, then pointed to what looked like gills along her neck. "SeaWings can breathe underwater. So we'd swim until we got tired, take a nap at the bottom of the sea, eat some fish, and then keep going. It felt like heading off the edge of the world. For most of the trip, we couldn't see any land in any direction — maybe an island in the distance, unless we were hallucinating those. But we were trying to stay on a course due west, following the stars if my brother has any idea what he's talking about.

"It took us about four days of almost nonstop swimming, but I bet I could have done it in three by myself. I'm not sure if Turtle is really sick or just still recovering from all that exercise."

"Oi," Turtle protested weakly. "Right here! And really sick!"

"That's a long time to swim without knowing anything was out here," Sundew said. *They must be out of their minds. What kind of lunatics would swim off the edge of the world for no reason?*

"But we did know this continent was out here," Tsunami said, surprised. "Didn't you tell her, Willow?"

"I thought you should," Willow said.

"A Pantalan dragon washed ashore on our coast several days ago," Tsunami said. "She got caught in a storm and blown over the sea to us."

"In a storm?" Sundew echoed, her ears perking up. "Does she have pale green wings and glowing wrists?"

"Whoa . . . you know Luna?" Turtle said from the corner.

"I thought LeafWings and SilkWings didn't talk to each other," Tsunami said to Willow. "For example, Luna didn't say *anything* about this jungle."

"Or about dragon-eating plants. Or dragon-eating giant snakes. Or dragon-poisoning rivers," Turtle mumbled.

"I only met Luna briefly," Sundew said, "when we rescued her from the flamesilk cavern."

Turtle and Tsunami exchanged significant glances. "So that part of her story was true," Tsunami murmured. "Willow had never heard of a flamesilk cavern."

"I'm sure it was all true!" Sundew said. "Luna's feisty for a SilkWing, but she's still a SilkWing, and they're a pretty simple tribe. Whatever she told you, you should believe it."

"Really?" Tsunami said. "She was very worked up about the plight of the SilkWings. She wanted us to gather an army and charge across the ocean and destroy the HiveWings to save her tribe."

Sundew leaped to her feet, her eyes shining.

"Uh-oh," said Tsunami.

"YES!" Sundew cried. "Do that! DO THAT!"

"Hang on," said Turtle.

"How big is your army? What kinds of weapons do you have? How soon can they be here? Are they on their way? Are you the advance scouts?"

"Sundew, don't get too excited," Willow said, reaching out to touch one of Sundew's shaking wings with hers. "They're not sure they should get involved."

"Why WOULDN'T you?" Sundew yelped. "Don't you care about fighting injustice and — and — and evil? EVIL? YOU COULD STOP EVIL, DID YOU THINK OF THAT?"

"Hey!" Tsunami protested. "I've stopped PLENTY of evil! And so has Turtle!"

Sundew gave him a skeptical look but decided to refrain from asking how that was possible. "Then stop this one!" she said to Tsunami. "The HiveWings are the worst and they deserve to be wiped out!"

Tsunami's face closed down suddenly, like a dragon-trap slamming shut.

"We don't wipe out entire tribes," she said firmly. "And we will never help anyone who'd be willing to do that."

"But don't you know what they did?" Sundew cried. She felt like all her hope was slipping away, like chocolate in a dream, melting through her claws before she could eat it.

At that exact wrong moment, Hazel poked her head in the door.

"Wow," she said. "Can't you all hear that?" She jerked one claw over her shoulder. In the pause that followed, Sundew heard the unmistakable roars of a horribly familiar voice, somewhere on the jungle floor outside.

"Oh no," she said, looking at Willow. She didn't even realize she'd held out one of her talons until Willow took it and squeezed it reassuringly.

"What is that?" Tsunami asked.

Sundew sighed. "My mother is here."

— CHAPTER 10 —

Willow, Sundew, and Hazel reached Sequoia's throne room first. The LeafWing queen was sitting on her throne with her eyes closed and her forehead furrowed, as though she had a massive headache. *That's only going to get worse*, Sundew thought grimly.

"Your Majesty —" Willow said.

"We heard Belladonna outside," Sundew finished for her. "I don't know how she guessed I was here! I often leave the village at night or in the early morning to hunt. I didn't think she'd come looking for me so quickly, or that she'd ever think to check among the SapWings."

"Ah," Queen Sequoia said, opening her eyes. "She didn't think of it. I summoned her."

"SUMMONED her?!" Sundew said, flabbergasted. Nobody *summoned* Belladonna. Also, how dare the queen! "Why didn't you ask me? Or at least warn me? I don't want to see her! I mean — here, now, like this." She forced herself not to glance at Willow, not to give away too much with a look. She wasn't ready to tell her mother everything yet. She didn't want Belladonna to ruin this, the way she definitely would.

Queen Sequoia looked faintly incredulous. "*I* don't want to see her either, but we don't have time for my peace of mind or your family drama. Wasp is about to throw her entire brute force at us, every claw and tooth and venomous stinger. We need a plan and we need all talons ready . . . *all* LeafWings, no matter what our differences have been in the past."

"Well, talking to *her* isn't going to help," Sundew grumbled.

"I don't exactly have a choice," Sequoia said. "I need to know what else she's done and what she's going to do next. I told her to bring your captives, or else I wouldn't release my hostage," the queen added. "That's you." She let out a snort of laughter, as if she was picturing Belladonna's reaction to that threat, and Sundew had to admit to herself that it was kind of hilarious to imagine.

It was slightly less hilarious when Belladonna swooped in, though, in her towering cloud of rage. She came straight through one of the balconies and slammed her talons on the polished wood floor, scattering raindrops everywhere. She was only wearing a few of her pouches, as though she'd thrown them on in a hurry, but Sundew could hear ominous hissing and clicking coming from a couple of them. It sounded as though Belladonna had packed a few of her nastier insect weapons.

"What are you doing here?" she roared at Sundew. "You know you're not allowed to talk to SapWings! And you're definitely not allowed in their village!"

Sundew spread her wings and shrugged, hoping no one could hear her pounding heart. "What could I do? They caught me."

"CAUGHT you?" Belladonna snarled.

"And, um, dragged me back here," Sundew said. "Kicking and fighting the whole way!"

"*These* dragons?" Belladonna scoffed disbelievingly. "*SapWings* did that?"

"Yes, and then they *forced* me to tell them everything," Sundew said. "It was barbaric, really. You should be mad at her." She pointed at the queen, who rolled her eyes.

"Something about this feels highly unlikely," Belladonna growled.

"It doesn't matter," Queen Sequoia said, standing up. "Belladonna, I should arrest you for treason. You did *everything* I told you not to do. You were seen by HiveWings. You stole their sacred property. And you set one of their Hives on fire!"

Belladonna lifted her chin and narrowed her eyes. "I see you really did tell them everything," she said to Sundew.

"Did you bring her captives?" the queen asked. "The flamesilk and the others?"

"I brought the others," Belladonna said, flicking her tail at the window. Outside, Sundew caught a glimpse of Wolfsbane and Byblis hovering on either side of Cricket. No wonder the trees were starting to fill up with curious dragons, gathering to stare at the HiveWing in their midst.

"But not the flamesilk. You cannot have my flamesilk," Belladonna added.

"Even in exchange for your daughter?" Sequoia asked lightly, almost as though she was just curious.

"My daughter could escape and kill you all anytime she wanted to," Belladonna said with a stern look at Sundew. "The only reason she hasn't yet is she's trying to infuriate me."

"That's right, Mother," Sundew said with a theatrical yawn. "It's all about you. You're the only reason I do anything. I think about you *all day long*."

"Stop it, you two," the queen ordered. "Belladonna, bring the other captives inside. Hazel, please go retrieve our strange guests."

Hazel nodded and hurried out of the room.

"What if I don't —" Belladonna started.

"I don't care what you don't want to do! I am not going to let your dragons die," Queen Sequoia said fiercely. "You may have been apart from us for fifty years, but you're still *my* tribe. If we don't work together now, we don't stand a chance." She closed her eyes and muttered, "One . . . two . . . three . . ."

Belladonna huffed her way over to the window and signaled to Wolfsbane.

"Are you going to tell us the truth about that mind-control plant?" Sundew asked the queen.

Sequoia opened her eyes, gave her a strange, clouded look, and hesitated, but only for a moment. "Yes," she said. "I have to."

Sundew wanted to press her further, but just then Hazel came back in with Tsunami and the unfamiliar SilkWing behind her. The SilkWing was very tall, with huge indigo wings dotted here and there with iridescent green. She had an alert, defiant expression on her face, but she didn't seem worried to be surrounded by so many LeafWings.

"Oh, thank goodness," Swordtail's voice came loudly through the window. "I was wondering how long we'd have to wait out here in the rain! I am *completely* soggy! Ack!" he said as he landed on the balcony and squelched inside. "I'm so sorry about your floors! Aw, man, look at these footprints; I didn't even know I had this much mud on me! I mean, how did that even happen, we were *flying*, right? And yet —"

"Swordtail?!" the purple SilkWing gasped.

He looked up, and his jaw dropped, and he stared at her for an astonished moment. "IO!" he finally shouted, bounding across the room toward her. All thoughts of his wetness seemed to fly out of his head, much like the shower of droplets that covered everyone in the room as he threw his wings around the other dragon.

"Swordtail, by all the trees," Sundew huffed, shaking herself off. She glanced at the balcony and saw Cricket coming in, carrying Bumblebee. Their eyes met, and Cricket gave her a tentative, worried smile.

"This is my sister!" Swordtail crowed. "Sundew! Cricket! This is Io! My sister!"

"How did you get here?" Io cried.

"That's the longest story ever. How did *you* get here?" he asked as Cricket sidled across the room to Sundew's side. Sundew noticed that Bumblebee was asleep, and then noticed that she found that disappointing for some completely inexplicable reason.

"Well, my plan was to hide with some friends in the Yellowjacket Hive Chrysalis," Io said to Swordtail, "but when I got there, I was spotted by guards, who chased me pretty much all the way to the jungle. I flew inside to escape them and almost immediately got caught by this enormous horrifying insanely sticky plant. It was going to eat me,

Swordtail! With, like, its goo or something! How wild is that? But these dragons rescued me, and they said I could lie low here for a while."

"That is bonkers," Swordtail said. "I got eaten, too! By a giant mouth plant!"

"Another Swordtail," Sundew whispered to Cricket. "Just what we need."

Io seized Swordtail's front talons. "Have you heard anything about Blue?" she asked. "Did the HiveWings catch him, or did he find the Chrysalis?"

"Neither!" Swordtail said. "He found her." He pointed at Cricket.

Io saw the HiveWing for the first time, and her face underwent an extraordinary transformation from excitement to fury in seconds. She took a step forward, her ears flattened to her head, but Swordtail bundled himself into her path and shook her by the shoulders.

"No, no, calm down. Cricket's on our side," he said. "She saved Blue. Like, more than once. He's here, in fact, in the other LeafWing village right now."

"Oh," Io said. "But . . . what about . . ." She flicked her tail at Cricket, pointed to her head, and rolled her eyes back until almost only the whites were showing.

"Doesn't work on her," he said. "No evil queen in her head, not ever."

"Oh. Well . . . great." Io waved politely at Cricket. "Nice to meet you. Thanks for saving Blue."

"Excuse me," Tsunami interjected. "Did you say Blue? It's just, we were told to find a —"

"Oh my gosh," Cricket gasped. She gripped Sundew's arm and pointed at Tsunami. "Oh — oh my gosh. Do you see that? What is happening? Who is that? Why is she amazing and blue and look at her wings and are those webbed talons? Are they for swimming? Is she a water dragon? What is she and where did she come from and OH MY GOSH SHE'S FROM THE DISTANT KINGDOMS, ISN'T SHE?"

"If you're going to faint, hand me Bumblebee first so you don't squash her by accident," Sundew suggested.

"I should visit new continents more often," Tsunami said with a pleased expression. "I wish everyone was that excited to see me!"

"Wait until you tell Swordtail that you met Luna," Sundew said.

Swordtail whirled toward Tsunami, his face incandescent with hope.

"Yes, she's all right," Tsunami said. "She washed ashore on our continent. She's the reason we're here — she says you all need help. She asked us to look for Swordtail and Blue to tell them she's OK."

Io put one wing around her brother as he buried his face

in his talons and burst into tears. "Aw, Swordtail," she said. "She'll find a way back here. You'll always find your way back to each other."

"Sappy," Tsunami commented, "but that's basically what Luna said, too."

"How does she speak our *language*?" Cricket breathed. "Is it *magic* that we understand her? Is she a magic super-powered dragon like Clearsight? Oh my gosh, can you see the future?"

"I can see *a* future," Tsunami answered. "One where it takes me the next three years to answer all your questions."

"REALLY?" Cricket gasped.

"Calm down, Cricket," Sundew said. "If this dragon could see the future, she wouldn't have almost been eaten by an anaconda."

"True," Tsunami said. "I also wouldn't have eaten that thing this morning that looked like a slug and turned out to be a slug."

The queen clapped her talons together, and everyone fell silent, turning toward her.

"Listen. There's a lot to cover," she said, "and we don't have much time, so we must save the introductions, reunions, and questions until after our urgent business. As I understand it, two days ago, Belladonna and the PoisonWings committed an act of war by burning one of the HiveWings' cities. During the course of that mission, LeafWings were seen, so there will be no doubt in Queen Wasp's mind that our tribe is still alive, and that we are the ones who started the fire."

"Can't we tell her it was them and not us?" Hazel asked, jabbing one of her claws at Belladonna.

"Yeah, give that a try," said Wolfsbane darkly. "I hear she's quite reasonable."

"Sorry, Hazel," said the queen. "She hates all LeafWings equally, and she'll be even more furious when she discovers I'm not dead. There's no chance she'd let half of us just carry on living quietly in the jungle." She flared her wings and looked over at Wolfsbane and Belladonna. "There's also no chance I'd let her kill the other half of our tribe, even if she did promise the rest of us our safety. Those are our dragons, too."

"We don't bow to you!" Belladonna snapped. "We don't have a queen!"

Sequoia narrowed her eyes and took several long, deep breaths without saying anything. Finally she spat, "But you do have a problem. An incoming army problem, and you won't be able to fight them with only half the tribe. Even a full LeafWing tribe wasn't able to stand against them last time . . . and our numbers are much smaller now."

"How do you know we have an incoming army problem?" Belladonna scoffed. "Maybe we scared them! Maybe they're licking their wounds and wondering if we're vengeful ghosts."

The queen shook her head. "I know Wasp. She strikes back the moment she's struck. I estimate we have a day, maybe two, while they put out the fire, tend to their wounded, and relocate their eggs and dragonets. Then perhaps a day to gather her horde and travel here — more likely less. If they're not on the border of the Poison Jungle by tonight, they will be by tomorrow morning."

"Tonight!" Willow gasped.

"That's ridiculous," Belladonna growled. "She can't organize her army or get war-ready that quickly."

"Yes, she can," Cricket said. "She doesn't need to waste time sending messengers or waiting for dragons to say their good-byes or any of that. She'll just slither into all their heads and *make* them come to her, whether they want to or not."

"I told you about the mind control," Queen Sequoia said with a sigh, "but you never quite believed me." She stood up, lifted the vine off the back of her throne, and held it out for everyone to see. "This is the other reason she won't waste any time. She needs this plant to keep her hold on her tribe, but Sundew and her friends burned up her supply."

"Which was a *good* idea," Swordtail objected. "Just so we're clear. It was very heroic and a blow for justice and freedom and I was definitely involved."

"She might have more of the plant," Cricket said. "We burned one greenhouse, but she could have a backup somewhere, couldn't she?"

"Maybe," said the queen. "But she also knows where to find as much as she needs." She pointed out the window. "Right here. In the Poison Jungle, where it came from."

"It came from here?" Sundew said. "Are you sure? I haven't been able to sense it anywhere."

"That's because it's quarantined." Queen Sequoia frowned at the vine, as though it didn't deserve to live. "It only grows in one particular corner of the jungle, guarded by a dragon named Hawthorn who is forbidden to let it escape."

"Really?" Hazel breathed, her eyes wide. "You've never told me about this."

"I've never heard of it either," growled Belladonna.

"It's not a secret we want anyone to know," said the queen. "It's the most dangerous plant in the whole Poison Jungle." She plucked one of the wilting flowers off the vine and held it before her eyes. The pale white of the petals was starting to fade to brown, but at the heart of the wilting flower was a glistening dark red seed, so dark it was almost black.

"Have any of you," asked the queen, "heard of the Legend of the Hive?"

Tsetse Hive
Beetle Lake
Vinegaroon Hive
Hornet Hive
Cicada Hive
Mantis Hive

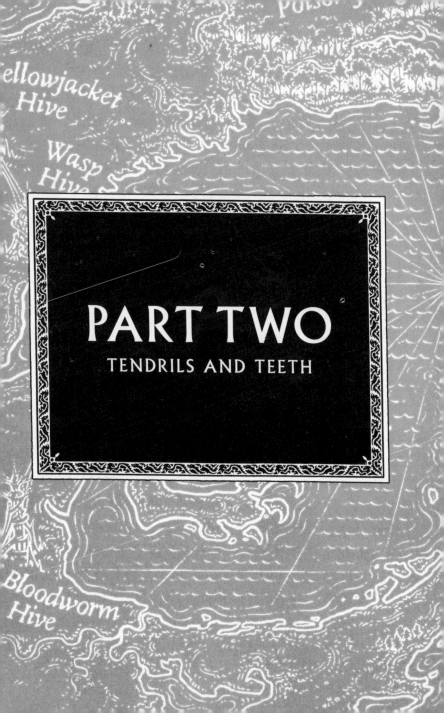

PART TWO

TENDRILS AND TEETH

—— CHAPTER 11 ——

"The what?" Belladonna barked. "Legend? Is it story hour now? I don't care about an old legend!"

"This is important," said Queen Sequoia. She held out one talon to Hazel, who went forward to take it. "Do any of you know it?"

Sundew glanced around, but all the other dragons in the room were shaking their heads, too.

The queen sighed again. Sundew kind of wanted to poke her in the snout with her sharpest claw, once for every sigh. What did she have to be so tired about, after fifty years of cowering in the jungle and *not* fighting the bad guys?

"It was a story from long before Clearsight's time," Queen Sequoia began, guiding Hazel to sit at her feet. The princess looked up at her great-grandmother with wide-eyed awe. Sundew wondered if Bumblebee would look like that when she could understand stories. *Not that I care; I certainly won't be the one telling them!*

"The legend begins with the earliest days of dragons arriving on this continent," said the queen. "Back when the LeafWing tribe and the BeetleWing tribe were new, and they came to these shores to escape trouble in the Distant Kingdoms."

"The what?" Swordtail broke in. "What's a BeetleWing?"

"That's what SilkWings and HiveWings used to be, before Clearsight came along and her ancestors split them into two tribes. The BeetleWings were more like SilkWings, according to the stories, except that some of them had deadly weapons like the ones you now find among the HiveWings . . . shooting deadly venom from their fangs, in particular, according to the old stories."

Tsunami gave a little jump, as if she'd been startled by something.

"Whoa." Swordtail looked at his claws as if he was hoping venomous stingers might suddenly pop out of them.

"What was the trouble that they had to escape from?" Cricket asked.

"Probably the same trouble there always is," Io said. "Dragons being cruel to other dragons because they don't look or act exactly like themselves."

"The legend doesn't say. What it does say," the queen went on, "is that the first dragons who landed on Pantala encountered something . . . very strange." Her voice dropped so low

Sundew could barely hear her over the sound of the rain outside. "The night they arrived, as they all slept, the earth below them began to seethe with motion. Tiny legs crawled across their scales — and then more — and then more of them. The dragons awoke suddenly, from their dreams into a true nightmare. They were covered in fire ants.

"Their shrieks rose up to the three moons and they ran to the ocean, but even as they ran, more colonies of ants boiled up out of the ground and attacked. They marched up the dragons' legs and burrowed between their scales and dug their mandibles into their skin. The ants didn't let go as the dragons plunged into the sea; they didn't try to save themselves. They held on like grim death, until at last the ants drowned."

"Yeeeeesh," Swordtail said with a theatrical shudder.

"But the ants were only the beginning," said Queen Sequoia. "The next morning, as the dragons were limping back to their campsite, they heard buzzing in the air, getting closer and closer. When they looked up, the sky was dark with bees. So many bees they blotted out the sun. The bees descended and attacked, all at once, just as the ants had done. And again, the dragons were forced to flee into the bay and hide below the water.

"The legend says they were saved by their flamesilks, who burned the bees out of the sky."

"So the Legend of the Hive is about creepy ants and bees?" Io asked.

The queen shook her head. "It got worse . . . and stranger. The swarms of insects kept coming. And the next attacks came from insects that normally don't work in groups — imagine armies of venomous centipedes, battalions of tsetse flies, swarms of bombardier beetles.

"They killed dragon after dragon with mindless, unwavering ferocity. Some of the dragons vanished in the night, never to be seen again. Others went down right in front of their friends, suddenly covered in assassin bugs.

"Of course, the dragons fought back. They'd come too far to run away, and according to the story, they were refugees who could never return to the Distant Kingdoms.

"So they fought to stay, but it seemed that whenever they struck down one group of attackers, another would instantly appear in its place. The insects were followed by coils of rattlesnakes, a vast pride of lions, murders of crows."

The queen lowered her voice again, staring into the heart of the pale flower. "These were not ordinary attacks. The animals moved like a single organism. If a crow was struck on one end of the battlefield, the crows at the far end somehow knew instantly. The snakes attacked simultaneously, targeting their victims with coordinated precision."

"But how?" Cricket asked. "This sounds like a myth that's gotten a little warped over time. Are you saying this plant works on *anything*? Reptiles, birds, insects, *and* mammals? How is that possible, scientifically?"

"Um, I have a more important question," Sundew interjected. "Who was controlling them?" She realized she'd twined her tail around Willow's at some point during the story, probably while the ice was trickling down her spine. But Belladonna's eyes were riveted on the queen, and Sundew couldn't make herself pull away from Willow's comforting warmth.

Queen Sequoia closed her front talons around the flower and looked straight at Sundew. "Nobody knows."

"WHAT," said Swordtail.

"Three moons. I think my chills have chills," Tsunami said, shaking her wings out as though she couldn't feel them anymore.

"How could nobody know?!" Cricket asked. "Didn't they find the dragon behind all the attacks?"

"The tribes never found anyone," said the queen. "They searched far and wide for years, but there were no other dragons on the continent, as far as they could tell."

"But . . ." Hazel started, then trailed off.

"What they found was this." Queen Sequoia opened her talons to reveal the flower again. The seed inside it glistened like a wicked little eye, watching them. "We call it the breath of evil."

"Seems a little dramatic," Belladonna muttered.

"This vine covered everything," said the queen. "The legend described it exactly — it is the part of the story that has survived the most intact, as though the storytellers knew how important it would be for us to recognize it if it ever appeared again. This plant was wound around every tree, through every meadow, in every marsh. No matter the landscape, it thrived across all of Pantala.

"But the dragons from the Distant Kingdoms soon discovered that when they destroyed this plant, the attacks waned. When they cleared all the vine from an area, that area gradually became safe to live in. No more attacks. The animals began to behave like normal animals, so long as they lived within the perimeter the dragons made, where there was no breath of evil."

"I don't like this name," Swordtail said. "OR this plant. I just want that on the record: I don't like it at all."

"I can see why Queen Wasp doesn't let us hear that story," Io said. "It might ring a few bells, even inside a dense HiveWing skull."

Sundew saw Cricket wince and tuck the sling a little tighter around Bumblebee.

"But . . . how does it end?" Willow asked. "The Legend of the Hive, I mean."

"There's not much more," Queen Sequoia said, spreading her front talons. "It's all garbled from millennia of being passed down. This is how I understand it: something here tried to kill us when our ancestors arrived, using mind control to turn the wildlife into weapons. But destroying the breath of evil took away its power. Once they realized that, the tribes organized expeditions to uproot the plant across the whole continent."

"Hang on, can we go back to the thing breathing the evil?" Sundew said. "The dragon — or dragons — that controlled everything. Even though the tribes never found it, it must have died, too, right? Once the plants were destroyed and it realized it had lost." She paused and looked around at the range of frightened expressions. "Right?"

"Of course," said the queen. "This was a very long time ago. Thousands of years."

"But I guess the plants weren't all destroyed after all," said Cricket, lifting her head to face Queen Sequoia.

The queen rested one talon on Hazel's head and sighed. "No. Some of it survived, hidden deep in the Poison Jungle."

"Where Wasp found it," Cricket said slowly. "She must know the Legend. She must have gone looking for it, hoping she could use it herself. I wonder how she figured out what to do with it. And if it once worked on any animal, why does she only use it on HiveWings? Why bother with the Tree Wars if she could also mind-control the LeafWings and SilkWings?"

Queen Sequoia shuddered.

"I'm sure she tried," Belladonna spat. "Probably doesn't work on a superior species like LeafWings."

Sundew caught Io rolling her eyes.

"The point is, this is where she got it from," Sundew said. "So this is where she'll come to get more of it, if we really burned up her whole supply."

"Not if we strike her first," snarled Belladonna. "We're going to burn all their Hives. I'm planning our next attack now. We just need a little more flamesilk, and Yellowjacket Hive will be a pile of ash before you can blink."

"Wasp isn't going to wait for you to do that," Cricket said. "Queen Sequoia is right. She's gathering her army right now. She'll be here before you can convince Blue to give you any more flamesilk . . . before you could even get to Yellowjacket Hive, if you already had it."

"We must act quickly." Queen Sequoia rose from her throne with a commanding expression, and Sundew could suddenly see why a whole tribe would have followed her into battle over and over, no matter how often they lost.

"Belladonna, Wolfsbane, and the SilkWings," the queen said, pointing to Io and Swordtail. Wolfsbane looked slightly startled that she knew his name. "You four will come with me. We will gather our strongest warriors — from both villages — and fly to the Snarling River to prepare for Wasp's attack. We need to strengthen the jungle's defenses and hold them off as long as possible."

"Um," Swordtail said. "I mean, that sounds awesome. But . . . how exactly are *we* going to help?" He pointed to himself and Io.

"By talking to the flamesilk," Sequoia said. "I understand his reluctance to burn down Hives, but I hope you can convince him how much we'll need him in battle when Wasp attacks. Also, one of you must contact the Chrysalis. If they want to rise up and overthrow Queen Wasp, *now* is the time. They must bring their dragons to fight alongside us, or Wasp will win, and they will never have a chance to be free."

"What about me?" Hazel asked. "Shouldn't I go with you?"

The queen's face softened, looking down at her great-granddaughter. "No," she said. "I won't be able to think clearly with you there. I need to know you're safe here, and that the rest of the tribe is safe, too, because you'll be in charge of them. If Wasp gets past us, you'll need to decide what to do . . . fight her, or run."

"Run where?" Cricket asked.

"Deeper into the jungle," answered the queen. "Or . . . perhaps farther." She turned her gaze to Tsunami.

"That's what I've been saying!" Cricket yelped. "Right, Sundew? I said we should escape to the Distant Kingdoms!"

"Hey, whoa," Tsunami said, spreading her wings and looking alarmed. "It's not that easy. Can any of you swim? Or breathe underwater?"

"We can swim," Willow said. "In the river. Maybe not like you swim, though. All right, probably nothing like you. Not, like, swim-across-an-entire-ocean-for-days-and-days kind of swimming, no."

Sundew realized that her mother was glaring narrowly at Willow, and also realized, a half second later, that she still had her tail twined with Willow's, and oh dear, that probably had something to do with the look on Belladonna's face.

Well, too bad, she thought defiantly. *I'm not letting go now. I'm not ever letting go of her again. If this is it, all our truth spilled over the table, then this is my truth: I choose Willow. Even if she is a SapWing, and not Mandrake. MOM.*

"Right," Tsunami said to Willow. "So how would you all get there? Sorry, it just . . . it seems unlikely. I've been trying to think about how we could bring other dragons over here to help you — *if* we decided to do that," she added quickly, glancing at Sundew, "and I can't think of anything. Maybe if my friend Starflight were here . . . or Qibli.

Hmmm." She crinkled her snout. "I might have a way to ask them, though."

"What?" Swordtail asked. "HOW? HOW WOULD YOU DO THAT?"

"Distant Kingdoms super dragon magic," Cricket whispered, her eyes shining.

"Ahem," the queen said, taking over the conversation again. "So. Hazel and Tsunami, you'll stay here and try to formulate a plan. A way to get to the Distant Kingdoms, if we need to, or another solution in case Queen Wasp reaches the village. Belladonna, you may send a few of your dragons to work with them. Byblis, perhaps; I understand she's quite clever."

"Yes, I see how much information your scouts have gathered. No need to rub it in," Belladonna snapped.

Queen Sequoia closed her eyes, lifted her chin, paused for about the amount of time it took to count to ten, and then turned her gaze directly on Sundew.

"The rest of you," she said. "Sundew, Willow, HiveWing. You must seek the guardian of the breath of evil vine. Hawthorn has had fifty years to work . . . it's a long shot, but maybe he finally found the one thing that could truly save us."

"An antidote!" Cricket blurted.

Sequoia arched an eyebrow at her. "Yes," she said. "That was *my* dramatic line, young dragon. An antidote."

"Something that could break the mind control?" Cricket said, too excited to be chastised. "A way to free the rest of my tribe?"

"That was our hope, and his quest," said the queen, "but he never returned. I have heard nothing in all these years. So perhaps it was impossible . . . or perhaps he is dead."

"Or perhaps we'll find him and save everybody!" Cricket bounced on her talons so enthusiastically that Bumblebee woke up with a snort.

"Don't get your hopes up too high," the queen warned. "After all this time on his own, I'm not sure he could possibly still be alive."

"Not to mention," said Io, "that even if you do cure all the HiveWings, they might still decide to fight for Wasp with their own free will."

This finally did make Cricket's wings sink. "They won't," she protested. "I'm sure they won't. Some of them won't, anyway . . ." She trailed off, worrying one of her claws.

"Where is this dragon?" Sundew asked the queen.

"In the Eye of the jungle," Sequoia answered. "I'll give you a map. It'll be a dangerous journey, but I think you're the right dragons to undertake it."

"You might want to leave the dragonet with us, though," Hazel offered.

Cricket closed her wings protectively around Bumblebee, who shoved them aside to peek out again. Her eyes were enormous, and she was quieter than Sundew had ever seen her.

"I'd rather keep her with me," Cricket said.

"She'll be fine," Sundew agreed. "We'll keep her safe."

"Just a moment," Belladonna hissed. "I'm not letting my daughter stroll off on a suicide mission with only these two . . . these two *strangers* alongside her." She cast a vicious look at Cricket and Willow (especially Willow, Sundew thought). "I insist they take two of my dragons with them."

Sundew guessed immediately where this was going. "Ugh, *noooo*, Mother, why?" she protested.

"Either you don't go," Belladonna said firmly, "or you take Mandrake and Nettle with you."

— CHAPTER 12 —

"I think I should be in charge," Nettle announced as Sundew spread the map out on a tree stump in the center of the SapWing village. The rain had finally stopped, so the stump was slightly damp, but the map was drawn on a large waterproof leaf. It was also, in Sundew's opinion, not the most helpful map she'd ever seen, but Queen Sequoia said this was all the information she had.

"Ha," Sundew said without looking up at Nettle. "No."

"But *I'm* the oldest," Nettle hissed. "So I have the most experience in the jungle and I have been training for a mission like this my whole life *and* I am a natural leader."

"Ha HA," Sundew snorted. "Outvoted. Four to one."

"You didn't even ask them! They might vote for me!"

"Nope," said Willow.

"Sorry, no," said Cricket.

"Meboo bope!" Bumblebee chimed in enthusiastically from her sling.

"Oh, whoops, five to one," Sundew said. "Maybe she is smarter than she looks," she added to Cricket. She held out her palm and the dragonet whacked it delightedly.

"MANDRAKE," Nettle demanded, swelling up with indignation. "TELL HER I SHOULD BE THE LEADER."

"Sundew, why would you do this to me?" Mandrake asked plaintively.

"Because if she's mad at you, maybe she'll stop harassing me for a nanosecond," Sundew pointed out. "Willow, what's the farthest you've been on this map?"

Willow pointed to a cluster of squiggles northeast of the village. "The manchineel grove. I got too close to it once on a hunt, and my father dragged me back here and lectured me for a week about it."

Willow's father had turned out to be a kind-eyed pale green dragon with a lot of nervous energy. Sundew had only met him for a moment as the queen swept him into her entourage and he paused to wish Willow good luck. Sundew had noticed with a twinge of disappointment that Willow hadn't said *my girlfriend* in that introduction. Of course, that probably required a slightly longer conversation, involving some confessions about sneaking off into the jungle at night.

Sundew needed to have a similar slightly longer conversation with Mandrake, but not in front of Nettle, and not when they only had a day to find the antidote and bring it back to stop Queen Wasp.

Priorities, Sundew. Focus on the mission.

Totally not just avoiding something enormously awkward, no.

"There's not a lot of detail in this map," Sundew observed. She wished she'd had time to restock her pouches. They felt unfortunately light for such a dangerous expedition. She rechecked her list in her mind, hoping what she did have would be useful.

"Most of us haven't gone past the manchineels," Willow said. "They're scary death trees."

"I've read about them, but I've never seen one," Cricket said, pushing up her glasses. Her tail was doing its so-curious-I-can-hardly-stand-it twitch-dance.

"Don't even think about it," Sundew said. "No time for research today, Miss Brainy. We'll go around them." She rolled up the leaf again and glanced up at the trees. The SapWings were frantically busy, hopping from tree to tree, shouting suggestions at one another, and gathering in small worried groups to whisper before splitting up again. But there were still a few of them who had stopped to peer down curiously at Cricket and Bumblebee — the first HiveWings most of them had ever seen.

Which is thanks to us, the real LeafWings who scared off all of Wasp's raiding parties . . . or tricked them into getting eaten.

"Find something more productive and less nosy to do!" she shouted at the closest peeping LeafWing. He jumped and scurried away up the tree like a startled squirrel.

"Oh my goodness," Willow said. "Must you be so terrifying?"

"It's my special skill," Sundew said. "And he deserved it."

"*Did* he, though?" Willow said thoughtfully.

"Could you please keep being the one dragon I'm not furious at right now?" Sundew said. "Come on, everyone, let's go. Willow, you lead the way for now, since you're the most familiar with the jungle around your village."

Willow hesitated for a moment, as though she was thinking about pressing her point a bit more, but instead she nodded and headed into the trees, to Sundew's relief. Sundew followed, with Cricket a half step behind her. The HiveWing was like a shadow, staying as close to Sundew as she could, although she kept twisting her head to stare at weird plants as they went by.

"*I'm* familiar with this area, too," Nettle complained from the rear. "I've been scouting in SapWing territory since before Mandrake was born. I know *every* kind of tree around here."

"Meh meh *meh* meh meh," Bumblebee said in a hilariously similar tone of voice.

Sundew smothered a laugh and glanced over her shoulder for the joy of catching Nettle's furious scowl.

"ExCUSE me," Nettle demanded. "WHY are we taking a HATCHLING with us? A nasty HIVEWING hatchling, no less? Oh, is it because we're hoping something will eat her? A snack for the dragon-traps, what a good idea."

"Maybe you should shut *your* trap," Sundew suggested.

"BurrMRRBRRGRR," Bumblebee agreed. She seemed to be feeling saucier now that they were heading away from the villages full of staring dragons.

"Mandrake!" Nettle cried. "Are you going to let her talk like that? If you don't stand up to her now, she's going to walk all over you when you're married!"

"Oh, I have no idea what that feels like," he grumbled.

Willow turned to arch her eyebrows at Sundew.

Don't panic, Sundew. Don't blurt out something idiotic. This was not the end of the world. Willow knew about Mandrake. She knew Sundew was supposed to marry him in some distant future. She knew Sundew didn't want to and didn't plan to and wasn't going to, and she knew that Sundew had been figuring out how to explain that to him for years.

Willow did think "years" was a bit of a long time for Sundew to hang on to that explanation.

But she also thought Sundew would eventually leave the offshoot tribe and come live with the SapWings. She'd always hoped that one day Sundew would magically stop feeling so angry, and that she'd give up the vengeful life of a

"PoisonWing" on her own. Willow had expected that to be the inevitable end of any marriage plans with Mandrake.

Sundew had a different endgame in mind, however. In her plan, she'd fulfill her destiny, destroy the HiveWings, prove to her mother that she could do it herself, and return a hero. Then she'd be able to choose her own future. She'd be able to do anything she wanted, once that was done.

She hadn't expected her destiny to be quite this *awkward*.

They walked and climbed and whacked their way through the undergrowth for a long time, mostly in silence, apart from Nettle complaining and Bumblebee chirping at things. Willow moved confidently, pointing out things to avoid, like snake nests and low-hanging strangler vines. Dense clouds of moss covered the tree roots all around them, dotted with sprouts of deadly mushrooms that looked like eyeballs growing out of the earth. *Eat me*, the mushrooms chortled. *Just try*. Ferns brushed their scales and whispered back along their stems, *Strange strange why why beware beware creatures out of place,* in their vague feathery fern way.

Nettle was on a rant about how she'd have found a better route by now, when they reached a slope that slanted sharply down ahead of them, riddled with lumpy roots and pricker bushes. A slick layer of rotting leaves made it tricky to stay upright. Sundew found a branch that wasn't covered in thorns or toxic sap, held on to it with one talon, and reached out to support Cricket with the other.

"You know, you can go ahead and ask all the annoying questions buzzing around in your head," she said as the HiveWing slipped and slid past her, clinging to her arm. Bumblebee leaned out of her sling to gawk at the fuzzy orange monkeys in the tree overhead. Sundew wasn't sure how Cricket could balance at all, with the dragonet wriggling around like that. "I'd rather listen to you than Nettle."

"Oh, REALLY," Nettle spat. "Leave the jungle *once* and suddenly you're a HiveWing-loving traitor to the tribe. I should have seen this coming. I always —"

Her diatribe turned into a shriek as she took a wrong step, lost her balance, and plummeted down the steep hill. Sundew yanked Cricket out of the way, and Nettle hurtled past, plowing a canyon through the wet leaves. Willow managed to leap into the air and hover before she got knocked over. She tried to catch Nettle, but the dragon was sliding too fast.

"Wait, come back and tell us again about how you're the smartest dragon in the jungle!" Sundew called after her.

Nettle screamed back something about killing Sundew, and then her voice abruptly cut off as she vanished over the bottom edge of the hill.

"Uh-oh," Mandrake said.

It was difficult to fly between the low, tangled branches, the hungry dragon-traps, and the surprise cobwebs full of poisonous spiders, but they finally managed to hop-hover-skip down the slope to a flat spot at the bottom, which turned out to overlook a large, brackish lake.

Cricket peered over the edge. "It's not that far down," she reported. "But I don't see Nettle anywhere."

"Wow," said Sundew. "I was hoping we'd lose her, but I didn't think it would happen quite that fast." Mandrake gave her a look, and she rolled her eyes. "I'm kidding! I'm sure she's fine. She can handle anything, remember?"

"What if she fell in the pond and drowned?" Willow asked anxiously.

"Get me out of here!" Nettle's muffled voice screamed from somewhere below them.

"That doesn't sound like drowning," Sundew said. She found a spot where she could spread her wings to their full length and hopped over the edge, floating down to the muddy banks of the lake.

Her talons squelched into slimy black mud and nearly flattened a squashy-looking toad, who let out an alarmed *blart* and scooted away. Sharp hollow reeds poked out of the marsh all around her; some of them were broken near the bottom and nearly hidden by the mud, stabbing her feet as she picked her way closer to the water.

From down here, it was obvious what had happened to Nettle. A huge cluster of pitcher plants was gathered right below the hill, gaping maws ready to swallow any animal that tumbled down it. Each one looked like a long green sack, tipped with stripes of dark pink around the open mouth at the top.

Sundew had a collection of much smaller pitcher plants growing outside her nest to catch flies before they buzzed in and bothered her. She really didn't like this big kind, though; it was *super creepy* to look at a giant pitcher plant and wonder whether there might be a dragon corpse decomposing inside it.

Or, in this case, a dragon that was still very much alive and spitting mad.

"GET ME OUT! GET ME OUT OF THIS THING!" Nettle shrieked. One of the plants wobbled as she slammed herself into the side.

"Whoa," Cricket said, landing beside Sundew. "She's . . . *in* there? Why doesn't she just fly out?"

"Meeebomorp," Bumblebee added, wide-eyed.

"The inside walls are covered in slime," Willow answered as she and Mandrake joined them. "It coats the wings of its prey as it falls in, making it harder to fly and impossible to climb out. There are also sharp hairs lining the walls, pointing down so anything that tries to fly or climb up will get stabbed."

"And if we don't get her out soon," Mandrake said, "she'll either drown or get digested by the acid pool at the bottom of the pitcher. Which would be bad," he added, almost as though reminding himself.

"I wish Blue were here," Cricket said, pressing her talons to her forehead.

"I'm not sure setting it on fire would improve Nettle's situation," Sundew pointed out.

"Oh — I didn't mean for his flamesilk," Cricket said. "It would just . . . make me feel better." She glanced down, looking embarrassed.

Sundew understood that. She had wished for Willow's company a million times during her mission to the Hives. She stole a glance at Willow, caught her looking back, and had to smother a smile.

"We'll have to cut her out," Sundew said briskly. "Willow and I will start with our claws; Mandrake and Cricket, look for anything else around here that might be even sharper."

They had to wade into the thicket of pitcher plants to get to Nettle's, which was extra creepy because Sundew could sense them all thinking, in essence, *Mmmm yummm come in yummm delicious want it mmmmmm mine*, like a creepy background chorus of hungry ghosts. Their stems were cold and clammy, and the pitchers bumped against them, some of them skin-crawlingly heavier than others.

Don't think about what might be in there. Do NOT think about it.

The plant Nettle was in had a particularly smug, plummy vibe to it, as though it wanted all its neighbors to notice that it had caught the best prey and no one else could have it. *Hahahrmmm, look at my yums, all mine my yums*, it smirked.

Well, it wasn't going to be so pleased for much longer.

Willow stabbed her claws into its side, and Sundew felt the plant snarl with fury. Chilly vibrations echoed through the roots and leaves all around her, and she thought some of the plants were leaning closer. *Mmmm yummm climb in here little yums dangerous delicious eat before it hurts us eat it now yummmmm.*

She added her claws to the grooves Willow was making, dragging them up and down, digging deeper each time. They carved a square in the side of the pitcher, big enough (she hoped) for Nettle to crawl through. But the walls of the pitcher were thick and rubbery and oozed with slime that made their talons sting and stick together. It felt like their progress was too slow, as though they might look up any moment and find that night had fallen. Also, it was incredibly hard to focus with Nettle shrieking bloody murder the entire time.

Sundew took a step back and shook her aching talons. *I can't believe I'm doing this for Nettle, of all dragons!*

"Here," Cricket gasped behind them. She leaned between two pitchers and passed them a wickedly sharp thorn almost as tall as Willow.

"Ack, watch it!" Sundew cried. "You nearly stabbed Willow!"

"Not that nearly," Willow said. "This is perfect, Cricket, thank you." She wrapped her arms around the wider end and thrust the thorn at the plant like a spear.

To Sundew's surprise, it pierced right through one of the lines they had carved.

Nettle's shriek instantly went up an octave. "WHAT ARE YOU DOING?" she screeched. "ARE YOU TRYING TO KILL ME?"

"We're getting you out!" Sundew yelled back. "Like you've been screaming about this whole time! Just get out of the way!"

"As if there's anywhere to go!" Nettle bellowed. "It's cramped and dark and things are stabbing me and this goo on my tail REALLY HURTS and . . ."

But while she was shouting, Willow had been dragging the thorn along the outline of the square, and suddenly a whole piece of the pitcher wall fell off and Nettle came tumbling out after it.

"EW," Bumblebee declared, in perhaps her most accurate observation so far.

Nettle was dripping with pinkish-green slime from horns to tail, and the acidic, rotting smell coming from her and the sliced-up plant was nearly as bad as a corpse flower in full bloom.

"That took you long enough!" she yelped, struggling to her feet. Her wings were plastered to her side.

"You're welcome!" Mandrake called from outside the pitcher plant cluster.

"I cannot BELIEVE this!" Nettle stamp-squelched past Sundew and Willow, shoving pitcher plants viciously as she went by, and marched over to the edge of the lake. The muddy water made the slime look even more dreadful, but as she scrubbed it all over herself, hints of her own green scales started to peek through again.

"Are you all right?" Cricket asked.

"As if YOU care!" Nettle spat. "Do NOT talk to me right now! I don't want anybody talking to me!"

That sounded like an entirely fine plan to Sundew. She pulled out the map and held it up, squinting at the lines in the semidarkness. She knew the sun was high in the sky, but only a little of its light filtered down to them here at the bottom of the jungle.

"It looks like we need to cross this lake to avoid the

manchineels," Sundew said. "Nettle, while you're there, could you poke your nose in the water and see if a bladder-wort tries to eat you?"

"I'll feed YOU and your stupid little STRIPED MONSTER to the bladderworts!" Nettle snarled.

"Ta-daaaaa!" Bumblebee declared, working two of her wings free and flinging them out to either side.

"Could you two please stop yelling at each other?" Willow asked. She was standing at the edge of the water, squinting at the cloudy surface that stretched ahead of them. "It's only making this harder."

Sundew blinked at her in surprise. It didn't feel harder to her; in fact, yelling at Nettle gave her energy, and it stopped her from worrying about all the really big things she had to worry about.

Moreover, couldn't Willow see the difference between Nettle's yelling (unproductive, vicious, out of control) and Sundew's (hilarious and morale-boosting)?

"Look," Willow said. "There are plants floating right below the surface all the way across the pond. Bet you any-thing there are waterwheels everywhere."

"Yeeeeesh," Mandrake said with a shudder, and even Nettle took a step back.

"Waterwheels?" Cricket asked Willow.

"They're like aquatic dragon-traps," Willow said. "Same

idea — touch one, and it closes around you, drags you under, drowns you, and digests you."

"Ooooooooooo," said Bumblebee.

"No, Bumblebee," Cricket said sternly. "Not 'ooooo.' More like 'ack yikes terrifying'! Although, speaking purely scientifically, that is pretty amazing. Plants that can drown you! Plants that slime you and eat you! I can't believe they didn't teach us any of this at Terrarium Academy. This is WAY more interesting than how to grow radishes!"

"I'm glad you're so fascinated," Nettle said in an icy voice. "Perhaps we could switch places, and *your* tribe could try growing up in a habitat where everything is trying to kill you."

Can't I yell at her when she's being mean to Cricket? Sundew wondered, glancing at Willow again. She was studying the trees overhead now. *Although . . . I guess I've said things almost exactly like that to Cricket, too.*

She nudged Cricket, who was looking pretty deflated. "I bet you're dying to ask about the manchineels," she said.

The HiveWing wrinkled her snout. "I've been restraining myself!" she whispered.

"You can see them over there," Sundew said, pointing to the grove of trees that crowded all the way up against the left bank of the lake. "The fruit looks edible but will make you insane and then kill you. Also the sap is poisonous. If you stand under one while it's raining, poisonous sap will drip on you and you will die. Also they are covered in wicked thorns."

"Like I said," Willow chimed in, "scary death trees." She pointed up. "I think we have enough room to fly over the lake, if we're careful, go one at a time, and avoid the dragon-traps, trumpet flowers, and Roridulas."

"Roridulas?" Cricket said alertly.

"Do you know *anything*?" Nettle demanded.

"Nettle, stop it," Willow said in her most extremely Very Stern voice. "Roridulas are like . . . sticky death shrubs," she said to Cricket. "If you brush up against one, you'll be stuck there until assassin bugs come and eat you."

"Urk," Mandrake said faintly. "You know, I'm really not sure why Belladonna wanted me to be on this mission."

"So you could keep an eye on Sundew, of course," Nettle snapped.

Sundew bristled. "NOBODY needs to keep ANY EYES on me! Gross! How dare you!"

"Sundew, *stop*," Willow said, resting her tail gently on Sundew's shoulder. "Just let it go. We have more important things to worry about."

Sundew scowled at Nettle. It was bad enough when Nettle

was just irritating, but there would be justifiable murder involved if Nettle kept making Willow talk to Sundew like that.

"I'll fly across first," Willow said, "to make sure there's a safe path."

"No, I'LL fly across first!" Nettle said. "I'm not scared, if that's what you think!"

Willow held out her talons, palms up. "I do not think that. Of course you can go first, if you want to."

"That's right," Nettle muttered, shaking the last bits of slime off her wings. There was mud caked between her scales and trails of dried slime along her neck and tail, but at least she was able to fly again. She stamped her feet a few times and then took off.

They all squinted after her, watching her path as she zig-zagged and maneuvered around the obstacles that hung over the lake.

"It must be exhausting to be that angry all the time," Willow commented.

"I'm not, though," Sundew said. "You know that, right? That I'm not like *that*?"

"I know," Willow said, but her smile seemed a little hesitant.

Sundew thought for a moment, and then said, carefully,

"But it's not *bad* to be angry. Sometimes there are things a dragon *should* be angry about."

"I guess," Willow said, looking down at her claws. "It's just not usually my first reaction to anything. Like everything about the HiveWings and what they did . . . it makes me really, really sad. If I think about it too much, I want to curl up in a pile of leaves and cry. But what good would it do to be mad instead? I mean, whenever I *do* get mad, I usually end up feeling guilty or really tired, or both."

"It's not like that for me," Sundew said. "Maybe the guilty part, sometimes. But being mad makes me want to get up and *do* something. It makes me want to *fix* the bad things. Isn't that better than curling up under a pile of leaves and hoping the bad things go away?"

Willow looked into her eyes for a long moment, as if she was really thinking about Sundew's point. "Yes," she said finally. "That makes sense."

"It does?" Sundew said, startled. In her tribe, arguments went all day and nobody ever admitted that the other dragon had said something sensible.

Willow glanced sideways at Cricket and Mandrake, but their gazes were riveted on Nettle as she negotiated a tricky spiral under a strangler vine.

"I like that you want to fix the bad things," Willow said

softly, touching one of Sundew's talons with her own. "But are you only mad at the bad things? Or are you mad at everybody, all the time?"

Sundew bit back a snappy retort. That wasn't fair! She wasn't mad *all* the time. And when she *was* mad, the other dragon *clearly* deserved it.

"She made it!" Mandrake shouted. He jumped up and down, flapping his wings. "We can do this!"

"Do you want to go next?" Cricket asked him.

"I'd rather watch someone else one more time," he said. "If that's all right."

"I'll go," Willow said. She brushed Sundew's wing lightly, with an expression that might have meant *Sorry, don't be mad* or *We'll be all right* or *I'm totally falling out of love with you right now.* Sundew wasn't sure, but she wished she had something to stab to make herself feel a little better.

Willow's crossing was smoother and more graceful than Nettle's (objectively true, not at all Sundew's biased opinion). Mandrake went after her, swerving wildly around a Roridula and swooping low enough that he nearly fell in the lake a couple of times, but at last he made it safely to the other side.

"All right," Cricket said, taking a deep breath. "I can do this."

"Let me take Bumblebee," Sundew said. "I'm more used

to this kind of flying than you are, and she might throw you off."

"Snudoo!" Bumblebee cheered. She lifted her little talons up and did a very good impression of something cute. Something more like a tamarin and definitely not like a HiveWing.

"Are you sure?" Cricket asked. "I thought you didn't want her getting attached to you."

"Well, I'm not planning to glue her to me," Sundew said. "I just figured I'd marginally increase both your odds for survival."

"I do like that goal," Cricket said, smiling as she untied the sling. She passed Bumblebee into Sundew's arms and started rewrapping the scarves around Sundew's shoulders, readjusting her pouches as she did.

Bumblebee was lighter than Sundew had expected, a warm little ball of scales with lots of spiky bits. Her elbows and wings and horns and tail all seemed to poke Sundew at once as the dragonet wriggled around, burbling with joy. But after a moment, she settled with her wings tucked in and nudged her nose under Sundew's chin. One of her tiny talons wrapped around the pouch with the jade frog in it.

It felt weirdly comfortable and mildly alarming at the same time. This was definitely a small living thing that might die if Sundew did anything wrong. But it was also a small living thing that apparently completely trusted her. Plants did that, sometimes, but plants weren't exactly cuddly.

"We're fine," Sundew said to Cricket. "Stop fussing and get flying."

She watched Cricket dart and hover through the obstacles, pausing now and then to peer at a plant she didn't recognize. One of them turned out to be an iridescent pink beetle instead of a flower, and it shot a blast of acid at her that she just managed to duck before heading down to land on the opposite shore.

Sundew tugged the scarf a little higher up Bumblebee's neck. "Our turn, little bug. Stay very still and do NOT distract me, understand?"

"Ooobeegoo," Bumblebee said sternly. She patted Sundew's face. "Do NOBBY splamflamp."

"I wasn't planning on being splamflamp," Sundew retorted, "whatever that is."

She lifted off, wobbling a little as she adjusted to Bumblebee's weight. Her claws skimmed the lake's surface as she flew under a crisscrossing tangle of vines, and below her she saw blurry waterwheels snapping shut on the ripples. A knobbly reptilian head rose from the depths to stare at her with yellow eyes, but she didn't stop to figure out what it was.

Up a little higher, over a knot of dragon-traps, wings tucked to fit between a loop of dangling snakes and a glittering web of poisonous sap. Now she had a straight line of sight to the four dragons waiting on the far side. Nettle was twitching her tail impatiently; Willow looked anxious.

"Not much farther," she said to Bumblebee.

She beat her wings once and turned into a dive.

And then suddenly Bumblebee shrieked, "BEEBUF!" and flung herself upward, grabbing Sundew's horns, pulling them down, and smacking her little body over Sundew's entire face.

Sundew yelped and fell, momentarily blinded. Her wings flailed to catch the air.

And instead she felt one of them catch on something else.

Something sticky and prickling that caught and held her wing fast, slamming her to a stop. Her momentum spun her toward the caught wing. She flung out a talon to stop herself and felt it smack straight into the same gluey ooze.

She was trapped, and so was Bumblebee, and she could already feel the other tendrils closing in.

Mmmmmine, whispered the plant. *Sssso delicious mine . . .*

CHAPTER 13

"Sundew!" Willow screamed.

Sundew couldn't see around the black and yellow scales draped over her snout. She didn't even know exactly which kind of sticky plant had caught them.

"Bumblebee," she said, trying to keep the panic out of her voice. "Are you all right?"

"Yim," Bumblebee said in a small voice.

"Good," said Sundew. "Then WHAT IN THE NAME OF ALL THE TREES WAS THAT?"

"Eep," Bumblebee said in an even smaller voice. "Beebuf?"

"Get off my face," Sundew snapped. "CAREFULLY. I am REALLY MAD AT YOU."

"Beebeebeebee*bee*buf," Bumblebee protested, wiggling down until she was hanging from Sundew's snout with her tail around Sundew's neck. She managed to scoot herself back into the sling and leaned into Sundew's chest, patting her heart under the jade frog. "Meesnugoo."

"Goo is right," Sundew said, studying their abductor. She was stuck on one of the towering leaves of a plant that sprawled across a small island in the lake below her. The leaf was bright lime green, with hundreds of thin red stalks poking out of it that made the entire plant look fuzzily scarlet from afar. At the tip of each stalk was a glistening drop, like a translucent murder pearl.

"Oh no," Sundew muttered.

"Isn't this amazing?" Nettle called, with an undeniable note of triumph in her voice. "The great and wonderful Sundew trapped by an *actual sundew*?"

"That's a sundew?" Cricket said. "Huh. I thought they'd be prettier. That thing looks like a giant spider got turned into a plant and sprouted weird red hairs all over it. But you can get away from it, right, Sundew?"

"Sundew!" Willow cried. "Don't move!"

That was an unhelpfully obvious piece of advice. Sundew knew that struggling would only trap her worse. But she didn't exactly have many options at the moment. Three of the sticky dewdrops had snagged Sundew's left wingtip; her right front talon was caught on another two, and her back talons were snared in still more below her, as she tried to brace the rest of her body away from the plant.

Huddled in her sling, Bumblebee was trapped between Sundew and the sundew, but she hadn't touched the sticky substance yet. She peeked at it with wide eyes, more still than Sundew had ever seen her, as though she understood the danger of moving.

The other tentacles on the leaf were creeping toward them, leaning, drooping, closer and closer. In a few moments, new beads would reach her scales, latching on with gummy ferocity. Soon after that, the tentacles would wrap tighter, drawing her inescapably into their embrace, until they held her and Bumblebee as close as they could . . . until they suffocated and died and were consumed by the plant.

She summoned all the power of her leafspeak. *STOP!* she screamed at the tentacles.

The sundew froze. Each red stalk tentacle paused where it was, as though the plant was staring at her with a hundred glistening beady eyes.

Let us go, she ordered it.

A long pause as confused messages fired up and down the sundew's synapses.

Can't, it finally whispered back, not so much a response as an observation echoing through the leaves. *Hungry*.

Want this.

Mine.

One of the tentacles reached for her face and she roared *STOP!* again.

It froze once more, but it was so close to her eye now that

she couldn't stop the panic thundering through her heart. The plant sensed it and flickered something curious and malevolent back at her. Her fear tasted delicious to it.

"I'm not scared," she snarled out loud. "I want to rip you out by your roots and burn you to ashes."

Malevolent flicker. *Mmmore.*

It liked the taste of her anger, too. She shuddered despite herself and felt a tentacle snag on her tail.

She had to stay calm. Especially for Bumblebee. The rotten little bug face had gotten her into this mess, but she didn't have to die for it.

You do not want this prey, she thought forcefully in leafspeak. *It will sicken you.*

Hmmmshhhh, the sundew responded with skepticism.

"Sundew, I'm coming to get you!" Willow called.

"No!" Sundew shouted back. "You'll only get stuck, too! I can get out of this! Stay there!"

"Maffib?" Bumblebee asked, wiggling her head up closer to Sundew's. She poked the jade frog pouch with one of her claws. "Smeebuf?"

"Smeebuf?" Sundew echoed. "Are you trying to annoy me to death before the plant eats me, you wretched little lizard?"

"Buf!" Bumblebee insisted indignantly. She leaned under Sundew's left arm and jabbed another pouch. "Buf! Buf! Buf!"

Sundew was about to yell at her to shut up, when a realization hit her like a falling tree. "Wait," she said. "Are you trying to say *bug*?"

"Dazameezacco!" Bumblebee shouted, as though she couldn't believe how thick Sundew's head was. "BUF!"

"I do have a couple of bugs in there," Sundew said. "That might . . . shush and let me think."

"Smusha *mee* smush," Bumblebee grumbled. She draped herself around Sundew's free arm and glared at the tentacles. Most of them were still hovering as the plant decided what to do, but a few were stealing closer at a snail's pace as if hoping no one would notice until too late.

Bugs.

Buf . . . wait . . . beebuf . . . what if that actually meant something?

"Willow," Sundew called. "Did you see why Bumblebee freaked out? Did she see something?"

"Yes!" Willow called back. "Didn't you see it, too?"

"Obviously not! What was it?"

"It was the biggest tsetse fly I've ever seen!" Cricket exclaimed. "It was like three times the size of Bumblebee!"

"All the insects are oversized here," Mandrake said. "At least, that's what my father says."

Now Sundew had a vague memory of something buzzing nearby, right before Bumblebee grabbed her face. She *hated* tsetse flies. One of her favorite teachers had been killed by a tsetse fly bite. After that, she'd made it her personal mission to tell every carnivorous plant near the village to eat as many tsetse flies as possible, and they hadn't been seen in her part of the jungle ever since.

But this wasn't her part of the jungle.

"Willow! Where did it go? Can you still see it?"

"No," Willow said. "Nothing . . ."

"Maybe there?" Mandrake's voice said nervously.

"Oh! Yes — I think so! Sundew, to your right and above you, on the vine!"

Sundew carefully inched her head around and looked up. She glimpsed the shimmer of wings and a huge blackish-brown body, nearly hidden by leaves.

She tried to think, but it had been a long time since she'd studied them. "What attracts tsetse flies?" she yelled to her friends.

"Attracts them?" Nettle shouted. "Why would you want to do that?"

"Maybe the smell of blood?" Willow guessed.

"Bright colors!" Cricket shouted. "Especially blue!"

"Really?" Mandrake said. "How do you know that?"

"I read a study," Cricket said. "From a while ago, way before the Tree Wars. I kind of . . . like reading studies."

"Worth a try," Sundew said, thinking quickly through

the items in her pouches. The only problem was that she couldn't reach most of them with her only free talon — at least, not without probably getting more stuck.

She took a breath. "Bumblebee," she said. "Are you listening? Can you do something important for me?"

"Yim," Bumblebee said in her most solemn voice. Patches of black scales circled her yellow-gold eyes, making her look a little like a tragic panda as she gazed up into Sundew's face.

"I need you to climb onto my back," Sundew said. "*Really carefully*. Hold on tight and find the leaf pouch under my left wing that's a darker green than the others. Do *not* open it yet."

"Beemish," Bumblebee said grandly. She crawled up onto Sundew's shoulder and started inching her way down Sundew's back, clinging to the pouch straps and the other side of the sling as she went. Sundew could hear her singing softly to herself: "Beemish Snudoo, Bumpbump snableday, beemish Snudoo, Bumpbump snableday . . ."

The dragonet tugged at the fiber ropes wound around Sundew's left wing, and one of the tentacles above them curled forward and glommed on to Sundew's wing scales next to the others.

Yuck dragon, Sundew thought frantically at the plant. *Dragon so very yuck. Sick the plant that eats the dragons.*

Shhhhhh . . . the sundew thought, but then, shivering along its leaves from the central core: *Sick . . . sick?*

Poisonous yuck dragons, Sundew tried. *Maybe kill the sundew.*

Mine the meal, the plant whispered to itself. *Danger . . . but hunger . . . but danger . . . but hunger . . .*

"Zob," Bumblebee announced, holding up the dark green pouch.

"In the inner fold you'll find butterfly wings," Sundew said. "Pick out the blue ones and throw them at the tentacles right above us."

The dragonet hesitated, and Sundew realized that was too many instructions at once.

"Do you know the color blue?" Sundew asked.

Bumblebee glanced around nervously, then pointed up with a "maybe?" expression. Except up could be the sky, which was in fact blue, or the tree canopy that mostly hid it from view, which was not, or any of the various bright flowers and curious monkey faces watching them.

"Find a blue wing in there and show it to me," Sundew ordered. Her arms and back ached from the strain of pressing herself away from the sundew, and her mind was getting very tired from trying to keep the leafspeak orders going at the same time.

The little HiveWing dug into the pouch for what felt like an age, and finally emerged with a talonful of bright blue morpho wings.

"That's right!" Sundew said, twitching more than she meant to in her excitement. Another tentacle latched itself to her tail. "Now —"

But Bumblebee wasn't waiting for more directions. She threw the morpho wings up at the stalk of the sundew that was slowly curving down toward them. The blue stuck where it landed, covering the scarlet and green with a small window of bright azure beauty, like Blue's wings.

Bumblebee squeaked with delight at herself and immediately pulled out another talonful. This one, when she threw it, turned out to have a few other colors mixed in, but it still looked like a shining mosaic, most of it a blue that shone in the dark green jungle. The plant twitched around the scattered wings, bewildered by the new sensation that didn't match the others.

Bzzzz. Bzzzz.

The tsetse fly was moving. Only a little at first, hopping to a closer leaf, turning in a circle, flaring its wings and zipping them closed again.

"Bumblebee," Sundew whispered. "Get back in the sling."

Bumblebee clambered rapidly over Sundew's shoulder again, no singing or burbling this time. She crawled into the sling and wrapped it around herself with a little shiver.

Bzzzzzzzzzz.

The tsetse zoomed past, close enough for Sundew to feel

the wind of its passing against her free wing. She held still as it circled and dove again. It was studying the blue shapes with its huge, horrible eyes.

Come on, Sundew prayed. *Please let this work.*

With a final, decisive buzz, the tsetse fly swooped down and landed squarely on top of the blue wings, just above Sundew's head.

She lunged forward and slammed her free talon into its back, smashing the fly into the sticky tentacles. It jerked and spasmed, but the sundew held it tight. More tentacles closed in, faster the more the fly fought.

Yesssss, the sundew's leaves hissed.

Take the fly, Sundew commanded, matching her leafspeak to the sundew's sly, curling tone. *Delicious yes. Dragons yuck.*

Two of the stalks touching her wing pulled away and reached for the fly instead. Then another . . . then the ones trapping her talon let go . . . and gradually she felt the sundew releasing her, choosing the simpler, less argumentative prey instead.

As soon as she could, she threw herself back into the air, to freedom. She dove toward the lakeshore, where Willow was waiting with outstretched arms, and landed with a crash.

"Ha HA!" Bumblebee declared triumphantly. She rolled herself out of the sling and did a little shimmy dance in the mud. Her wings whisked around her, iridescent and sparkling like a dragonfly's. "Beebuf! I sabladay! Mee mish! Yim yim yim!"

"You wouldn't have *had* to save the day if you hadn't *gotten us stuck in the first place*," Sundew pointed out. She stretched her cramped wings and tail and neck and arms and tried to shake the feeling back into her toes. Her muscles were so confused. She decided to lie down in the mud for a moment and let them recover.

"Good work, Bumblebee," Cricket cooed. "You helped so much! You're such a smart dragon! What a good listener!"

"For trees' sake, Cricket," Sundew said. Belladonna had never given her that many compliments in her *life*, let alone all at once. "If my mother talked to me like that, I'd be —"

"Well-adjusted?" Willow guessed, with a crinkly-eyed smile that made it very hard to scowl at her.

"As soft as a SapWing," Sundew finished, sticking her tongue out at Willow.

"Aw, you can be soft," Cricket said to Bumblebee, still in her googly voice. The dragonet was curled in her arms now, preening and purring like a baby jaguar. "You don't have to be mean and scary, no you don't. You won't be like the other HiveWings. You're too cute and you have your *own* brain, don't you?"

"Snubble flump," Bumblebee agreed, let out an enormous

yawn, and drooped into Cricket's shoulder with her eyes closing.

"Blech," Nettle grumbled. "I'm going to be sick."

"So sorry I didn't manage to die for you," Sundew said.

She realized that Willow was lying down beside her, twining her tail around Sundew's and resting her wing across Sundew's back. "You scared me half to death," Willow said softly in Sundew's ear. "Are you all right? Can you please promise me you'll never die?"

"Yes," Sundew said, nudging her with her snout. "I promise." She was relieved to see that Willow wasn't still upset about their argument on the other side of the lake. It was scarier than a tsetse fly to think that Willow might see Sundew differently once they were around other dragons . . . that she might think Sundew was just another Nettle. But that wasn't what she saw in Willow's eyes. She saw herself, loved, just the way she was.

Nettle frowned down at Sundew and Willow, then turned and kicked Mandrake's ankle.

"Ow!" he protested. "I mean — uh, I'm glad you're alive, Sundew."

"Thanks," Sundew mumbled. "Just going to rest for a moment."

She closed her eyes and took a deep breath, filling her

lungs with Willow's scent and her mind with the murmurs of plants who weren't trying to murder her, at least not right that second. There were orchids nearby, each vying to be the most beautiful. She found the roots of sun lilies not far below the soil and quietly sang one up to the surface so it would peek through right between Willow's front claws. Sundew didn't have to open her eyes to feel Willow smiling.

"*I* nearly got eaten, too," Nettle complained, "and *I* didn't require a nap afterward."

With a sigh, Sundew pushed herself to her feet. Nettle was the worst, but it was true that they didn't have time to rest any longer. The sun had passed the midway point of the sky, and if Cricket and Queen Sequoia were right, the HiveWing army was almost certainly on its way.

Willow leaned over her shoulder as Sundew unrolled the map again. Nettle shoved Mandrake so he stumbled into Sundew's other side.

"This is where the map gets extra unhelpful," Sundew said, reaching out her wing to help him catch his balance. "I mean, what are all these small squiggly lines from here to the Eye?"

"They look like snakes," Mandrake offered. "Um. Someone tell me I'm wrong."

"They *do* look like snakes," Willow said.

"That's fine," Nettle scoffed. "I've killed *hundreds* of snakes. No problem."

"But . . . all at once?" Mandrake asked. "I mean . . . this whole section of the map is just . . . snakes. If those are snakes. Maybe they're not. Maybe they're very tiny rivers."

"It looks like there are words here," Cricket said, crouching closer to the leaf and squinting at it.

"You're right." Willow held the leaf up to the faint sunlight, and they all tried to read the miniature letters carved between the squiggle shapes.

"Does it say tiny rivers?" Mandrake asked hopefully.

"Den?" Cricket guessed. "Den . . . of . . ."

"Vipers," Sundew said. A shiver ran down her spine that felt like the sinister glee of a plant about to feast. "The last section of the jungle standing between us and the Eye is called the Den of Vipers."

— CHAPTER 14 —

Sundew couldn't tell whether the jungle had gotten darker because the sun was starting to go down, or because the tree canopy was denser here and there was less room to maneuver, or because it felt like beady eyes were watching them from every tree. They had been walking (clambering, squelching, slogging) for a long time since crossing the lake and still hadn't run into any snakes.

"You are all ridiculous," Nettle declared, shoving her way past Sundew as they climbed over a fallen tree. "Snakes are not scary."

"Nettle, you are very welcome to kill all the vipers for us," Mandrake said in exasperation.

"Do you think they're dragonbite vipers?" Cricket asked anxiously. "I read that those can kill one of us with a single bite. Have any of you ever seen one? I've never seen one. We don't exactly get a lot of snakes in the Hives. Not even in the greenhouses. I saw some little snakes in a pet shop in the market. Do LeafWings have pets?"

"Yes," said Willow at the same time as Sundew said, "No."

They glanced at each other. "SapWings do," Sundew added with a shrug.

"PoisonWings don't," Willow agreed.

"We're not PoisonWings!" Sundew objected for the millionth time. "That really makes us sound like the bad guys!"

"I'll stop if you stop," Willow offered. "I mean, SapWings sounds like a tribe that drips around sticking to everything."

Cricket giggled and Sundew smothered her own laugh. "All right, truce," she said.

"LeafWings," said Willow. "We're both LeafWings."

"But only the drippy sticky half of us have pets," Sundew pointed out. She ducked away from Willow swatting at her and thought she saw something dart by under the leaves. Something long and gold and black and green.

She froze, staring at the ground as the others kept walking.

But now the leaves were still. She didn't see any sign of whatever had moved. Maybe she had imagined it, as nervous as she was.

She hurried to catch up to her friends.

"I have a cockatoo," Willow was saying to Cricket. "Her name is Talkatoo and she's the smartest bird in the world SUNDEW STOP LAUGHING AT ME." She shoved Sundew's shoulder affectionately. "I was only a little older than Bumblebee when I named her! I'd like to see you come up with a better name at that age!"

"Wordibird," Bumblebee said sleepily from her sling, and Cricket laughed again.

"Could you keep the racket down back there?" Nettle shouted from up ahead.

They fell silent for a moment, navigating an uphill slope covered in ferns and moss-covered rocks and death cap mushrooms. Sundew glanced up at the looming trees. She'd never felt trees *loom* like this before. Even with her leafspeak, she couldn't connect well with them. These trees grumbled and muttered; they were unhappy about something that had gone on long enough to register even with them. But they couldn't articulate it — of course they couldn't, trees almost never could. They could only radiate discontent and gloom.

"Is it me," Cricket whispered, "or is it a lot quieter all of a sudden?"

Willow and Sundew both stopped beside her and listened.

Cricket was right. The constant chirping of cicadas and grasshoppers had fallen silent. There was no sound of monkeys swinging above them or calling across the jungle.

Sundew couldn't even hear any birds. The wind rustled the branches overhead; that was all.

Sundew was searching the treetops for any birds, when she saw the first dragonbite viper's head. She looked past it twice at first, because it was perfectly still. But the third time, something about the smooth, serpentine shape caught her eye.

The head was poking up out of a cluster of green weeds only a few steps from Willow. It was, most definitely, the head of a viper, attached to the rest of the body of a viper, as far as Sundew could see . . . but it was not moving. It seemed frozen there, like a statue of a snake.

She noticed that Mandrake and Nettle had fallen silent, too, and stopped where they were, at the top of the slope. They both had their eyes fixed on something near their feet, and Mandrake looked close to fainting.

"That is really weird," Willow said, answering Cricket's question. She clearly hadn't seen the snake. With a shrug, she stepped forward, and Sundew reached to pull her away from the viper — but it still didn't move.

"Willow," she whispered, poking her tail. "To your left. Ominous paralyzed viper or something."

Willow saw it and started back in alarm. But it *still* didn't move.

"What's wrong with it?" Cricket whispered. "Can't it see us? Is it dead?"

"No," Sundew whispered as the snake's tongue slithered out, tasted the air, and slithered back in. Its lidless bright yellow eyes seemed to be staring right at them. But when they edged forward together, its eyes didn't follow. It stared directly into space, head raised, completely still except for its tongue.

"Should we try to kill it?" Sundew asked quietly as they stepped forward, keeping their gaze on it.

"That might wake it up," Willow whispered. "I say as long as it's not moving, don't touch it. Let's just get away from it."

They moved softly but quickly up the hill, staying on the rocks and away from the long weeds as much as they could.

Another snake was poised near the top, staring at Nettle and Mandrake. This one was coiled around a thorny shrub, its green-and-black head jutting out into the air like an extra-creepy branch.

"Has it moved?" Sundew whispered from a boulder behind them.

"Not yet," Mandrake answered through his teeth. "But neither have we."

"See if you can slide away," Sundew suggested. "We saw one below that stared at us but didn't attack. Maybe this one is frozen in place, too."

"I should wring its neck," Nettle growled. But she didn't make a move toward it, and after another moment, Mandrake cautiously sidled a step away, and then another.

The snake's tongue flickered in and out, but it stayed poised in place, enormous yellow eyes glaring. Sundew guessed it was as long as a dragon, if you straightened out all its coils.

"Let's go," Willow whispered. "Watch where you step."

She led the way as they paced single file with careful steps along the ridge of the hill and down the other side. Sundew kept her wings tucked in close and her tail lifted off the ground. Each time her talons came down on a slick of wet leaves, she expected to see a blur of motion and feel fangs sinking into her ankle.

"There," Cricket breathed, inclining her head to the left.

Two more snakes were looped around the branches of a tree with their heads reaching toward the path, staring and still.

"Over here, too." Mandrake flicked his tail slightly. They were passing a patch of tangled ivy, vines, and long grass that appeared to have strange plants growing up from the center of it . . . but they weren't plants. They were more snakes, six or more, smooth heads curled up like cobra lilies with their menacing dandelion eyes glittering.

"Why aren't they moving?" Cricket asked. She hesitated at a large tree root, inspected the shadows around it, then gingerly stepped over it.

"Stupid question. We obviously don't know," Nettle muttered. "Never seen snakes act like this."

"Maybe they're watching for better prey than us," Willow whispered.

Sundew could hardly stand it. Her sore muscles protested at the slow, tense pace. She wanted to scream; she wanted to seize a tree and shove it over on top of the snakes; she wanted to throw exploding seed pods at them. She would rather fight than deal with this . . . this awful creeping, this prickling feeling of *waiting* for something to attack.

They reached the bottom of the slope and found a stream, its muddy water trickling slowly over stones. Willow began to pick her way across, silently pointing to branches that were actually snakes, rocks that were actually snakes, and glimmers of fish that were actually underwater snakes. There were a *lot* of snakes in the stream.

"Maybe we should fly," Mandrake suggested, halfway across. "We could go over the whole Den of Vipers, couldn't we?"

Nettle snorted and jabbed one claw at the trees overhead. Sundew looked up.

The branches above them were dripping with snakes. Scales gleamed between the leaves; hundreds of yellow eyes watched them, unblinking. There were so many coils wound around each branch that it was impossible to tell where one snake ended and another began.

Sundew glanced back at Bumblebee, asleep in her sling. *Maybe we shouldn't have brought her out here, after all.*

The water was very cold around her talons, colder than she thought it should be.

I wish we knew how much farther we have to go.

They waded out of the stream on the other side and kept going, between trees that pressed closer and closer, below more and more frozen, watchful snakes. Sundew reached out tentatively with her leafspeak and felt the presence of plants so dangerous her tribe had cleared them out of the area around the village. Malicious blistering hogweeds chuckled nearby, spiking through the murmur of the other plants. A hungry gurgling hum underneath everything told her that kudzu vines were wound throughout this area, devouring and choking the quieter trees.

But there was something worse . . . something much creepier. Something that reached out to her mind with cold tendrils.

She hissed softly. Willow paused to look back at her.

"The breath of evil," Sundew whispered. "It's here. I can feel it."

She could smell it now, too, the same peppery rotting smell that she'd encountered in Queen Wasp's greenhouse. She had examined that vine while they hid there, but it hadn't spoken to her at all. Nothing like what was currently reaching back toward her, as though it was trying to plant little seeds in her brain and slither through the cracks in her scales.

"Look," Mandrake said, pointing. There was a light up ahead — a break in the trees where full sunlight was shining through to the forest floor.

"Maybe that's the Eye," Cricket whispered. "Where Hawthorn lives?"

"How can he live here?" Willow whispered back. "Surrounded by all these vipers and the breath of evil?"

"Maybe he doesn't," Nettle said. "Maybe he's dead."

"That's the spirit, Nettle," Sundew said. "Let's go check it out."

They headed toward the light, and as the jungle became easier to see all around them, Sundew spotted the scarlet-and-green vines overhead. It *was* here, growing freely, hardly a day's walk from Queen Sequoia's village. She shuddered. Why hadn't any scouts encountered it? Why didn't everyone know about it? Was it too well hidden behind the vipers and the manchineel trees, so no one ever came this way?

They were almost at the edge of the clearing when the snakes suddenly moved.

An enormous one dropped straight out of the tree in front of them, blocking their path. Five more glided out of the bushes behind them; others slithered down from the branches. They were surrounded, and the vipers began to hiss.

"Sundew?" Willow said, taking a step closer to the group. "Any ideas?"

"Why bother asking her?" Nettle demanded. "*I* have a great idea. Let's kill them!" She lunged toward the one in front of them. It bared its fangs and darted at her, fast as lightning, and Mandrake screamed, and Sundew felt Willow grab one of her talons as they threw their wings out to form a shield around Cricket and Bumblebee.

A gust of wind billowed from the clearing as something gigantic swooped down, and then wings blocked the sunlight and giant claws stabbed into the snake, stopping it barely a heartbeat away from sinking its fangs into Nettle's throat.

The snake writhed in its death throes, and as one, all the vipers around them rose up like cobras about to strike, glaring with their yellow eyes.

"Begone!" shouted the new dragon. "Leave these travelers in peace!"

The hissing intensified, slipping along Sundew's nerves and all through her bones, but after a horrible, heart-pounding moment of stillness, all the snakes dropped to the ground and slithered away into the underbrush.

"Well, *you* very nearly just died!" the giant LeafWing said, smiling down at them. He shook the snake's corpse to make sure it was dead, then tossed it away like a weed he'd just yanked out of the dirt. "What kind of idiots come to a place like the Den of Vipers?"

"Desperate ones," Sundew admitted. "We're looking for a dragon named Hawthorn."

"Thank you for saving my sister," Mandrake interjected.

"I didn't need saving!" Nettle barked. "I was about to kill it myself!"

"If you had, then the others would have immediately killed all of you," the stranger pointed out. "I mean, only reasonable, right? You did come into our territory. No one ever does that! So they tend to be a bit overprotective."

"They . . . I'm sorry, who? The vipers? They're *protecting* you?" Cricket asked. "They're protecting *you*? What?"

"Oh, yes," he answered. "I'm Hawthorn, and those were my vipers. Who wants tea?"

CHAPTER 15

Hawthorn turned and sauntered cheerfully off into the sunlight. Mandrake followed him, blinking in confusion. Willow stopped Sundew with her wing as she stepped forward.

"I feel like we should be really careful," she said softly.

"Me too," Sundew agreed.

"Same here," Nettle said unexpectedly.

"But this is the dragon we're looking for, right?" Cricket asked. She adjusted her glasses. "The one with all the answers? Who knows everything about this vine and the mind control?" Her tail was twitching with nervous excitement.

"Yes," Willow said. "And he seems nice enough. It's just . . . everything else."

"We'll go with him," Sundew said to Cricket. "But carefully."

Cricket nodded, and they edged out into the clearing, squinting in the much brighter light here.

All the low-hanging vines had been cut back along with

sections of the canopy overhead, leaving space for grass to grow in the patches of sun. A small vegetable garden covered a quarter of the clearing, with the undergrowth cleared away all around it. And in the center of the clearing was a house shaped like a cell in a hive, not a nest or a hammock or a platform in a tree. Someone, presumably Hawthorn, had taken the time to turn tree trunks into smooth, flat boards; someone had fitted them together; and someone had woven flax curtains for the door and windows, then dyed them pale red.

Sundew pivoted to study the entire space, but she saw no sign of the breath of evil within the perimeter of the clearing. She could still hear it, though, and feel it curling around the edges of her mind.

"Come on in," Hawthorn called from the doorway.

They stepped up onto a covered porch that ran along the front of the house. One end of it seemed to be a small woodworking studio, where a little half-carved dragon sat on a stump. Honeysuckle vines adorned the roof of the porch, adding a sweet smell to the air and a tranquil murmur to the chorus in Sundew's head.

Inside, Hawthorn's house was breezy, warm, and full of a rose-colored light from the sun filtering through the curtains. It was all one room, but with a high ceiling and lots of space. Carved wooden dragons, snakes, trees, and orangutans perched atop the shelves on every wall. Sundew looked closely at one of the dragon heads and thought it looked a lot like Queen Sequoia.

"Did you make all of these?" Cricket asked, gazing around the room.

"Ah, yes," Hawthorn answered. "Lots of time on my talons, you know. No one else to talk to, so I thought I'd make some friends for myself. This one's my favorite." He patted a smooth egg shape made of honey-colored wood, with a delicate filigree of leaves carved around the top. It sat on a stand on a little table by itself, next to the window. "They're better company than you'd think. Thank goodness I have you, right?" he said to the egg.

Poor lonely dragon, Sundew thought. *But then, carving little figures to be your only friends is one thing — organizing a nest of snakes to be your bodyguards is quite another.*

"I can't help but notice that you're a HiveWing," Hawthorn said, wagging one claw at Cricket. "I hope you being here means peace has finally been achieved between the tribes? So . . . maybe I can go home?" he added hopefully.

Nettle snorted. "Peace! Not even close," she said. "This one's a bit of an ex-HiveWing, at least according to the morons who believe her."

"Ah, hmmm," Hawthorn said, crouching to dig in a cabinet. "Traitor to her tribe, eh?"

"No!" Cricket said. "The opposite! I want to *save* them!"

"Oh, right," his muffled voice responded. "I know that feeling." He emerged again, smiling. "I must say, if I'd known so many visitors were coming, I would have carved more cups! But these are all I have." He produced three ebony cups and a stone jar full of tea leaves; Sundew could smell the chamomile from across the room. "We'll just have to share, won't we? Yes, we can manage that."

"Oh, no, thank you," Willow said politely. "I'm afraid we don't have time for tea."

"We don't?" Mandrake said with a wistful look. Nettle stepped on his talon and he yelped.

"It won't take long," Hawthorn said. "There's a hot spring out back where I can get the water. I even have honey!" He started toward the door.

"Really, no," Sundew said, putting one talon over the tea jar. "The tribe is in danger. We must get back before Queen Wasp attacks, which might be as soon as tonight."

"Oh," Hawthorn said, looking startled. "That does sound serious! Really worth mentioning, I must say. Yes. I'd call that relevant news. How *do* you know that? Someone is quite clever, I see." He put one talon on his wooden egg and frowned down at it thoughtfully. "Ah," he said after a moment. He looked up at them, his brow clearing. "You know about the breath of evil."

"We know it's linked to Wasp's mind control," Sundew said. "We were hoping —"

"Did Queen Sequoia send you?" he interrupted eagerly. "Does she want me back at last?" He hesitated. "That is . . . Is Sequoia still queen?"

"She is," Willow answered.

"She *is*!" he said, clasping his front talons together. "That's . . . that's *wonderful* news. After all this time. Still alive! I can hardly believe it. And she did send you? What did she say about me?"

"That you've been working on a cure for Wasp's mind control," Sundew said. "She said you know more about it than any other dragon alive."

"Ha!" he said. His long green wings dipped and folded back. "That is certainly true, isn't it? I mean, that was her intention, sending me here. Quite a long time it's been, for me to be here studying it, all alone. I really should be an expert by now." He laughed.

"Are you using it on the snakes?" Cricket burst out. "Is that why they listen to you?"

"Well, of course," he said. "Rather hard to study something without doing a few experiments."

"So they obey you?" Nettle said curiously. "You can just order them around?"

"Are you in their heads, like Wasp when she controls her subjects?" Cricket asked.

"So many questions! I really don't know if I can do this without tea!" Hawthorn said, grabbing a teapot and bustling out the back door. Willow and Sundew exchanged glances while he was gone, but for once, Sundew couldn't guess what she was thinking. Sundew wasn't even sure what *she* thought of the eccentric old dragon.

Hawthorn scooted back inside, steam rising from the water in the teapot. He shook out a pile of tea leaves into each cup and poured the water over top of them.

"See? All ready," he said. "Please do have some; I'm quite proud of this tea." He set a jar of honey on the table as well, with a pleased expression. "No visitors in decades. This is so splendid."

"Hawthorn," Willow said gently. "We really are short on time."

"Of course," he said, his expression clouding. "I am surprised it took Sequoia so long to send you. I was beginning to think none of my messages got through."

"Messages?" Mandrake asked.

"Well," Hawthorn said. He took a sip of his tea. "I was forbidden to return to the village myself, wasn't I?"

Sundew gave Willow a puzzled look. "You were?"

"So I sent messages however I could," he said. "In coconuts down the river. Tied to the legs of monkeys and birds. I even sent a few of my vipers, but they were killed before they could reach the village. Such a shame; they were smart little snakes, just doing what I'd asked."

"I . . . don't think she got any of those messages," Willow confessed.

"What did they say?" Sundew asked, leaning forward. "Did you find an antidote?"

"I did," he said. His eyes suddenly glistened with unshed tears. "That is, I believe so."

"But that's amazing!" Cricket said. "Why are you sad?"

Hawthorn rubbed his eyes with his knuckles. "Oh, it's only . . . you know, the time I've lost . . . all these years I could have spent with Sequoia."

Cricket sat down beside him and put one talon over his where it rested on the table. He twitched slightly, as though his instinct was to pull away from a HiveWing, but he left his talon in hers.

"I'm sorry for what you've been through," she said. "I can't imagine what it was like to be alone for so long. But what you were doing is *so important*. You're going to save so many dragons, Hawthorn. When all the HiveWings are freed, you're going to be a hero. The LeafWing who devoted his life to freeing them! Your antidote will save my sis — my mother. It means everything to me. Not to mention it'll stop another war."

He sniffed and pulled his talon away to swipe at his eyes again. "That is something," he said. "If it works . . . I'm glad to know this wasn't all for nothing. And don't get me wrong. I know I deserved this. I told the queen I understood, and I meant it. This was the right punishment for me, the only punishment."

"What?" Cricket said, glancing at the other LeafWings as though they might have the answers.

Willow spread her wings, equally puzzled. "What do you mean?" she said to Hawthorn. "I thought you volunteered for this — how could you deserve it?"

"What were you being punished for?" Sundew asked.

He blinked at them, surprise written in every crease of his face. "Didn't she tell you why I'm here?" he asked.

Sundew shook her head. She didn't know why she suddenly felt so full of dread, as though the earth was about to collapse underneath her.

"Because I'm the one who found the breath of evil, after everyone thought it had been wiped out centuries ago," he said. "And I'm the one who gave it to Queen Wasp."

── CHAPTER 16 ──

"What?" Willow cried. She staggered back a step, and Sundew reached to catch her, their wings sliding together like falling petals.

Hawthorn's words didn't seem to fit inside Sundew's brain. She couldn't link them properly to reality. They just didn't *make sense.*

"You gave it to her?" Cricket said. "The breath of evil? What do you mean? When? You didn't really . . . why would you do that? Why would you make her more powerful? Why would you give *anyone* the power to control other dragons like that?"

"I don't understand," said Willow.

"Me neither," echoed Mandrake.

"I understand that someone's been lying to us! And keeping things from us!" Nettle snarled. "I may not under-stand what those exact things are, but I know that I'm angry about it!"

Hawthorn held up his front talons, palms out. "I'm sorry, I thought you knew! I thought Queen Sequoia would have told you. Wouldn't you think she would share the whole story before sending someone on a quest this dangerous?"

"I WOULD think that!" Nettle snapped. "She SHOULD have!"

"Maybe she thought Hawthorn was dead, and if he was, then no one would ever have to know the whole truth," Mandrake suggested.

"That is not better!" Nettle cried. "That is worse! Talk about cowardly!"

Sundew was angry, too, but she mostly felt as if she'd been walking along a strong branch and it had suddenly snapped off and sent her plummeting to the ground and the ground was extraordinarily far away and her wings weren't working, and it was difficult to focus on being mad and trying not to plummet at the same time.

"I think *you* need to tell us the whole story," Sundew said to Hawthorn. *I must have misunderstood something. He didn't mean he went* looking *for the breath of evil. He can't possibly mean that we did this to the HiveWings.*

Hawthorn looked down at his tea and fiddled with the handle on his cup. "All right," he said. "But can I please start by saying I know you'll hate me at the end of it. That's all right. If you could hold back a little bit, though, I'd appreciate it. Fifty years of carrying this guilt has really been a lot. If you can imagine."

"More explaining, less self-pity," Nettle hissed.

He nodded again. "Yes. Well. Let's see. Queen Wasp was dangerous from the moment she inherited her crown. Her mother, Queen Cochineal, was deceitful and power-hungry, but at least she respected the separate tribe monarchies. Wasp, though . . . she looked at SilkWings and LeafWings and only saw more dragons to crush under her talons. She wanted everyone to bow to her. That became clear very early on.

"But that wasn't the worst of it. She thought our power came from the trees, and she thought that if she cut them down, we'd become weak. She did it stealthily at first. Stretches of forest cleared in faraway corners where we might not notice. 'Accidental' forest fires that wiped out hundreds of trees. Another hundred cut down to build her first Hive, and a dramatic performance art piece when we tried to object: 'Oh, are LeafWings the only ones allowed to use Pantalan resources now? Why shouldn't I build *my* tribe a city to live in?' And so on."

He paused to sip his tea again, then nudged one of the other cups toward Nettle and Mandrake with a hopeful expression. Nettle scowled at him, and he sighed and returned to his story.

"By the time we figured out what she was doing, it was too late for countless trees. We tried to stop her in all the diplomatic ways, but she would lie to our faces, promise to stop, and then turn around and keep doing it. Or she'd have her guards throw us out — the queen of the LeafWings, tossed out of Wasp Hive like a spider that crawled in the wrong window! Can you imagine?!"

"I can imagine tossing *you* out a window," Nettle offered.

"And then she became even worse," he continued hurriedly. "She announced that according to the Book of Clearsight, the time had come for us to consolidate the three tribes under one queen: her. She sent Queen Monarch and Queen Sequoia instructions for formally stepping down and handing their subjects over to her control."

"We know this part," Sundew said. "Queen Monarch said yes, Queen Sequoia said no, and the Tree Wars began."

"Not immediately," said Hawthorn. "First we tried to talk her down. And second . . . we tried something else." He cupped his claws around the teacup and closed his eyes. "I thought we could stop her. I thought we could save everyone."

"By giving Wasp the most powerful weapon in the world?" Cricket asked.

"Yes, please do explain the logic there," Sundew said.

"It wasn't supposed to make her powerful." Hawthorn looked down at his talons. "I thought, if I found the plant and we used it on her . . . that *we'd* be able to control *her*."

Willow turned her face in toward Sundew's shoulder, hiding it for a moment as she breathed in a small, hiccuping way. Sundew wound her tail around Willow's and tried to think straight.

We were trying to turn the HiveWing queen into our mind-controlled zombie.

We would have done that to her — the same terrible thing she's done to her subjects.

Instead we made her stronger than any other dragon. We gave her a way to keep her claws on her tribe's necks, and the power to use them against us.

She glanced over at Cricket, who was staring at Hawthorn in horror.

I thought we were the good tribe. How could we do something like this?

"When did this happen?" Cricket asked, questions suddenly exploding out of her like flamesilk erupting from Blue's wrists. "And how did you give it to her? How did she get her talons on more of the plant? How did she figure out what to do with it?" She stopped, pressing her talons to her temples. "Why would you *do* this?"

"She threatened our trees, HiveWing," Hawthorn said, with a hard note in his voice that told Sundew he still thought his actions were justified. "The trees we loved, our homes and souls. We saw the war that was coming. We knew how dangerous she was, and we knew we couldn't give her the LeafWings.

"So we held a peace summit and I . . . I put it in her food that night."

Willow took one of Sundew's clenched talons, smoothed it flat, and looked up at Hawthorn again. "Did the queen know what you were doing?"

He made an inscrutable face. "I told her what I wanted to do. She didn't *stop* me. But I can't say she exactly told me to do it. She *could* have stopped me, though. I was so loyal. I always listened to her. If she had told me not to do it, I wouldn't have. She never said no! This is really —"

Hawthorn stopped himself, lashing his tail for a moment. "I mean," he continued in a calmer voice. "Of course it was my fault. I found the plant; I slipped it into Wasp's food. That was me. Even if I did it with the noblest of intentions."

He really does still think he did the right thing, Sundew thought. *And that it just . . . went wrong.*

"At first, it seemed like nothing happened. It clearly

didn't work," Hawthorn said. He put one talon on the wooden egg again, tracing the leaves with one claw. "Wasp behaved exactly the same, both that night at dinner and the following morning during negotiations. We tried to steer her onto a peaceful path. We tried subtle suggestions, and when those didn't work, we tried to order her to back down. She hissed at us and promised war, just as she always did. So we thought we had failed. No harm done . . . a long shot attempt at salvation that didn't work.

"It wasn't until later, when I saw her mind control, that I realized we must have caused it. I don't know how she figured out what to do, or where she got the plant." He tapped his claws on the top of the egg.

"That's what you get for sneaking and half measures!" Nettle growled. "It should have been poison in her food instead. That would have saved hundreds of dragons."

Nobody argued with her, but Sundew could see the consternation written all over Willow's and Cricket's faces. *She's right, but she's also wrong*, Sundew thought. *Even I don't think anyone should poison dragons at a peace summit.*

"The good news," Hawthorn broke in, slicing through the tension, "is that now I know what we did wrong. We needed to ingest the plant ourselves. Otherwise there was no connection between our minds and hers."

"But if you both ate it," Cricket asked doubtfully, "who would control who? Why wouldn't she be the one controlling you instead?"

"Ah!" said Hawthorn, his expression lightening. "Those are mysteries I solved with science! Experimentation! Research! Investigation! All the careful procedures I wish I'd had time for back then. It's amazing what you can discover when you're alone for fifty years with nothing else to do. Yes, I know, not completely alone."

Sundew tilted her head at him. "Not completely alone?" she echoed. "Do you mean the snakes?"

"The snakes, the foliage, my wooden friends," he answered, waving his claws around the little house. "I have extremely strong leafspeak, so I can always chat with the jungle if I get lonely."

"So you've been experimenting on the snakes," Cricket said, "and you've figured out how to mind-control them? Is that also how you found the antidote?"

"Yes, exactly!" Hawthorn said. "I tried everything, and I finally found this!" He darted across the room to a wooden chest, ornately carved with hundreds of tiny leaves. Sundew couldn't even imagine how long it had taken him to carve it. He lifted off the lid, grunting slightly at the weight of it, and laid it on the floor beside him, then beckoned Cricket to look inside.

Sundew edged closer so she could see as well. The chest seemed to be full of tiny gnarled bits of roots — they looked like ginger root but smelled more like old oranges. From the look on Cricket's face, though, they might have been made of gold.

"This is the antidote?" she said to Hawthorn in a hushed voice. She reached in and lifted out one of the roots, turning it between her claws. "What is it?"

"It's another plant I found growing in the jungle," he said. "I call it 'heart of salvation.'" Nettle snorted and he shot her a half smile. "I figure if we're going to be all dramatic with our plant names, I might as well join in."

"Wow," Cricket said reverently. "And it really works? It breaks the mind control?"

"As far as I can tell," he said. "It works on snakes . . . but who knows about dragons? I haven't exactly had any test subjects for that, have I? Oh! Maybe you could eat one, and we'll see if it works on you!"

She shook her head ruefully. "I'm not susceptible to the mind control," she said. "Queen Wasp never injected my egg, so it doesn't work on me. Which means we wouldn't learn anything from me eating this." She sighed and put it back in the chest. Hawthorn watched the movements of her claw intently, as if he was trying to think of a way she could still be useful to the experiment.

"So to test it out," Sundew said, "we'll have to find a HiveWing who *is* all zombie-brained, force them to eat it, and see what happens."

"I'm afraid so," he said, wringing his claws together.

"Well, luckily for us, there's probably about a thousand of them heading this way right now," Sundew said. "Pack all the weird knobbly salvation roots you have and let's go."

CHAPTER 17

It took a while to convince Hawthorn that, yes, they really meant it, he should come back to the village with them. That, yes, Queen Sequoia would be happy to see him, now that he'd found the antidote. That, no, nobody would yell at him, probably, and in fact nobody had any idea what he'd done except for the queen, as far as they knew.

Then they had to deal with him being miffed about everyone completely forgetting him, and *then* they had to talk him out of packing every single one of his carvings.

"There's no time!" Sundew cried as Hawthorn scooped up an armful of little wooden Sequoias and glanced around frantically for a box. "Hawthorn, you can come back and get them later. Right now the only thing we can bring is the antidote. We need to move as quickly as we can, not cart a houseful of nonsense all over the jungle."

"They're beautiful carvings," Willow interjected soothingly. "Maybe just bring one, for now?"

Hawthorn's expression relaxed, and he dropped all the others, reaching for his egg-like favorite. "Yes, we can do that," he said. "As long as I have this friend, I'll be all right."

"Wonderful," Nettle said, rolling her eyes. "You carry that; Mandrake and I will carry this." She waved one wing over the chest full of roots.

Sundew had misgivings about that plan. Leaving the antidote in the talons of those two . . . but Cricket was carrying Bumblebee, and Sundew wanted a chance to talk to Willow out of everyone's earshot.

It'll be fine. They'll be careful with it, I'm sure.

"What about my vipers?" Hawthorn asked as they stepped out the door. Sundew cast a glance at the sky. She guessed it was late afternoon.

"Uh . . . what *about* your vipers?" Mandrake echoed. They started across the clearing, back into the snake-spangled jungle.

"Should I bring them?" Hawthorn said brightly. "I should bring them, shouldn't I?"

"Your army of poisonous snakes? To a village full of dragonets?" Willow said. "I vote . . . definitely no?"

"But they might be useful," Hawthorn argued, his face falling. "Aren't we about to go to war? Yes, so I hear. So maybe Queen Sequoia would like a few zombie vipers on her side this time!"

"Please don't!" Cricket said. "We don't want to make killing dragons easier. We don't want to kill *anyone* — we're going to free them all with the antidote and then there won't be any war."

Nettle snorted extremely pointedly.

"If it works," Hawthorn said sadly. "And if we can figure out how to give it to all of them. Ooh, vipers might help with that!"

"Sounds like a decent backup plan to me," Nettle chimed in. She'd wound vines around the trunk and looped one end over her shoulder and one over Mandrake's so it hung between them. They were both already huffing from the weight of it. "I mean, no harm done having an extra secret weapon around, right?"

"Exactly!" Hawthorn said, beaming. He flapped his wings once and gazed through the trees, his eyes going weirdly still. "I'll just have a few of them follow us."

"Willow," Sundew whispered. "Should we stop him?"

"I don't know," Willow whispered back. She furrowed her brow at the rustlings in the leaves. "It feels wrong, but then, I'm not even sure I know what's right and wrong anymore. Queen Sequoia was always my moral compass. I thought she'd always do the right thing, and I wanted to be like her so much. But what she was going to do to Wasp . . . and the fact that she lied to us about it. I don't know how to feel right now."

"Mad!" Sundew suggested. "Really mad! You're allowed to be angry about this, Willow." She brushed Willow's wing lightly.

"I don't want to be mad," Willow protested. "What good would that do? If I let myself be really angry, I might do something terrible like yell at Queen Sequoia."

"Maybe she *should* be yelled at," Sundew pointed out.

"But how would that help? Then she'd feel awful and I'd feel guilty and we'd be distracted from more important things."

"The point is to make sure she knows she did something wrong! So she won't do it again . . . and maybe she'll try harder to fix it."

"I'm sure she already knows it was wrong," Willow said.

"I'm not sure *he* does," Sundew said, nodding toward Hawthorn. He was walking at the front of the group, chatting with Cricket. A pair of snakes was slithering along right by his talons, but he barely even glanced down at them.

"Getting angry will only make me feel worse," Willow said firmly. "But I am upset. And just . . . really, really sad." She shook herself from head to tail. "That's what this is. I'm sad."

"Well, I'm pleased for you that you're that good at choose-your-own-emotion," Sundew said. "I'm *definitely* mad and I can't just smush that into feeling sad or something else instead. So you can go eat chocolate or whatever being sad leads to; I'm going to yell at the queen."

Willow shot her a troubled look. "I hope you won't be too mean. We need her on our side for the war ahead. I mean . . . I want her to keep listening to us. To *you*. So I just hope you won't drive her away."

"She still talks to Belladonna after all this time," Sundew said. "And she's a queen. She should be tough enough to handle it."

Their trip back to the village seemed faster than their trip out, partly because they were able to move much more quickly through the Den of Vipers, and partly because this time they went around the other edge of the lake, which was lined with sharp marsh reeds and cobra lilies, but nothing that actually managed to catch them.

They reached Queen Sequoia's tree palace shortly after nightfall. Sundew's leafspeak kept picking up strange murmurs from the jungle around Willow's village. *Trouble* . . . they'd whisper one moment, and then the next, *All is well*. She wound her mind through the roots and whispers, but she couldn't pin down what they were feeling or worrying about.

All is well, all is well.

Danger is coming.

All is well.

She shivered and pulled her mind back. It didn't make sense, so she'd have to ignore it for a while until it did. Trees could be ridiculously maddening sometimes.

Hawthorn had pulled his wings in close and gone quiet as they entered the perimeter of the village. He kept looking up at the trees, perhaps sensing the LeafWings who had come out to watch them pass by. Sundew hadn't seen any sign of more vipers beyond the two at his feet, but she wondered if they were out there somewhere, too, a small deadly army trailing along behind their leader.

They flew up to the throne room and found Hazel there, pacing in a circle around Tsunami, who was lying down with her eyes closed and her front talons clasped. If the SeaWing was asleep, she didn't look very peaceful; her brow was furrowed and her tail twitched furiously as though she might be lashing it inside her dream.

They landed as quietly as they could, and Willow signaled *what in the world?* to Hazel.

"She said she could communicate with the Distant Kingdoms somehow," Hazel whispered, hurrying over to them. "I have no idea what she's doing! Maybe all the dragons over there are delusional."

"Or *magic*," Cricket breathed.

"Where's your great-grandmother?" Sundew asked.

"She left with Belladonna and half the village," Hazel said. "They're at the Snarling River by now, I'm sure." She picked up a book from the throne, fiddled with it for a moment, then put it back. "I haven't heard anything. Hoping for a messenger soon. What did you find?"

"We found Hawthorn," Willow said, indicating the old dragon. "And he *does* have an antidote, but we need to test it to make sure it works."

"As quickly as possible," Sundew agreed.

"So we need a HiveWing?" Hazel asked sharply. She climbed onto the throne and tapped the small gong hanging above it. "Then let's get one." Three guards came swooping in from the level above them. "Go to the Snarling River," Hazel commanded. "Find the queen, and find out whether Wasp's army is there yet. If so, capture a HiveWing on his or her own and bring it . . ." She hesitated for a moment, her eyes scanning the village out the window. "Bring it to the hemlock grove on the banks of the Gullet River. As fast as you can."

"I want to go, too!" Nettle demanded. She dropped the chest and flapped herself loose from the loops of vines. "I want to abduct a HiveWing! I want to be where the fighting is!"

"You may go with them," Hazel said. "You can explain everything to the queen."

The guards bowed and flew off with Nettle, their flashing scales quickly swallowed by the darkness outside.

Hazel hopped down from the throne and untied the vines around the chest so she could look inside. "This is it?" she asked, looking up at Hawthorn. "Will this be enough?"

"It depends on how we give it to them," he said. "Ideally they would all eat a piece at least this big." He held up his claws to indicate a small cube. "But it might work if we could get it into their water supply."

Sundew shook her head. "We need a way to give the whole army the antidote at once, before Wasp realizes what's happening. Otherwise she'll stop them from taking it the moment she notices." She frowned at the pile of roots. She knew the jungle was enormous and probably contained hundreds of plants she'd never encountered, but she was still a little surprised that the heart of salvation didn't look more familiar.

"Oh!" Cricket said suddenly. "What if . . . would it work if we burn it, and they breathe in the smoke?"

Hawthorn scrunched up his snout, thinking. "Maybe."

"We could set the whole army free that way, couldn't we?" Cricket adjusted her glasses and patted Bumblebee absentmindedly. The dragonet had just woken up and was trying to clamber out of the sling, babbling to herself.

"I would think we'd need more than this," Hazel said.

"What if we plant a few of these and get our most powerful leafspeakers to grow them as quickly as possible, so we'll have as much as we need?"

Hawthorn reached past her and gently closed the chest. "I'd wait to see if it works on dragons first. The heart of salvation is rather a pain to uproot once it takes hold . . . you wouldn't want to overrun your village with it for nothing. Keep a few aside for planting; the rest should be enough for the army, and we can grow more for the rest of the Hives later."

Hazel lifted one eyebrow at the wooden egg wrapped carefully in its sling across his chest. She opened her mouth to argue with him, but just then an abrupt snort from Tsunami made them all jump.

The blue dragon let out a hiss and then grumbled, "Arrrrgh, FINE, but *I'm* still Head of School. Yeah, tell him hugs to him, too, and no, the cows are not bigger and more delicious over here. BYE." She snorted again, rolled over, and sat up, blinking and rubbing her eyes.

"Whew," she said. "I'll never get used to that."

"What did you just do?" Cricket asked eagerly.

"It's . . . I . . ." Sundew noticed Tsunami slipping something into a pouch behind her front left leg. Something she clearly wasn't comfortable telling them about. "I was . . . sort of . . . talking to a few of my friends back on the other continent."

"Oh my goodness, how? With Distant Kingdoms magic?" Cricket asked.

"Yup," Tsunami said, flicking her wings back. She looked troubled. "Hard to explain. Anyway. They didn't have any particularly helpful ideas, but Moon seems really sure that there must be a way for you to get there." She rubbed her forehead. "Something about a prophecy. Have I mentioned that I hate prophecies?"

"She had a prophecy about us?" Cricket yelped. "What was it? What's going to happen?"

"No," Tsunami said, pointing a stern claw at her. "Do not get excited. Prophecies are terrible and annoying. And this one sounds like a pile of wet seaweed to me, because there's no way you can all get over there!"

"Clearsight did it," Willow pointed out. "She wasn't a SeaWing, but she crossed the ocean safely, somehow."

They all looked back at Tsunami. "I guess that's true," she said doubtfully. "I have no idea how, though."

"Maybe there's a clue in the Book," Willow said, whirling toward Sundew. "Can we look at it? Maybe there's something in there that will tell us how she got here."

"I read the whole thing and didn't notice anything like that," Sundew said, but she pulled it out of its pouch and unwrapped it anyway. The faded blue cover and thin pages looked even more ancient in the glow from the firefly lamps.

"You can check for yourself, but it doesn't matter if you don't find anything. The LeafWings aren't going anywhere. I'm staying right here and fighting for our place on *this* continent, no matter what Wasp does!"

"And the antidote will work," Cricket chimed in. "So we won't have to run away. Although, I mean, I'd love to see the Distant Kingdoms someday, if there is a way to get across the ocean."

Hazel glanced out the window; the sky was fully dark by now, and the jungle was alive with the sounds of busy insects, grumbling frogs, and night predators.

"Let's get to the Gullet River and hope the guards return soon," she said. "Tsunami, you study the Book in the meanwhile. Sundew, Cricket, Hawthorn, and Willow, come with me." She opened the chest and picked out two pieces of the heart of salvation root.

"Not me?" Mandrake started. "I'll just . . . wait here, then."

"We'll be back soon," Sundew said.

There was no one at the hemlock grove when they arrived. Hawthorn lay down on the grass, cradling his wooden egg between his front talons, and one of his snakes slithered up to coil around his neck.

Cricket watched Hazel pace between the trees for a moment, and then she turned to Hawthorn. "Hey, I was wondering something," she said.

"You?" Sundew teased. "Really?"

Cricket ignored her. "According to the Legend of the Hive," she said, "the plant originally worked on everything, right? Bees, ants, lions, birds, snakes, anything. But it seems like Queen Wasp can only use it on HiveWings. I mean, she *must* have tried injecting the SilkWings, too, don't you think? Maybe even a LeafWing at some point? So why doesn't the mind control work on other tribes?"

"That is an excellent question," Hawthorn said approvingly.

"Thank you," Cricket said with delight, fluttering her wings.

"When I found the plant, it was barely hanging on," he said. "There was so little left, cut off from sunlight and slowly wasting away. I brought it into the sun. I nursed it back to health. And while I did, I used my leafspeak on it. I trained it, essentially. I altered it so that it would only work on HiveWings . . . those would be the minds it was drawn to. I wasn't sure how well I'd succeeded, but it seems I did well enough."

He looked horribly proud of himself. Sundew wanted to scratch his face off. How could he still be *pleased* about what he did, after all this time and all the damage he'd caused?

"Oh," Cricket said. Her wings sank to the ground. "I . . . guess that's very impressive."

"It is," he assured her. "Not many dragons could do it."

It occurred to Sundew that they should tell Hazel the whole story; the future queen had no idea what her great-grandmother and Hawthorn had done. But this wasn't the time. She could hear muffled yells getting closer and closer.

The LeafWing guards appeared in the treetops, carrying a HiveWing prisoner who was blindfolded and tied up with strangler vines like an insect in a cocoon. They flew him down to the damp earth by the riverside and Nettle threw him at Hazel's feet, grinning.

"That was GREAT!" she said. Sundew wasn't sure she'd ever seen Nettle so happy. It was, quite frankly, very unsettling. "I want more missions like that!"

But Hazel wasn't smiling. She took a step back and gazed down at the HiveWing, then up at Nettle. "I guess this means Wasp and the HiveWings are at the river already."

"Oh, yes we are," the HiveWing suddenly snapped. His fangs glistened in the moonlight. Even without seeing his pale white eyes, Sundew recognized the creepy extra layer to his voice: Wasp was inside his mind, using his mouth to speak to them.

"We're here, LeafWing, and this time we'll make sure to finish what we started. You're all dead!" The HiveWing twisted and writhed, trying to drag the blindfold off his eyes.

Nettle put her front talons on his ears and pinned him to the ground, ignoring his flailing. "There were thousands of HiveWings on the other side of the river," she said in a low voice. "And we could see more flying in. They're just . . . standing there, row after row of them, staring at the jungle with creepy white eyes. It looks like they're waiting for something."

"The rest of the tribe?" Cricket guessed. "It would take longer for the dragons from Mantis Hive and Cicada Hive to get here. Maybe she wants them all in place before attacking."

"Did you see Queen Sequoia?" Hazel asked softly.

"Is Blue with her?" Cricket chimed in.

"Yes," said Nettle. "She has the flamesilk and the other massively annoying SilkWing. They're working on —"

Hazel cut her off by putting her talon around Nettle's snout. She indicated the HiveWing; even with his ears covered, they couldn't risk Wasp overhearing Queen Sequoia's plans. Nettle scowled down at him and nodded.

"Let's do this quickly," Sundew said. She held out one talon for the heart of salvation root. Hazel used her claws to slice off a piece about as big as an eyeball (which was an image Sundew immediately regretted conjuring) and passed it to her.

Nettle lifted the prisoner's snout and pried his jaw open. He tried to bite her, but her grip was strong. Sundew stuffed the root into his mouth, and Nettle slammed it closed, holding it shut until he swallowed. Finally she let go and stepped back.

"That little worm Cricket is here, isn't she?" the dragon spat immediately. **"The one who thinks she's so very clever, with her pamphlets and graffiti and rumors. Guess what, Cricket? I figured it out. I know who your father is. And he's mine, all mine, and I could kill him in a heartbeat if I wanted to. Or I could let you meet him. Would you like that? Wouldn't you like to come back to Wasp Hive so I . . . can . . ."**

The HiveWing trailed off. His whole body went limp, and his head lolled back onto the grass.

Sundew reached out and took one of Willow's talons between hers. She could feel Willow's heartbeat in her palm. For once, it was as fast as Sundew's.

Hazel turned to Hawthorn. "Does that mean it worked?" she asked.

"I think . . . maybe?" he said.

The HiveWing jerked once, twice, like a fish pulled up on land. He rolled on his side and gasped several times, as if there wasn't enough air in the world to breathe.

"What is happening?" he croaked finally. "Where am I? Why does everything smell wet?"

Cricket motioned the others back, crouched beside him,

and removed his blindfold. From the shadows behind him, Sundew couldn't see his face, but she could hear the hitch in his voice.

"What's your name?" Cricket asked him.

"Inchworm," he answered. "From Vinegaroon Hive. Who are you?"

"Cricket," she said. "Cicada Hive. How do you feel?"

He hesitated for a moment. "Weird. Empty? And I seem to be all tied up."

"Do you know why you're here?"

"No!" he blurted. "I don't even know where here is!"

"Try to think back," Cricket said. "You were going about your day in your Hive, when suddenly the queen was in your head. What did she make you do?"

"Ohhhh," he said. "Right. The summons. I was getting Glowworm ready for school — Glowworm!" He tried to surge upright but fell back, straining against the vines.

"Is that your dragonet?" Cricket said, touching his shoulder with her wing. "We'll make sure she's safe, don't worry."

"She was summoned, too," he said, his voice racked with worry. "Everyone was. I think Wasp called the whole tribe. Are we going to war? My dragonet is out there . . . she doesn't know how to fight! I have to find her." He began struggling again.

"We're not going to war," Cricket said. "We're going to stop it. If I untie you, will you help us stop it?"

"Us?" he said warily.

"Me and the LeafWings," she said. "You'd have to promise you wouldn't hurt any LeafWings."

"I promise," he said. "I promise! I don't want to fight anyone! I just want to get Glowworm and go home!"

"That's what we want, too," Cricket said.

Sundew felt a jolt of familiar anger. *Is that what we want? All the HiveWings get to go home and keep living their happy lives as though they didn't nearly destroy us? Where's the punishment? The justice?*

She knew what Blue would say: *These HiveWings are not the enemy. Queen Wasp is the enemy. Focus on her.*

But the HiveWings had benefited from everything Wasp did, and they never lifted a claw to stop her. They were part of the problem, too. They needed to learn a lesson and atone, not carry on as though nothing had happened.

She didn't have a chance to say anything — not that she had any idea what she would say — before Cricket was standing in front of Hazel, spreading her wings.

"I think it worked!" she whispered, pushing up her glasses. "Wasp is gone! Hawthorn, you did it! He's free!"

"Unless he's faking it," Nettle growled.

"I don't think he could," Willow said.

"And Wasp wouldn't miss a chance to be scary to my face," Cricket agreed. "If she was in there, she'd show herself. Can we untie him?"

"Let's get the antidote on its way first," Hazel said in her queenly voice. "Nettle, I assume you want to go back to the front lines?"

"Yesssss," Nettle hissed with glee.

"I'll go, too," Sundew said. She wanted to see for herself what they were facing. And if they were able to use the antidote, she wanted to see it work. She wanted to see Queen Wasp's reaction when all her power evaporated.

"Can I come?" Cricket asked. "To check on Blue?"

"Very well," said Hazel. "Willow and Hawthorn, you can help me figure out how to get this HiveWing back to his dragonet. The three of you, go collect the antidote and fly it to the queen. As fast as you can — we have no idea when Wasp will decide it's time to attack."

Sundew found herself starting to bow and felt ridiculous; she had barely known Sequoia and Hazel for a day and yet she kept instinctively treating them like real queens. But then, out of the corner of her eye, she caught Nettle doing the same thing. Nettle! Of all dragons! So maybe Sundew wasn't that ridiculous, after all.

Willow grabbed one of her talons as Sundew took a step

back. "Please be careful," she said. "Remember you promised me you'd never die." She choked out a half sob, half laugh.

"You be careful, too," Sundew said, wrapping her wings around Willow and pulling her close. "I'll see you really soon. Like, immediately after we save the world."

Willow laughed again, and then they let go of each other, and Sundew lifted into the air to follow Nettle and Cricket.

The war was waiting for them. And one small plant might be the only thing that could stop it.

Tsetse Hive

Beetle Lake

Vinegaroon Hive

Hornet Hive

Cicada Hive

Mantis Hive

PART THREE

LEAVES IN A STORM

— CHAPTER 18 —

"I know something," Cricket sang, nudging Sundew's wing as they flew through the village.

"You know entirely too many things," Sundew observed. "But you are very welcome to keep them all to yourself."

"*I* know who your one true love is," Cricket whispered. "It's *not* Mandrake. I knew it wasn't!"

"Yes, because I told you that," Sundew snapped. "You're very clever."

"Well, I just wanted to say I like her, and I like the look on your face when she talks to you."

"I AM NOT EVEN REMOTELY INTERESTED IN WHAT YOU LIKE," Sundew barked, landing on a branch behind Nettle. Cricket thumped down behind them, and they all hurried along in silence for a moment. "But thank you," Sundew finally grumbled.

"I figured it out, too," Nettle said suddenly from the lead. She swung her head around to glare at Sundew and Cricket before moving on. "I don't understand falling for a SapWing at *all* or when *that* could have possibly happened, but I also don't care, and as far as I'm concerned, not having you for a sister-in-law would be a stellar development."

"Well, not being related to you is one of my favorite things about her!" Sundew growled back.

Nettle harrumphed and hopped to the next tree. A dewy pine leaned hopefully toward her, and she hissed fiercely at it.

"Sorry," Cricket whispered to Sundew. "I didn't think she'd hear me!"

"I have very sharp ears," Nettle declared.

"This conversation can be over now," Sundew suggested. She saw the tree palace up ahead and darted out in front, swinging out of the tree and flying down to it. Inside, Tsunami had been joined by the other SeaWing, Turtle, who looked much less queasy than he had before. They both had their phosphorescent scales lit up and were leaning over the Book of Clearsight, studying each page.

Mandrake came hurrying over as Sundew landed. "Did it work?" he asked.

"As far as we can tell," she said. She stepped into the loops of vines that Nettle had abandoned next to the chest and started tightening them around herself. "We're taking this to Queen Sequoia now."

"We should leave a few here," Cricket said, opening the chest and scooping out a talonful of roots. She glanced around for a moment, then went over to pile them on top of the throne.

"What about you?" Sundew asked Tsunami as Nettle tied the other side of the looped vines around her shoulders. "Any luck?"

The blue dragon shook her head. "Nothing much about Pyrrhia so far. But Moon said *a secret hides within their book* . . ."

"She did?" Cricket asked. "Was that part of the prophecy?"

"Part of the gibberish," Tsunami muttered.

"The big secret in there is that the HiveWings have been lying about it for hundreds of years," Sundew pointed out. "That's got to be what that means. That all the 'prophecies' about uniting under Queen Wasp were fake."

"Yeah, probably," Tsunami said with a sigh.

"Let's *go*," Nettle said, hopping from foot to foot. "Mandrake, you too. Not that you'll be useful, but you can at least try to look like it."

"Tsunami," Cricket said hesitantly. "This is a lot to ask, but . . . could I leave Bumblebee here with you?"

"EKNO!" Bumblebee objected, throwing her arms around Cricket's neck. "NOBYNOBYNOBE!"

"That does look like fun," Tsunami said wryly.

"Bumblebee, be reasonable!" Cricket yelled over her wails. "There might be a war where I'm going! Dragons all stabbing each other! Very bad things! I don't want you near that. I want you here and safe!"

"STABEEBAD," Bumblebee argued. "YUUUUsafe."

"I will be careful and I'll come back soon. I promise." She disentangled Bumblebee and the sling and handed them over to an extremely skeptical-looking Tsunami.

"GROWLFACE!" the dragonet shouted. "ARGNORAW RGRUMPHLE!"

"I'm actually very cool," Tsunami pointed out to her. "I run a school for dragonets on my continent. Bigger, less noisy ones, though."

Bumblebee glowered at her as though she did not find this information endearing whatsoever.

"Bye, little bug," Sundew called as they lifted off. "Be good!"

"HAAAA!" Bumblebee shouted after her, which boded ill for the rest of Tsunami's night.

It turned out to be extremely annoying and unwieldy and exhausting and aggravating to carry the antidote chest with Nettle on the other side of it. Every time Sundew tried to go down, she went up; every time Sundew tried to hop over a stream, Nettle would hop the other way at the exact same time and they'd both end up in the water. It was lucky that the chest was so sturdy and thick, or it would have been covered in dents and scratches in no time, or possibly collapsed. But it was also unlucky, because its sturdiness made it REALLY STUPIDLY HEAVY.

But finally, sometime close to midnight, Sundew guessed, they reached the border of the jungle and Queen Sequoia's makeshift camp, which took them a little while to find. Sundew had to use her leafspeak to track down the area where the plants were complaining the most about activity and disruption.

A platform had been hastily set up high in the canopy, balanced between a few trees and lashed to their branches. It was close enough to the thin uppermost branches that the three moons could shine through, illuminating most of the encampment. Sequoia stood in the middle of it with Belladonna, issuing orders and consulting with a flow of incoming and outgoing dragons. As Sundew and Nettle struggled toward them, Sundew saw a few warriors she knew receive an order from Sequoia. They looked at one another as though they might not obey, but then Belladonna barked something furiously, and they backed away, nodding.

She also noticed the activity in the trees around them and sensed it down on the jungle floor as well. Her leafspeak told her that several dragons were gathering plants that could be used as offensive weapons — blister bush seeds and sand-box tree fruit in particular. She could hear dragons sending whispered messages through the trees.

They lowered the chest to the platform and landed beside it. Sundew realized that Blue and Swordtail were there, too, huddled in a corner that was nearly hidden by leaves, argu-ing in hushed voices.

I'm not sure I've ever seen Blue argue before, Sundew thought. She wondered if he felt betrayed by her. Would he still help them fight the HiveWings? They'd need his help to burn the antidote . . . Sundew realized that she'd been tak-ing his flamesilk for granted as a weapon they could use. *But it's not our flamesilk. It's his.*

As she watched, Cricket landed and ran over to him, and his face lit with joy at the sight of her.

"What is this?" Belladonna demanded, stalking up to the chest.

Sundew waited until Queen Sequoia had dismissed the dragon she was speaking to. The queen turned toward her with a slightly anxious, slightly disbelieving look on her face.

"This," Sundew said, "is the antidote to the breath of evil." She rested one talon on the lid. "Hawthorn was still alive. He told us a very interesting version of the events that led up to the Tree Wars, Your Majesty."

Queen Sequoia flicked her tail from side to side, studying Sundew's face. "He really found an antidote?" she said quietly.

"We think so," Sundew said at the same time as Cricket blurted, "Yes!"

"It's called heart of salvation," Mandrake added.

The queen let out a long breath. "Then we can finally atone for what we did," she said.

Sundew heard the echo of her own thoughts like a stab in the heart. She'd wanted the HiveWings to atone . . . she *still* wanted them to. They were *much worse* than the LeafWings.

But Hawthorn and Sequoia did terrible things, too. The HiveWings would be right to want them to be punished . . . but they would be wrong to want the same for the whole LeafWing tribe.

So maybe . . .

Maybe I need to think about that, too.

Hawthorn, Sequoia, and Wasp. I should be angry at them — I can be furious at them. I can fight Wasp without hating the entire HiveWing tribe.

I can free the HiveWings and spare their lives without betraying my quest. Because Wasp is the real enemy: Wasp and her mind control.

She dragged the vines off her wings and off the chest so

she could throw it open. "Here's what we need to do," she said. "We take these roots down to the Snarling River and build a bonfire with them, as close to the HiveWing army as we can safely get. Then we set it on fire, they breathe in the smoke, and we cross all our claws that this works." She hesitated, then turned to Blue, who had stepped forward to listen.

"Which means we need flamesilk," she said, "*if* Blue is willing to give us some."

"If he's willing!" Belladonna spat. "Who's giving him a choice?!"

"I am," Sundew said, frowning at her. "It's his choice. He doesn't belong to us, any more than all the other flamesilks belong to Queen Wasp. If we force him to do what we want, we'll be just like her." She turned back to Blue. "But I'm hoping you'll choose to help us," she said. "This isn't like burning a Hive. This should free the HiveWings, like we hoped."

Cricket leaned into his shoulder and twined her tail around his. "Please?" she whispered.

"Of course I will," Blue said. "I'll fly down there and light it myself." He looked up at Queen Sequoia. "But I want you to promise me you won't take any part of my fire to hurt any dragons. I don't want to find out in three days that some piece of my flamesilk was saved and then used to burn any more Hives."

Belladonna hissed and lashed her tail, which Sundew guessed meant that she'd been planning on doing that exact thing.

"I promise," said Queen Sequoia. "Belladonna?" The way she looked at Belladonna made it clear that wasn't actually a question.

"I promise, too," Belladonna said sulkily.

"Then let's get to work," said the queen. "I'll have my soldiers build the pyre tonight, under cover of darkness, while the HiveWings are still frozen out there. As soon as the sun rises, Blue, I want you to fly down to set it aflame."

"Why not right now?" Nettle asked. "Why wait for the sun?"

"Because I want to see their eyes," Sequoia said. "I want to be sure it works. With luck, the queen will wait to make her move until morning as well, although we should be prepared to fire it at once if she starts to do anything tonight."

Blue nodded, looking terrified.

"I'll help build the bonfire," Sundew offered.

"No." The queen reached one of her wings out to Sundew's shoulder. "I want you to rest."

"Rest!" Sundew protested. "The night before a war?! Or a not-war, whatever happens," she amended, glancing at Cricket's face.

"Yes, absolutely," said the queen. "You've been traveling

all day and for many days before this one. You need to sleep, because first thing in the morning, I want you to take some of these roots and grow more heart of salvation. We need as much as we can get. There are thousands of HiveWings out there."

Sundew hesitated, tempted to argue . . . but exhaustion was beginning to set in as though her eyelids were stuck together with sundew goop. It had been a long day, a long several days.

It was also kind of a weird nice feeling to have someone notice and care. She couldn't remember Belladonna ever telling her she needed to sleep.

"All right, but only for a little while," she said.

She took a few roots from the chest and tucked them into one of her pouches. The rest were carried off by Sequoia's soldiers, out through the canopy and down to the battlefield. Sundew felt strangely apprehensive, watching them fly away. The trees were troubled, but they couldn't tell her why, and it tangled up her leafspeak, adding tendrils of worry to every thought.

Is this really going to work?

What if something happens to the antidote?

What if Wasp figures out what we're up to and manages to destroy it?

Or what if we free the HiveWings from her mind control, but they decide to fight for her anyway? Then there really would be war tomorrow. A war where the dragons Sundew grew up with would all be out in front, with HiveWing weapons pointed at them.

Sundew had spent her whole life being furious with the HiveWings for trying to wipe out her tribe . . . but she hadn't ever quite felt the danger of what would happen if they tried to do it again. She'd been mad about dragons who died half a century ago, but now she had to picture her friends, her tribemates, her parents as the targets, and suddenly she understood, painfully and forcefully, what Sequoia and Willow had felt, and why they hadn't wanted to restart the war.

But we can still stop it, she hoped, she prayed, as she climbed up to a sheltered curve in the branches and lay down next to Cricket and Blue. *If the antidote works.*

Please let it work.

She closed her eyes and drifted into an uneasy sleep.

—— CHAPTER 19 ——

Sundew woke before dawn, her heart pounding. She couldn't remember her dreams, exactly, but she felt as though insects had been crawling all over her. Wasps, perhaps, thousands and thousands of wasps with eyes fathoms deep.

She slipped away from Cricket and Blue, who were still asleep, curled together like intertwining vines. Swordtail was sprawled on Blue's other side, snoring lightly.

The tree branches shook as she climbed to the top, swaying in the breeze. Up here, she could smell the ocean; she could hear the cries of seagulls and birds of prey as they swooped by high overhead. Away from the jostling noise of the jungle plants, her leafspeak could discern the faraway murmurs of savanna grasses.

But this morning, there were other smells, other sounds. This morning she could smell dragons; she could hear hundreds of talons shuffling; she could sense the plants under their feet being smothered, struggling to survive.

And from the very top of the tree, she could see them. Columns of HiveWings lined the plain on the other side of the Snarling River, stretching to the horizon. Orange and gold and black scales, diaphanous wings flickering, each dragon in its place, an exact distance from every other dragon. They looked too precisely placed to be real, but they were real. The HiveWing prisoner had been right; it seemed as though Wasp had summoned every HiveWing in the tribe for this.

She's hoping to wipe us out with one fell swoop, Sundew realized. *She's going to throw everything at us. She wants to finish this today.*

Finish us.

"It's terrifying, isn't it?"

Sundew turned to find Mandrake perched on another high branch nearby. His eyes were tired, and she wondered whether he'd slept as poorly as she had, or maybe not at all.

"We'll stop them," she said. "We have to."

The sky was shading toward pale gray, streaked with pink. The sun would slip over the horizon behind Sundew very soon.

If there's a chance we're all going to die today . . .

"Mandrake," she said. "I'm not going to marry you."

"I know," he said, giving her a real smile for once. "I've always known that."

"Really?" she said. "Because it's not about you. You're one of the few dragons I actually like. But you're not Willow. And she's the only dragon I want to marry."

"I hope you do," he said. "I hope the antidote works. I hope this whole horrible thing ends and we all get to live happily ever after."

His smile faded as he returned his gaze to the vast army below them.

Sundew squinted down at the river, searching for the bonfire pile. It looked pitifully small from up here, especially next to all those thousands of HiveWings.

"Does that look like enough antidote to you?" she asked him.

He shook his head, looking grim. "No. Not even close."

It's not going to be enough. The smoke might reach the first few rows of dragons . . . but that will leave thousands more still behind them, still under Wasp's control.

Thousands more still coming for us.

Panic surged through her like a jolt of toxin.

"I'm going to make more," she said. "Come with me and help!"

He nodded and followed her. She scrambled down the tree until she found an open gap in the branches where she could spread her wings and drop down to the jungle floor.

It was still very dark down here, but Sundew let her leaf-speak reach down into the soil and out through the root systems, tracing them along until she found water. A stream, a tributary of the Snarling River. That would be the best place to grow more heart of salvation, in the mud along the banks, where the damp earth could help it along.

She heard cracking branches overhead and looked up to see Cricket flailing her way down, catching on every vine and cobweb as she did. Mandrake ducked out of the way as the HiveWing landed in an ungraceful sprawl. She hopped to her feet, shaking herself off.

"You don't have to come with us," Sundew pointed out.

"Sure I do," Cricket said. "I can help carry roots! I can harvest them while you make more grow! Also I really want to watch; I didn't get nearly enough of a chance to watch that chokecherry grow, and I imagine it'll be really awesome. I mean, scientifically speaking. I wish I could make plants grow just by thinking at them!"

"Well, it's slightly more complicated than that," Sundew said, "but all right, come along."

They hurried through the jungle until they reached the stream, which wound between small pitcher plants and gurgled over smooth stones. Long feathery ferns leaned over the water, as if plotting how to steal it all for themselves.

Sundew found a patch of dirt, dug a hole, and planted a piece of the root in it. It looked pale and ghostly against the dark wet earth, like a grub that had wiggled its way up from the depths of the underground, or the haunted spirit of a real plant. She could still see patches of its white skin winking through the dirt as she covered it up, until finally it was completely buried.

Mandrake took another piece and moved farther upstream to do the same thing. Cricket stayed beside Sundew, with her tail wrapped around her talons, watching curiously. She wisely (and surprisingly) kept quiet as Sundew dug her claws into the earth and closed her eyes, summoning all the power of her leafspeak.

Hello, little plant. We need your help.

Hmmm, the plant murmured back softly.

You want to grow, Sundew told it. *Let me help you grow. You can grow big and grand and wild, with so many roots you won't need them all . . .*

Grow wild spread far . . . the plant echoed, more or less, stretching its tendrils like a centipede unwinding. *Grow far spread wild . . .*

There was some kind of block between Sundew and the plant; she could reach it, but she couldn't wrap herself all around it. She could feel it growing, but she couldn't latch on to its exact voice. She felt as if she was hearing it reflected off another surface. It was hard to describe . . . like a sound just out of range that she knew she'd recognize if she got a bit closer.

Come forth, Sundew called. *Be here. Let me see you.*

The plant's response felt like rustling in the back of her brain. *Yessss*, it whispered, *yesss, coming, growing, spreading, taking*, and then suddenly it was as loud as a waterfall *YESSS HERE NOW*, it roared, as vines shot from the earth and blasted across the ground all around them.

Sundew recoiled, her leafspeak recognizing them before her eyes did. She stared in disbelief as the vines kept growing, spreading, *laughing* inside her mind, red-and-green leaves unfurling, white flowers and evil-eyed seeds everywhere.

The antidote wasn't a new plant. There was no "heart of salvation."

She was looking at the breath of evil.

— CHAPTER 20 —

"Mandrake, stop!" she cried.

Too late, too late, the plant hummed. *Spread grow far wild conquer consume all mine . . .* The vines had stopped growing outward as soon as Sundew pulled back, but they were already huge and covered the bank of the stream. Cricket was nearly caught in a tangle of them, but she'd jumped into the air and hovered above, her talons pressed to her mouth and her eyes wide with shock.

Mandrake came stumbling back toward Sundew. She could see that his root had grown as well, not as vigorously as hers, but enough vines had sprouted to show him unmistakably what it was.

"What is this?" Mandrake asked plaintively. "It looks just like the breath of evil! Sundew, what is happening?"

"We were tricked," she said. "I think. I don't know! Why would anyone —? But look at it. The antidote is a *lie*."

"M-maybe not," Cricket stammered from above them. "Maybe another piece of the plant could be an antidote for the rest of . . . no, it doesn't make sense. Maybe Hawthorn got mixed up and gave us the wrong thing?"

"No," said Sundew. She felt frozen in place, as though the plant had hypnotized her. "He knew what he was doing. But I don't understand why." She tried, tentatively, to reach out to the plant again with her leafspeak. Maybe if she understood it . . . maybe if she spoke to it, she could turn it *into* an antidote? Perhaps that was what Hawthorn had done.

But she found nothing healing about this plant. It felt as sinister as the ones in the Den of Vipers, far worse than the ones in Wasp's greenhouse. And when she tried to investigate it, it reached right back, a sensation like freezing tentacles plunging into her brain. She closed herself off quickly.

"We have to warn Queen Sequoia," she said. "She needs to know that burning the roots won't help."

"But Inchworm —" Cricket said. "He was cured! It worked on him!"

"I think perhaps it didn't," Sundew said. She felt a new cold fear, like her skin turning inside out. They'd left Inchworm with Hazel and Willow. If Wasp was still inside him . . .

"If the antidote doesn't work, Blue is the first dragon they'll come for," Cricket said in a panicked voice. "He'll be out there where everyone can see him!"

"We'll go stop them," Sundew said, lifting into the air. "Mandrake, stay here and destroy all these vines. I mean *really* destroy them."

"He can try," said a voice from the other side of the stream, "but it won't make much difference. We're spreading through the jungle as we speak."

Hawthorn stood on the opposite riverbank, twitching pitcher plants away from himself with his tail. Beside him, with a dragonbite viper coiled around her neck, was Willow. Its fangs were bared and Willow's deer-brown eyes were fixed on Sundew, terrified and defiant at the same time.

Sundew hissed and started forward, but Hawthorn raised one claw and made a patronizing "ah, ah, ah!" sound. She could kill him for that sound alone, but she was *definitely* going to kill him for threatening Willow.

"If you hurt her," Sundew growled. "If you *dare* —"

"I know, I know," he said. "You'll do something terrible and violent to me. But it will be too late, because she'll be dead. So how about you stay on your side of the river while we have our little talk, and maybe she'll survive this, more or less. You too, little gnat. And you, disposable LeafWing, I can still see you; don't even think about sneaking away."

Sundew sank back down to the ground; Cricket and Mandrake did the same on either side of her. The moment they touched the earth, the breath of evil vines slithered around and around their talons, snarling them in place so they couldn't move.

"There," Hawthorn said. "After all, it would spoil everything if you went to warn Sequoia. My whole brilliant plan, ruined by a trio of idiots? I think not."

"What brilliant plan?" Sundew asked. "So you tricked us into burning a pile of roots; great work! If you think that means Queen Sequoia won't be prepared for Wasp's attack, *you're* the idiot. She'll be ready even when the bonfire does nothing. We're stronger than you think, and so is this jungle!"

Hawthorn chuckled. "Oh, I know how strong this jungle is. It's been my home for thousands of years, after all. It came so close to killing me at last, after so many had failed . . . but then Hawthorn came along and rescued me. Gormless lovely dragon husk. He's been so useful. I think I'm going to keep him forever, or at least, until his bones rot and I can't move him anymore."

Silence fell, chilling and horrible, like a dragon-trap closing its jaws around them. Sundew couldn't breathe. She couldn't think. She could only stare into Willow's frightened eyes, her pulse pounding *how do I save you, how do I save you, how do I save you from* this?

". . . What?" Mandrake said finally.

"Is Hawthorn — aren't *you* Hawthorn?" Cricket asked.

"Hee hee," said the dragon in front of them, a sneering sort of wheeze. "The outer bark is Hawthorn, yes. All these years, he thought he was in control. He thought I was merely one of the voices in his head, his beautifully carved seed just whispering back to him." He took out the carving that Sundew had thought was an egg. *But of course it's supposed to be a seed. The breath of evil's seed.*

Hawthorn cupped the seed in his talons. "Such a clever scientist. Left to test his experiments on himself, poor fellow. Imagine what he might have figured out if he'd had other test subjects. Aren't I lucky he didn't."

The vines tightened around Sundew's talons.

"Wasp," she growled. "So you've been here, in our jungle, this whole time. You knew we were still alive."

Hawthorn threw back his head and laughed, an awful slithering noise that sent cold vibrations through Sundew's leafspeak.

"Wasp, *really*," he said when he finally caught his breath. "No, no, no. She's a perfect ally, all poison from her core out, but in the end, she's my puppet, too. I let her do all her great evil things because it pleases me. But one day she'll realize I've hollowed out her brain and she has no more control than her lowliest worm of a subject."

"Then who are you?" Cricket burst out.

Hawthorn's face went very still, his eyes flickering white-green-white-green.

"I am the rightful owner of this continent," he growled in a low voice. "It was mine, all of it mine, every insect and blade of grass and grain of sand. I ruled it all. And then *you* came, with your outsized brains and your clumsy crushing talons and your fire. And you *stole it from me.*

"All these thousands of years, I've waited to recapture my home and destroy you all. I bided my time and planned my vengeance. Even trapped in the jungle, I knew I'd find a way one day. I had no idea how easy it would be, in the end. You foolish, shortsighted dragons. You came looking for me! You fed me to your enemies! You let me spread and infect you, and soon every one of you will be no more trouble than my obedient snakes here."

"I will always be trouble," Sundew said. "You can't control LeafWings, and you'll never control me." *Or you,* she tried to say to Willow with her eyes.

"Hee hee hee," Hawthorn said again, his grin widening so far it looked as though his face might split in half. "You are pleasantly stupid. You really haven't figured out the next stage of my plan? Let's see, how did you put it . . . 'when the bonfire does nothing.' But of course the bonfire does *something,* you splintery twig."

Cricket gasped, apparently guessing it before Sundew did.

"What? What does it do?" Mandrake asked.

"Well, Hawthorn did have very powerful leafspeak," said the thing inside the dragon facing them. "He almost managed to put a cage around me. He took advantage of one of my weak little shoots, who would have done anything to survive, and he really did adapt that branch of me to only work on HiveWings. Aggravating monster." He abruptly stabbed himself in the neck, then chortled as blood trickled down from the wound. "I could work with it, though. It was a good start, but not what I needed. Not what I *wanted*. I wanted *everyone*.

"So once I was finally inside him, I had him fix me. All his little chains are gone. And now . . . I will have what I want."

He stretched his wings and closed his eyes, breathing deeply.

"The fire has been lit," he murmured. "The smoke is rising. They are breathing it in, and me along with it. All those brave LeafWings, ready to fight. Oh, there's your mother, Sundew. The queen will be mine soon. It's too bad the Chrysalis didn't make it here in time . . . but I will get to them eventually. For now, at least I have these two sweet little SilkWings to infect."

"Blue," Cricket said softly, tears rolling down her snout.

And Swordtail.

And Queen Sequoia. Nettle. Belladonna. Wolfsbane.

Those poor dragons.

Thorn-sharp rage surged through Sundew. She had never been so furious in her life. She felt like the vines around her should erupt into flames, like she was a white-hot sun about to set the entire jungle on fire. She sank her claws into her rage, holding it close and letting it build. Her anger would get them out of this. Her fury was a weapon, and she knew where to point it now.

"Next important question," said the thing inside Hawthorn. "Which of you four should I infect first?"

CHAPTER 21

"Come, now," Hawthorn purred when nobody answered him. "Make this easy on yourselves. Eat a tiny piece of the root or one of the seeds, and all your worries will be gone! Wouldn't you like that? Who'll go first?"

Sundew's eyes were locked with Willow's. The viper's fangs were so close to Willow's neck. No matter what Sundew tried, the moment she made a move, those fangs would sink in and Willow would be lost. Even if she could somehow kill Hawthorn in an instant — which wasn't likely — she wasn't sure that would stop the viper. As far as she could tell, the thing controlling all the dragons was also controlling the snakes.

So killing Hawthorn . . . even killing Wasp . . . might not be enough to stop it.

Willow blinked once, twice, three times. She slowly rolled her eyes down and to the left, at the mud between her and Hawthorn. Then she looked back at Sundew meaningfully.

"Wait, I have more questions first," Cricket babbled. "Why aren't your eyes white, like the dragons who are controlled by Wasp? Or your voice; why isn't it all double weird like when Wasp talks through another dragon?"

Sundew shifted her gaze to Cricket, trying to look as though she was listening, when really all her attention was focused on her leafspeak. She had to weave it past the creepy shivering tangle of the breath of evil, burrowing through the earth around and below it. Her awareness slipped out of the nest of vines and across the stream, tiptoeing through the waterwheels.

The earth between Willow and Hawthorn . . . what had Willow seen there? What did she think Sundew could use? The pitcher plants here were too small to swallow a dragon; they had to content themselves with insects, frogs, and occasional small monkeys, but they were still very smug about it. *Do you know what I ate today? Well, do you know what I ate?* Self-important, like all pitcher plants everywhere. Even if Sundew made them enormous, they couldn't attack Hawthorn or the snake for her. They caught their prey by sitting there with their gaping mouths open.

Sundew reached farther and found mushrooms, water lilies, and arrowroot — none of that would be helpful.

Wait . . .

There was a tiny sprout buried among the pitcher plants.

Normally it wouldn't survive another moon cycle; the self-satisfied plants around it would crowd it out of existence and steal all its prey until it wasted away.

But Sundew could save it, and maybe it could save them in exchange. She had to be precise, though . . . and fast.

Hawthorn was explaining something about cells and fungi to Cricket. Something about the hosts (or playthings) of hosts having the white eyes, but not the hosts themselves. She asked another, even more scientific question. She was stalling, whether she guessed what Sundew was doing or not.

Hello, beautiful plant, Sundew whispered with barely a shimmer of leafspeak. She didn't want the *thing* to notice what she was doing, and she wouldn't be surprised if it could overhear leafspeak conversations.

Oh, she realized suddenly. *That's what I was hearing in the trees. They sensed the breath of evil — they were warning one another of trouble — but Hawthorn was talking over them with his own leafspeak, telling them all was well. He was confusing them and me.*

Frllp, the little plant said in a teeny-tiny voice.

Would you like to be bigger? Sundew asked in the plant's own language. She sent it visions of sunshine pouring through its leaves, all the pitcher plants bowing before it, first choice of all the prey that wandered through. All the creatures it could eat.

Ooooooooo, the plant murmured.

I can make you strong, Sundew whispered, *and big and tall, if you will eat one thing for me.*

She showed it the viper. The slithering feel of it, the flickering danger of it, its exact location in space relative to where the sprout could be.

Oooo would love to eat that yes give please, the plant said, more or less.

It's yours. Take it. Take it fast . . . NOW! Sundew shoved all her power through the systems connecting them, flooding the little plant with strength.

A swarm of sundew tentacles erupted from the earth near Hawthorn's feet, bright red and green like the daylight version of the evil vines. The sundew shot up and out, all its arms growing as thick as anacondas in the space of a heartbeat, and one aimed straight and true for the viper around Willow's neck.

The sticky droplets caught the snake's tail, body, head, mouth all at once, yanking it up into the air. The viper writhed furiously, snapping at the tendrils of goo, but the sundew sucked it in and rolled it up fast, like a frog catching a fly on its tongue.

Or a grasshopper.

"How dare you!" Hawthorn roared.

Several of the tentacles had snared around Hawthorn as

well as they shot from the ground, but Sundew could see that he was fighting them off with his own leafspeak. A few of them were withdrawing, reaching toward Willow instead as she backed away.

No! Sundew commanded. *Eat that big one. The infected one. Leave the other. I helped you; listen to me.*

Loud strong loud, whined the sundew. *So loud hurts.*

Even with her strength behind it, the sundew would give up soon; it was never meant to be an aggressive predator. She needed something else to fight Hawthorn with, and the vines were getting tighter and tighter around her.

Sundew looked around frantically and saw with horror that one of the vines had crawled up Cricket's leg and wound around her neck, squeezing. Cricket was trying to bat it away with her wings, but her breath was already coming in choked gasps.

"Maybe I don't need one more HiveWing," Hawthorn growled. "Especially a *deceitful, inquisitive* one who *won't shut up.*"

"Let her go!" Sundew shouted. "I'm the one who's all the trouble! Fight me, not her!"

"I know you are," the thing said. "But *you* will be useful to me. I'm going to use your leafspeak to retake my continent. Between you and Hawthorn — and I suppose this feeble worm over here," he added, indicating Mandrake, "we can spread across all of Pantala in a matter of days."

"I don't think so," Willow said from above him.

Hawthorn started to look up, but he was too slow to see the thorn as long as a dragon's tail in her talons. Too slow and still too tangled in the sundew to escape or move or fight her off.

The sharp end of the thorn slammed into the base of his neck.

And he fell, killed instantly, as all the breath of evil vines screamed with fury.

CHAPTER 22

Willow let go of the thorn and lifted herself up, her wings beating as she pressed her talons to her face.

"Willow!" Sundew cried. "Get to Cricket!"

The vines were seething with rage and confusion. As far as Sundew's leafspeak could gather, they were bewildered by the sudden loss of Hawthorn, like arms that had been cut off an octopus but still grabbed for prey. They'd lost their brain for a moment, but they were still deadly, and she was sure the brain was still out there, even with Hawthorn dead.

Willow snatched a branch from the ground and flew to Cricket, who looked close to passing out.

"Don't land," Sundew warned, "or it might get you, too."

Willow nodded, hovering over the mass of vines. She snapped the branch in half and stabbed the sharp, splintery end into the vine near Cricket's neck. Sundew could hear that tendril hissing, bleating to the others that it was wounded.

But the other vines couldn't help. The plant's voice was still loud, but the power to hold the dragons captive was fading. Sundew felt the bonds around her talons slacken and fall.

Cricket gasped for breath as the one around her neck dropped away. The moment the vines were loose enough, the three dragons all threw themselves aloft, out of reach in case they moved again. Mandrake took off across the stream and into the trees, and the other three followed him high up into the branches of a giant baobab.

Sundew threw her wings around Willow as soon as they landed. They held each other for a long moment without speaking, their necks curved around each other, their hearts beating as fast as rain in a thunderstorm.

"Why did the vines let go?" Cricket asked in a shaky voice. "I thought there was something out there controlling Hawthorn, and the snakes, and the vines, too."

"Maybe it's dead?" Mandrake said hopefully.

Sundew let go of Willow reluctantly and shook her head. "No. Willow killed one of its heads, but it's got more than one."

"It still has Wasp," Willow agreed.

They all fell silent, thinking of the other dragons it might have by now . . . the dragons near the smoke.

Sundew pressed one of Willow's talons between hers. "That was a pretty important head, though. I think the thing was using Hawthorn's leafspeak to make the vines attack us. Without his leafspeak to control them, the vines can't move any more than ordinary plants can."

"What do we do now?" Cricket asked.

"We fly to the border and try to save our tribe," Sundew said. "And our friends." She lashed her tail. "We fight that thing and kill it exactly the way Willow did. I don't know about you, but I'm ready to kill it A LOT."

"Wait," Willow said, pulling Sundew's talons toward her. "No. That's exactly what we shouldn't do."

"What?!" Sundew flared her wings. "We have to! We have to go now! I REALLY WANT TO DESTROY SOME THINGS."

"The four of us against the *entire* HiveWing tribe, Queen Wasp, all the best LeafWing fighters, and our friends?" Willow said. "We don't even know what to destroy!"

"She's right," Cricket said. "I'm all for killing Queen Wasp, but if that thing can be in any dragon, what are we supposed to do — kill *everyone*? We're not doing that and you know it, Sundew."

She did know it. Even if there was a way to kill all the HiveWings, she didn't think she could, after all. Not now that she knew HiveWings she cared about, or now that she'd learned the truth behind all of this and what the LeafWings had done to them. And especially not now that she'd heard the voice of their true enemy.

And of course, she could never hurt Blue, or Queen Sequoia, or Swordtail, or even Belladonna, who usually made her madder than anyone. If they were all lost to the thing . . . and she felt grimly certain they were . . . there would just have to be another way to save them.

"Fine, yes, but we still have to go see what's happening! We have to *fight*!" she argued.

"We will fight," Willow said. "We'll use this rage, I promise. We have to start by using it to save everyone else."

"I want to go to Blue more than anyone," Cricket said. "But I also need to make sure this doesn't happen to Bumblebee."

"Or Hazel," Willow agreed. "We need to protect the dragons who are left so we have someone to fight with us."

Sundew dug her claws into the branch and felt the tree wince. *Sorry*, she flickered through her leafspeak, sending a filament of comfort out to smooth over the scratched bark.

"All right. All RIGHT," she said. "Let's go."

They sped through the trees as fast as they could move, keeping to the higher branches where there was more room to fly, at least sometimes.

Sundew's village was first, closer to the Snarling River; Sundew reached out to the dome as they arrived and moved the plants to make a hole near the top. They hurtled through, startling all the dragons below them. It took several moments of confusion, hissing, yelling, and threats before the villagers realized that their savior Sundew was one of the "attacking" dragons, that Cricket was their erstwhile HiveWing prisoner, and that they weren't an advance party of invaders from Queen Wasp.

"But they are coming," Sundew said. "We have to fall back to the other — to the SapWing village and regroup with the dragons there."

"Fall *back*?" Cobra Lily objected. "Are you saying . . . we *lost*? Already?"

"Is Belladonna dead?" several voices asked in alarm.

"Not exactly, but she's lost to us right now," Sundew said. "I can explain everything, but I'd rather do it once, to everyone, and I'd rather do it after we get all our dragonets out of here."

"LeafWings don't run away!" someone shouted. "We stand and fight! We bare our fangs and raise our claws and —"

"And end up as mind-controlled zombies just like the HiveWings," Sundew snapped. "Don't be idiots! This isn't a normal threat! We have to find an un-normal way to fight it, and we need all the dragons we can gather! So we get to safety first, then make a plan."

"I'll round up the dragonets," Cobra Lily said unexpectedly. She loped gracefully off to the nursery area, and several other dragons followed her. Several more stayed to keep arguing with Sundew, but she ignored them and flew to the outer wall of the dome — the same spot where she used to sneak out to meet Willow. She rested one talon on the woven branches and nudged them apart, hoping they felt her love for them as she did. She loved all the plants that made up this dome, which she'd built to protect her tribe. She hated to leave it; she hated to imagine the breath of evil slithering over it, stealing its light and smothering it.

Dragons began climbing out through the hole; she tried to count them all but lost track around fifty. She guessed about a third of the village was here, most of them probably planning to be called up as the next wave of soldiers. A lot of them were carrying weapons of some sort. Many of them had pouches like hers slung around them, hopefully full of useful deadly things.

She wished she had time to refill her own pouches, but she'd have to do that later, when all the dragons were somewhere safer.

They moved a bit slower now, hampered by their numbers and the slowest among them, including two dragonets who couldn't fly yet, one elder who hadn't left the village in years, and three limping dragons who'd been recently wounded by various jungle dangers.

"Do you think Wasp and the army are right behind us?" Mandrake worried, pacing beside Sundew. "How soon could they get here?"

"I'm surprised we haven't seen anyone yet," Willow admitted in a low voice. "I would have thought the . . . the othermind . . . would have sent something to chase us down as soon as Hawthorn died."

"Maybe the smoke didn't reach all the LeafWings, and they were giving it a fight," Sundew guessed, feeling proud of them and horribly worried for them at the same time.

"Also, it doesn't know where to go," Cricket said.

"What?" Willow tilted her head.

"When Wasp takes over a dragon, she doesn't get his memories and thoughts and knowledge," Cricket said. "The othermind might have stolen our friends, but it doesn't know everything they know. It wouldn't know the way to Sundew's village."

"But it will know the way to mine," Willow said, "because it was there, inside Hawthorn."

"That's true," Cricket said, "although it might have trouble remembering the way, since it didn't come from the border before. And without Hawthorn's leafspeak, it won't be able to clear sundews and dragon-traps out of its way, like Sundew is doing for us right now."

Sundew was surprised that she'd noticed; she was doing it almost automatically, sending her leafspeak out ahead of the group to check for dangers.

"So, when we met Hawthorn in the Den of Vipers," Mandrake said slowly, "were we talking to the real Hawthorn? Or the thing inside him? It seemed like it had all of Hawthorn's memories."

"I think it was the real Hawthorn," Cricket said, "but he's spent the last fifty years being manipulated by that voice in his head. He might not have known what it was going to do — maybe he didn't even know the antidote wasn't real. But he was doing what it wanted him to do, even when it wasn't controlling him."

Sundew shuddered. *Imagine spending fifty years alone, with no one but an evil voice to talk to.* Perhaps Hawthorn had been more than adequately punished, after all.

"Do we need to talk about what . . . *it* is?" Mandrake asked. "What's using the plant to control everyone?"

"And is it the same dragon who used it all those thousands of years ago, in the Legend of the Hive?" Cricket asked. "If so, where is he, and why hasn't he come out in all these years? Or is it a group of dragons, and are they hiding somewhere?"

Sundew looked over at Willow, and she saw from Willow's face that she had come to the same conclusion as Sundew.

"I think it's not a dragon," Sundew said slowly. "I think . . . it's the plant itself." Willow nodded.

Cricket blinked at her. "The *plant*? But how? That's . . . plants don't have a consciousness, or a voice, or make sinister evil plans!"

"Some of them do, actually," Sundew said. "I can vouch for that. They don't usually have voices like ours, and I'm guessing this one didn't until dragons came along and it adapted to use us."

"Yeeeeeeesh," Mandrake said, stepping carefully over a fallen branch and eyeing it as though it might suddenly leap up to attack him.

"It's just a guess," Willow added. "We need to find out more so we can stop it."

It was late morning when they reached the other LeafWing camp. Sundew had seen the guards patrolling in the trees, watching them arrive, but nobody came out to stop them. *We'll have to warn them that not all LeafWings can be trusted anymore*, she thought with a shiver. *Now that anyone could have the enemy lurking inside them.* They left the dragons from Sundew's village gathered in a huddle in the biggest clearing, glaring up at the curious dragons around them.

Bumblebee came galloping across the throne room when Cricket and Sundew landed, her wings flopping to either side of her. To Sundew's surprise, she beelined straight for Sundew and bonked into her feet, bouncing and reaching to be picked up.

"Hey, little bug," Sundew said, lifting her. The dragonet's yellow and black stripes seemed cuter than they had the day before, and her snout was warm as she snuggled into Sundew's neck.

Sundew found herself feeling weirdly glad that they'd come back instead of going to fight. Saving Bumblebee from the othermind . . . that would be worth it.

What has happened to me?

Tsunami and Turtle were the only other ones there, both of them still leaning over the Book of Clearsight.

"Any luck?" Willow asked them.

Tsunami shook her head. "Not yet. I must admit I like this Clearsight a bit better than I did before, though."

"Why did you ever not like her?" Cricket asked, obviously shocked.

"Because I thought she was an idiot who nearly let her boyfriend destroy the world," Tsunami said. "Although, to be fair, I guess so did we."

"What?" Willow asked.

"Long story," Tsunami said.

They turned as Hazel swept into the room with a few LeafWing guards behind her.

"Where's Inchworm?" Sundew asked. If he was still here, in the village, with Wasp inside him —

"I had my guards take him back to the Snarling River,"

Hazel said. "Why? What happened? Where's the queen? Did the antidote work?"

Willow told her the whole story, as quickly and briefly as she could. By the end of it, Hazel was looking as shattered as Sundew felt.

"So you think this othermind got *everyone*?" she asked.

"I think we have to assume so," Sundew answered. "Even if the smoke didn't reach all the LeafWings, all it needed was Queen Sequoia. Once it had her, it could convince everyone else to take the 'antidote,' and no one would know that wasn't a normal order from our queen."

"So . . . we have to get everyone and hide somewhere," Hazel said, rubbing her forehead. She turned to the guards and put on her queen voice. "Gather the entire tribe. Tell them we're using the evacuation plan and moving out before noon. Pack lightly, if at all. Bring weapons. Try not to panic the dragonets. Tell them . . . tell them all is not lost, if we move swiftly. Make sure they know we can still save our queen and our friends, and that I'll tell them more once we reach safety."

"But where is that?" Willow asked as the guards nodded and flew away. "We can keep retreating farther into the jungle, but eventually we'll hit the ocean."

"So then we cross it," Cricket said. "I still think we have to get to the Distant Kingdoms. That's our only hope."

"How?" Tsunami said, slamming the Book of Clearsight shut. "This thing is no use. Turtle and I can't swim hundreds of you across."

"Let me see that book," Hazel said.

Turtle brought it over to her, and she flipped through it, brushing her claws across the pages.

Sundew tried to think. *Maybe we could build giant floating platforms*, she thought, *and pile everyone on to them . . . and take turns pulling them across the ocean?* She had a notion, although she wasn't sure where it had come from, that their earliest ancestors had arrived here that way, more or less.

But we don't have time to build platforms big enough for all the remaining LeafWings.

Maybe we do. Maybe we can buy ourselves time. If I go back and fight . . . with Cobra Lily and some of the others . . . while everyone else starts building . . .

"This book feels weird," Hazel said in her regular voice, turning it over and running one talon over the back. "I can't say I approve of whoever bound it."

Willow cracked a smile for the first time all day. "Trust you to care about the bookbinding of the ancient magical sacred text," she said.

"Well, look at how the back cover is thicker than the front cover. That's just messy. The end pages are sewn down with these perfect little stitches — it looks like gold thread, but maybe it's flamesilk, the kind that doesn't burn? So someone put all this effort into perfectly sewing down the endpapers around the edges, but left the middle all lumpy."

She stared at the inside back cover for a moment.

"Hazel! What are you DOING?!" Cricket gasped as the LeafWing sliced a long slit around the edges of the last endpaper. "You're destroying the Book!"

But Hazel wasn't listening. She reached two claws between the paper and the leather, and carefully, delicately slid out the folded page that was hidden inside.

It felt as if the whole world was holding its breath. Sundew wasn't sure why this felt so important. It would probably be something like the rest of the book — a prophecy about something that happened centuries ago, or another sentimental letter about being nice to one another.

And yet even her scales prickled with anticipation as Hazel carefully unfolded the secret note.

"It's . . . a map," she said wonderingly.

CHAPTER 23

Hazel spread out the map on the throne, and they all crowded around to look at it. The ink was faded but still legible. Sundew stared at the odd shapes and recognized the peninsulas that jutted into Dragonfly Bay. Willow leaned against her shoulder, her scales warm and smooth.

"That must be the Distant Kingdoms," Cricket said, pointing to the coastline on the far-right-hand edge of the map.

"Yes," Tsunami agreed. "That's the Ice Kingdom up here, the Kingdom of Sand all along here."

"And this is the eastern coast of Pantala," Hazel said, pointing to the coastline on the left. Even in a one-page drawing, the distance between the two continents looked immense. Uncrossable. Sundew's heart sank.

"So these dots in between . . ." Turtle said. "Could those be islands?"

"Yes!" Cricket cried, making them all jump. "That's it! They're islands! Look, Clearsight drew little arrows from one to the next. Start here, then fly here, then here next." Her claw hovered above the map as she pointed out the route.

"That's how she got to Pantala," Willow said wonderingly. "She must have used her future sight to see which direction the nearest island was so she could rest between flights. That's amazing."

"And then she wrote it all out so someone could follow the islands back across the ocean one day." Hazel's face was aglow with excitement. "Or a whole tribe of someones. This is what we need to get to the Distant Kingdoms."

"Oh wow," Cricket said. "We're going? We're really going?" She looked out at the trees, and Sundew could guess what she was feeling. On the one talon: the Distant Kingdoms and Bumblebee's safety. On the other: Blue.

If that were Willow trapped by the othermind, Sundew wasn't sure she'd be able to fly away, no matter what the stakes were.

"Yes. We're going, all of us, right now," Hazel said.

"Oh . . . everyone?" Tsunami said, sounding slightly alarmed. "I mean — right, yes, of course. Everyone. I'll just . . . come home with a whole other tribe of dragons."

"Make that two," said a voice behind them.

Sundew's heart nearly flew out of her chest before she spun around and saw that the speaker was Io. The tall purple SilkWing glided into the throne room with a few other SilkWings behind her. Sundew recognized Cinnabar from the Jewel Hive Chrysalis, who waved at her and Cricket.

"Oh," Tsunami said. "I mean, sure, what difference does seven more SilkWings make?"

"There are about two hundred more of us at the mouth of the Gullet River," Io said. "I thought we'd sneak in the back way to join you, but it sounds like we're too late."

"Two hundred . . ." Tsunami said faintly.

"*Two hundred* SilkWings came to help us?" Hazel said.

"Sorry — I only made it to Yellowjacket Hive, Wasp Hive, and Jewel Hive," Io said. "I didn't have time to get to the others, but I can round up more if I go back now. The Chrysalis is bigger than anyone thinks."

"Two hundred," Willow said to Sundew, her eyes shining. "I *told* you they were worth saving!"

"We've found a way to the Distant Kingdoms," Hazel said to Io. "We need to go before Wasp and her army get here."

"Aren't we going to fight them?" one of the SilkWings asked nervously.

"We will, but not today," Hazel said. "We're not ready. Wasp can infect LeafWings and SilkWings now. If we stay to try to fight, we could all end up under her control, with no chance of ever fighting back."

Io flared her wings and growled. "She can control *SilkWings*? Then I have to go warn the Chrysalis! We need to get everyone out of the Hives!"

Hazel hesitated, then looked at Willow as though she was hoping to find a plan in Willow's expression.

"What's wrong?" Cricket asked. "Io is right — someone needs to stay behind to gather the rest of the SilkWings and bring them over the ocean, too."

Sundew realized what Willow and Hazel had figured out. "The problem," she said, "is that we'd have to leave them a copy of the map. And if there's a copy left on this continent . . ."

"It could fall into the othermind's talons," Willow finished. "Or . . . tendrils, or whatever."

"Oh," Cricket said, her wings starting to droop.

"Hey, *no*," Io said loudly. "Come on! There's no way we're flying to safety and leaving hundreds of SilkWings to be zombified! Could you seriously abandon them all like that? SERIOUSLY? When we could save them?"

"But it puts our whole escape at risk," Hazel pointed out. "If we leave right now with the map, Wasp and the othermind won't be able to follow. We'd be completely safe over there. But if we leave a copy of the map, they could find it and come after us. They *would* come after us."

"Also, by the way, there are some other dragons over

there," Tsunami said in a rush, "who *might* not be super excited about you all arriving and, PS, also would *definitely* not like you to be followed by a creepy hive-brain army."

"They won't get the map," Io said fiercely. "I'll hide it somewhere safe, so even if they catch me and take over my mind, they'll never find it. You HAVE to let me save the SilkWings. Look, if Wasp gets them, it'll double the size of her army. You don't want that, right?! So this is practical, and also OBVIOUSLY THE RIGHT THING TO DO. I mean really!"

Hazel sighed and rubbed a spot over her eyes. "I wish Great-grandmother were here to tell me what to do."

"She's not," Sundew said. "Which means you're the queen for now."

Hazel gave her a wry half smile. "Unless Belladonna is right and it should be you."

"No, thanks." Sundew shook her head. "You're the exact right queen for us. You have the voice and everything."

"I do, I've been practicing it," Hazel agreed. She lifted her chin and turned to Io, her entire posture becoming majestic and imposing. "Very well. We'll make you a copy, and you'll go save the SilkWings."

"I can make the copy!" Turtle volunteered. He fiddled with his claws when everyone looked at him. "I, um . . . I have excellent penmanship."

"Do that," Hazel said, producing a sheaf of bookmaking

paper from a hollow behind the throne. "Just one copy, and make it perfect. Io, decide who's going with you."

"Me," Cinnabar said immediately.

"Um," Sundew interjected. "One small thing. If you happen to run into three LeafWings out there, please bring them with you. Their names are Bryony, Pokeweed, and Hemlock."

"Hemlock," Willow said. "Your father?"

Sundew nodded. They weren't exactly close, she and her father; he was usually too busy following Belladonna's orders, and he was terrible with words. But he was still her father, and she was leaving him here. She had no idea where he might be, or how to get him a message. She just had to hope Io found him before the othermind did.

Hazel was about to issue another order but stopped as they all heard crashing from overhead. Sundew felt all her muscles tense as she looked up. *They couldn't have reached us this quickly. They can't be here already.* Bumblebee squeaked, and Sundew realized she'd tightened her arms around her. The dragonet squirmed out of her grasp and clambered onto Cricket's back instead.

But it wasn't a HiveWing who came hurtling pell-mell through the trees; it was one of Hazel's LeafWing guards. He catapulted to a stop in the center of the throne room, gasping for air.

"Are they here?" Hazel asked.

"No," he said, shaking his head. "But something else is happening. They've set the jungle on fire."

Oh no, Sundew thought. She opened out her leafspeak and had to slam it closed almost immediately. The shrieking trees filled her head with rage and sorrow. She couldn't bear the entire jungle's panic in there along with her own.

She clenched her talons into fists. The othermind couldn't win. She couldn't run away and let it think it won!

"Get everyone to the coast," Hazel ordered the guard. "We'll gather on the north shore of the mouth of the Gullet River. Use the evacuation plan — everyone was assigned to a trio, and all the dragonets and elders have someone responsible for them. Tell them to go *right now*." He flew off and she spun toward Turtle. "Draw faster, dragon from across the sea."

"Our dragons don't have an evacuation plan," Mandrake interjected. He saw the look on Hazel's face and stammered, "B-but we can make one. Right now."

Sundew grabbed his shoulders. "You can organize them. You'll be great at this, Mandrake. It's just like sorting the insect collection."

"Yes," he said, his face brightening. "I'm good at that."

"So go sort LeafWings," she said. "Make sure they know where they're going or have someone to follow!"

He sprang away, leaping from the edge of the platform. Sundew turned and found Willow watching her, standing only a winglength away with a worried look on her face. Beyond them, the other dragons had all leaped into motion, flurrying about as Turtle bent over the throne, drawing the copy of the map.

"Why aren't *you* going to organize your tribe?" Willow asked.

"Because he'll be better at it," Sundew said.

Willow narrowed her eyes. "You're their natural leader."

"They should get used to following Queen Hazel's orders anyway," Sundew pointed out.

"Sundew." Willow hesitated, then took a step closer, spreading her wings. Sundew spread hers as well until the edges brushed together, encircling them in a small green bubble of quiet.

"Please don't do whatever you're thinking," Willow whispered.

"I can't run away!" Sundew protested. "I'm *so angry*, Willow! I want to go set all of *them* on fire! I want to set everyone in the *world* on fire! And drip poisonous sap on their heads! And pull out each of their claws and then stab them in their faces! And then set them on fire again!"

"I know!" Willow said. "So do I!"

That caught Sundew off guard. "You do?"

"Yes!" Willow said. "They set our trees on fire — the only trees we have left! They stole my queen! And that — that *thing* was going to use your leafspeak to devour all of Pantala. When it said that, I felt everything you're feeling, Sundew. I never let myself get mad like that before."

"And your anger helped you save us," Sundew said. "With the thorn."

"Right," Willow said. "Yes, fine, you can make the 'I told you so' face. But I'm going to make it right back at you. You're right that you should be mad. But I'm right that you should focus on who deserves your anger and when to fight."

"They all deserve my anger!" Sundew said, her voice rising.

"You know they don't! There's a monster inside them. There's a monster leading them. If you scatter your anger around like dandelion seeds, you'll hurt everyone, tire yourself out, and end up with a bunch of indignant dandelions. But if you summon it all together and aim for the monsters, you'll win. I know you will. Because you're Sundew, my forever dragon."

Sundew's eyes filled with tears, and she covered them with her talons. "Aaaargh. That's not fair. You're turning me into you! Look at my stupid leaking face."

"I think you mean, 'Aw, you're my forever dragon, too, Willow,'" Willow said in a rather terrible imitation of Sundew's voice.

"You know you are, twigs for brains."

"You're, like, *really* good at this romance thing," Willow observed.

Sundew laughed around her tears and thought, *How can I be this furious and this sad and this terrified and this full of love all at the same time?*

"Wait, I have one more really excellent point," Willow said. "If you go tearing off to fight the thing right now, fueled by super rage, it will one hundred percent gobble up your brain, and then it'll have Pantala's most powerful leafspeak. Without Hawthorn, that plant can only grow at whatever speed it normally grows at."

"Probably pretty fast," Sundew guessed. "Like a weed."

"But nowhere near as fast as it could grow if it had Hawthorn . . . or you. So *you* need to get far away from it more than anyone, if we want a chance of saving this continent when we come back."

Sundew sighed and leaned into her. "All right. You're right."

"As usual, Willow," Willow added in her Sundew voice, smiling through her tears.

When we come back.

Sundew kept those words close to her heart as they flew to the coast, as they gathered the bedraggled remnants of their tribes, as they looked west to the line of fire that rose toward the sunset, and then east over the beetle-dark ocean into apparent nothingness.

She repeated them to herself as they all lifted into the sky, following Queen Hazel southeast to the first island on Clearsight's map.

We're coming back. We'll get everyone to safety, figure out how to stop the othermind, gather some allies.

Sundew looked over her shoulder at the continent that was vanishing into the distance and the dusk.

And then we'll be back to deal with you.

EPILOGUE

The white dragon paced furiously over the snow-dusted grass. The sound of frozen blades cracking under her talons carried across the wide-open tundra.

Jerboa sighed and wheeled down toward her. She couldn't keep hiding in the clouds forever. Each moment she delayed would only make the young IceWing queen more hostile.

She landed on claws that were instantly freezing. Even though she'd been alive for so long, she'd never gotten used to cold temperatures. Her SandWing blood wanted to be out in the desert, rolling in warm sand.

"Finally!" Queen Snowfall shouted, bounding over. "I don't have time to wait around forever! I have an entire kingdom to run!"

"Sorry," Jerboa said. She inclined her head as politely as she could without actually bowing. "Queen Glacier usually arrived after I did."

"Well —" Snowfall dug her claws into the ground, scowling. Her wings gave a little tremor; Jerboa had noticed that happen before whenever she mentioned Snowfall's late mother. It made her think maybe there was a heart under Snowfall's icy exterior after all . . . one that mourned for Glacier. But there weren't many other signs of it.

"I guess I'm more punctual than she is," Snowfall blurted, "so you'll have to be, too!"

"I will try," Jerboa said, inclining her head again.

"Have you thought about what I asked?" The IceWing queen began pacing again. Before Jerboa could answer, she interrupted herself. "Well, I've changed my mind. I need something else instead."

Jerboa arched one eyebrow. "Oh?"

"The Great Ice Cliff," Snowfall said. "It's completely stupid."

"I've always thought so," Jerboa agreed.

"It protects our southern border from, I don't know, invading SandWings, if they were dumb enough to try that," Snowfall said. "I've only seen its animus magic work once."

"Shooting ice spears at any dragon who crosses the border that isn't an IceWing," Jerboa said. "That's why we meet on this side of it."

Snowfall rolled her eyes at the obviousness of this

observation. "But here's the problem. Maybe most dragons would try to attack that way, over land, and so we'd be protected. But what if Darkstalker comes back? Or another dragon like him comes along? And they try coming at us over the water instead? What if they fly around and come in our northern border? Or east?! OR WEST?!"

Jerboa sighed. "It's too cold for anyone to do that," she said. "The truth is, other tribes are not the slightest bit interested in stealing your kingdom."

"Maybe not, but they might be interested in killing all of us!" Snowfall said. "I can think of a very big scary awful dragon who was pretty recently interested in that exact thing!"

It was very unfortunate that Snowfall's reign had begun as a result of the plague Darkstalker had sent to wipe out the IceWings. He hadn't succeeded, and he was gone now, but as a result, Snowfall had ended up as an incredibly paranoid, perpetually anxious queen. Which made her exhausting for Jerboa to deal with.

"So I want you to expand the Great Ice Cliff for me," said the queen. She waved one talon at the kingdom behind her. "I want it to go all the way around, along the entire border of the kingdom." She paused, then gave Jerboa a narrow, suspicious look. "Something has happened. But you can't go tell Queen Thorn."

"I have never spoken to Queen Thorn," Jerboa said truthfully. That didn't mean she never would, but Snowfall seemed satisfied enough with her answer.

"I have scouts patrolling around our borders day and night," Snowfall said in a hushed voice. "I've told them to fly out into the ocean as far as they can to keep an eye on everything for me. Just in case someone DOES attack."

"Oh?" Jerboa said again. She had discovered that this was often the only contribution she needed to make to a conversation, especially when it was with a queen.

"And *guess what* one of them saw?" Snowfall whispered. Jerboa arched her brows again.

"DRAGONS!" Snowfall shouted. "Hundreds of dragons! Coming this way! Across the ocean! I don't know from where! But they're coming for my kingdom and I won't let them! Build me more Ice Cliff RIGHT NOW!"

"Maybe they're not coming for your kingdom," Jerboa pointed out. She had a pretty good idea of what dragons those were, from what Moon and Luna had said. She hadn't realized they were so close, though. "Maybe instead of shutting them out with magic, you should see if they're all right. Maybe they need help."

"AAAAAAAAAAAAAAAAAAAAAAAARRRGH!" Snowfall screamed. "No! It's an invasion! And you have to stop it!"

"Queen Snowfall," Jerboa said firmly, trying to cut off the tantrum before it got much worse. "Your mother and I had an agreement. She never abused my animus powers."

"And look how she ended up!" Snowfall cried, even more frantic. "She could have won the War of SandWing Succession! She could have protected the tribe from the plague!"

"No," Jerboa interrupted. "If she had come to me then — if I had known — we would have stopped it sooner and saved her. But she couldn't get to me . . . she was too sick. That's why she sent you." *And I rather wish she hadn't. Queen Glacier was a reasonable dragon to deal with. Queen Snowfall, on the other talon . . .*

"She should have told me about you sooner," Snowfall said. "Our own animus dragon is exactly what we need."

"I'm not *your* animus dragon," Jerboa observed. "And I have bad news." She saw the panic sparking in Snowfall's eyes and hurried on quickly. "Animus magic isn't working. Right now. Apparently."

Queen Snowfall stared at her, confusion and rage and alarm battling in her expression.

"Sorry about that," Jerboa added.

"WHAT?!" Snowfall roared.

Jerboa spread her talons. "It just isn't. It's not working for me or any of the other animus dragons. All previous spells are still working. But nothing new can be cast." She shrugged, her wings rising and falling in the chilly air.

"How is that possible?" Snowfall shouted. "Why is this happening NOW, just when I found you?! I NEED THAT MAGIC!"

"Or perhaps," Jerboa said, "this continent would be better off without animus magic for a little while."

Snowfall jabbed one claw at her. "Prove it. Prove that it doesn't work."

Jerboa agreeably snapped a frozen twig up from the ground. "I hereby enchant this twig to turn anything it touches green," she said. She held it out to Snowfall.

"Absolutely not," Snowfall snapped.

With another shrug, Jerboa tapped herself with it — shoulders, snout, wings. Her color stayed the same. She poked a nearby rock, but it remained as gray as ever.

Snowfall grabbed the twig out of her talons and glared at it, then threw it as far as she could. Jerboa kept quiet, resisting the urge to say, *See?*

"If you can't do magic," Queen Snowfall spat, "then what *good* are you? You're completely *useless*!"

Jerboa watched the queen spin and fly away, fury radiating off her like a cloud of ice particles.

Completely useless, Jerboa thought, allowing herself the smallest of smiles. *Yes. Just like I've always wanted.*